THE REST OF ME

ASHLEY MUNOZ

Cover Design: Jeanette Emerson- Net Hook & Line Design

Editing by C. Marie

Proofreader: Love Infinity Proofreading

❀ Created with Vellum

The Rest of Me

ASHLEY MUNOZ

SPOTIFY

Playlist

Goodbye John Smith- Barns Courtney
Some Kind of Lonely- Harbor & Home
How Not To- Dan & Shay
Known- Tauren Wells
No Saint- Lauren Jenkins
Grave- Thomas Rhett
Think & Drive- Seth Ennis
Wannabe- Dylan Schnider
Woulda Left Me Too- Ryan Griffin
Happier- Keith Urban

Click here for Entire Playlist

1

Layla

THEY SAY THE DEVIL IS IN THE DETAILS.

MAYBE THAT'S why I decided to make a deal with him.

It was nothing terrible, nothing horrible enough to keep me out of the pearly gates...at least I didn't think so. I merely asked to ignore all the details of my life for the past year. He could keep all the juicy specifics to himself and I wouldn't ask a thing.

I didn't want to know, didn't want to face or deal with any of the particulars.

I couldn't face them, not then anyway.

But now...

Now, my time was up.

THE SOUND of incessant beeping woke me, dragging me from a restless night of sleep. I quickly threw my arm forward, groping for the beloved snooze button, hoping and praying my children wouldn't wake up. I blinked open a blurry eye and squinted at the red numbers shining from my bedside table, but I was too blind to make them out.

"Come on," I groaned as I scooted toward the edge of my mattress. I moved my hand around the table until I found my glasses and shoved them on. Six fifteen in the morning, on a Tuesday. I looked around my room, ignoring how bare the walls still were after living here for six months, and wondered who'd set my alarm. I sure as hell hadn't.

After double-checking that my alarm clock was turned off, I tossed my glasses back on the end table and slumped back into my pillows. They'd hold me and hopefully keep me a little longer while I avoided what I needed to face.

I was nearly asleep when the sound of a rooster woke me. Not a real one from a nearby farm—no, this was a digitized, demonic fowl right there in my room. I sat up swiftly, reaching forward for my damn glasses again, knocking the alarm clock and a half-full glass of water onto the carpet in the process.

"Shit," I whispered, searching the room for my cell phone. The evil rooster was waking up every single one of my kids; I was sure of it. I fumbled forward until I was off the bed and crouching down on the floor, where the phone had fallen but was still attached to the charger. I swiped my thumb furiously over the snooze button and wondered again who the hell had set my alarms. "Very funny, Travis," I muttered to myself and stood, giving up on the idea of sleep.

I had promised myself this would be the day I'd face the things I'd been avoiding for the past year. It would be the day I started living again. I decided it'd be somewhat like riding a bike: slow, steady movements until they were consistent and familiar.

I moved away from the bed and, out of habit, pulled the collar of my t-shirt up, pressing the threadbare fabric to my nose, inhaling deeply. I paused, waiting for my memories to wake up and tell me I'd triggered something…but nothing came.

My stomach twisted into a painful knot as I stood barefoot on the tile of my bathroom floor. With my fingers pressed firmly to the black fabric at my nose, I took a shallow breath and inhaled again. I silently pleaded with the inanimate object not to do this to me, *not today*.

Eyes shut tight and fingers trembling, I slowly let the shirt drop back to my neck. Hot tears began to break through the dam I'd been haphazardly building for twelve months. I wasn't supposed to cry today. That was the plan. But *this* wasn't supposed to happen either... not so soon.

I angrily swiped at my face, discarded the t-shirt like it was on fire, and moved to my closet. I threw my hair up, pulled on some leggings and a tank top, and then shoved my running shoes on. My fingers shook as I tied the laces and, as much as I wanted to ignore it, my breathing was chaotic. This was why I avoided this shit, why I avoided details—because the truth hurts. It cuts deeper than a knife and hits harder than any fist.

I stood and glared at myself in the full-length mirror. My long blonde hair was pulled tight into a high ponytail, my freckled face was pale, and bags decorated the space under my eyes. I looked like hell, which was pretty fitting for facing the devil that lurked in all the details I had abandoned all year. I glanced at the discarded black t-shirt on my floor and felt a buzzing in my head.

Not today. Not yet.

I stalked out of my bedroom and jogged downstairs, no longer caring if anyone heard me. I secured the door behind me and eyed my long gravel driveway. I hadn't run in a long time. *Maybe I should stretch?*

My legs moved like they were on autopilot. I had no destination, no ideas of where I could go. I just needed to push the knowledge that Travis' shirts didn't smell like him anymore out of my mind, out of my broken heart. I had been sleeping in his shirts for the past year, rotating them, smelling him, keeping him. It just felt cruel that it'd been ripped away the day I needed it the most.

The yellow grass in the pasture on my right swayed in the morning breeze, which felt nice against my skin. Slick sweat had already started building at my temple, providing another uncomfortable detail I needed to confront.

I'd ignored my health over the past year. I'd traded jogging for chugging coffee, couch camping, and Netflix bingeing; they were my survival tools. Besides, running took energy, and for the past year, I hadn't had any.

I pushed my legs harder as a nearby farm crept up along the gravel road. I had no idea whose property it was or who lived there. So, when the woman in the large floppy hat waved at me, I cringed at the next detail that was surfacing.

I hadn't met a single person in this new town since moving to Wyoming six months ago.

Heavy breathing rattled my chest as I continued down the road without any direction. Images flashed through my head, tugging and demanding I stop and pay tribute to a ghost who still held my heart in his cold fingers. But I refused, because I'd been running from him and this day. I'd been running from what it meant for me and my grieving heart.

Namely, that it was time to move on.

My watch said I'd run a mile before I finally collapsed into a patch of dead weeds on the side of the road. My mind served up the shit I had been dodging on a shiny platter. If I could have seen the devil, I was sure he'd have been rubbing his hands together or eating popcorn while he cashed in on the debt I owed.

I lay on my back with weeds and cheatgrass jabbing into my shirt as I watched the sun shine against the blue sky. Tears mixed with sweat and frustration as I dropped my guard and allowed my mind to drift.

Back to the moment our lives ended.

To the stuffy, overfilled room, black suits, dresses, and too many red flowers.

To the silver casket that cradled my husband's body.

Images of Travis' life had flashed up on a screen against the pale white wall, making him seem like an already distant memory. Every time it shifted to a new one, my little four-year-old son would shake his tiny shoulders and cry into my side. His sobs would echo through the cramped room and I'd eye the hearse parked outside, and somehow, in that moment, I died a little more than I had when I'd been notified of his accident.

The preacher droned on and on about salvation and repentance, adding nothing about what an amazing man my husband was or how he'd been out late because of the city council meeting that went longer due to Margie complaining about her new pot-smoking neighbors. No one talked about how it was a fucking telephone pole that took his life. I suppose that's not entirely correct either, but that was one detail I wasn't ready to face.

I blinked, coming back to the dirt patch I was currently stalled on, and tightly shut my eyes, forcing the tears away, forcing my mind to readjust to the numbing sensation that came when I chose to forget and ignore.

The one-year anniversary of my husband's death...

I got to my feet and started the jog back home, feeling proud that I'd allowed myself to think about his funeral as long as I had. Usually, I capped it at about thirty seconds.

The jog back was easier. The sun was higher, the August heat enveloping me like an unwanted hug. Moisture coated my skin as I pushed toward my driveway, and shaky, uneven breaths caught in my chest as I slowed my pace and began walking. My side ached, my shins hurt, and my lungs burned, but it felt good. I used to run all the time, back when my husband was alive, when we were a cute little cookie-cutter family living in a two-story dream house just outside Portland, Oregon.

We had wanted a safer school district for our kids, so we'd planted ourselves in a small town, so tiny they'd all felt the need to talk to me whenever I left the house.

"Travis was such a good father," they'd say. "Such a shame about the accident," others would quip while I bought ice cream, pizza, and fish sticks. Our tiny town had a front-row seat to my avoidance of grieving properly. My kids didn't get a homecooked meal unless my sister or mother came over to make it. I just didn't have it in me. I was tired of the town talking about my sad loss like it wasn't really happening to me. I was tired of their constant desire to bring up what I wanted to forget.

My sister suggested I move closer to her, in Wyoming, and when I received a tip about a ranch for sale at a decent price, we did it. We moved to another small town called Douglas. We weren't exactly happy…we just were, but at least no one there would talk to me about the telephone pole or the other thing I wasn't ready to face.

My mother didn't approve of me moving. She'd have preferred I stayed closer to her, but I couldn't do that either. I didn't want to face the details she felt the need to shove down my throat or the "moving on" she said I needed to start doing.

No thanks.

I slammed the door shut behind me as I padded toward my kitchen in search of water. Jovi was up, chugging a glass of milk with the fridge still open. Her crazy blonde hair was sticking up and full of static, her brown eyes shifting until they landed on me. Her light eyebrows shot up in surprise as I filled a tall glass with water and threw it back.

"You went for a run?"

Her small voice caught on the tattered strings of my heart, the ones I had been ignoring. My words got stuck in my throat as I regulated my heart rate, so I nodded instead.

"That's good…" she whispered.

Somewhere inside of me was the mother I'd been before, the happy one, the one who would wake up early to make pancakes or French toast for my four children. That version of me hadn't shown up in a long time, but I missed her, and I was damn sure my kids did too. I wondered if they felt like they'd lost two parents that day, not just one.

Today, with the ugly truth I faced and knew I needed to keep facing, I decided I would start trying to find the mother my children deserved. I would start living again.

"Want to help me make some pancakes?" I hesitantly asked my daughter. I turned toward the cupboards and pulled out a glass bowl.

"Seriously?" Jovi asked, excitement tingeing her voice, betraying how eager she was. *Details.*

"Yeah, let's do it. Grab me the eggs and milk." I found the flour and other items we'd need. She stood next to me, her nine-year-old self only coming to just above my waist but clearing the counter just fine. She cracked the eggs then mixed in the butter and vanilla while I added the dry ingredients. I saw a tiny smile break out on her face, and whether the devil was in the details or not, that little lift of her lips was from Jesus himself.

"ARE YOU SURE?" My sister Michelle asked from her spot next to my son's horse, Thor. She was patting his neck and feeding him some kind of treat. Something like petty jealousy sparked to life in me as I watched her with him. Thor and I had a strained relationship. He didn't listen to me, and I didn't like him.

We both tolerated each other, but beyond that, we really didn't care for one another.

"I have to, Shell…it's the entire reason I bought this place and these horses," I explained, exasperated by my situation. I'd purchased five acres of farmland and filled the barn with three expensive horses. No one should have agreed to my request for one horse, let alone three. I had no idea what I was doing. Michelle was a veterinarian and helped when she could, but she lived an hour away so, for the most part, I was on my own.

"I know, but are *they* ready?" Michelle asked, toying with Thor's mane. I eyed the floor of the barn in frustration. I had no idea if my kids were ready for lessons; I just knew some of the details I'd been avoiding revolved around getting them through their grief. I'd read an article about a horse ranch in Oregon that rescued horses and paired them with troubled kids or kids who'd dealt with trauma. They had testimonials from children who had grown up in foster care or been injured in an accident; they talked about how working with and riding the horses changed them, how it healed them. So, I'd purchased horses for my children, to heal, but they wouldn't ride them. Hadn't for six months. They cared for them, but they refused to sit in a saddle.

"I think they're ready. I just need to find an instructor," I lied, grabbing a bucket of oats.

My sister scrunched her nose, which caused her thick, black-rimmed glasses to droop. She pushed them back into place with her finger. "I just hope you aren't suddenly rushing it. I know today is your big day. You gave yourself one year of being sad, one year to ignore everything…but I don't think grief works like that, sis." Michelle walked out of Thor's stall and clicked the door shut.

Frustration burned in my chest as I considered her words, and although I should have tamed my tongue, I didn't. I let my words fly like arrows, hoping they'd hit the mark because I hurt, and for one second, I wanted someone to hurt with me.

"What would you know about moving on too fast or too slow from grief?" I erased the chalkboard where we made notes about the horses and waited for her retort. My sister loved me, and I adored her. She'd been the only real support system we had when everything fell apart, but this pain inside me was hungry for company.

"You're right," she whispered, lowering her head. Her light brown hair shifted forward, covering her face. She was three years younger than me, and seeing her like that made me sick. I'd done that. I'd hurt her for no good reason.

"No, I'm sorry. I shouldn't have said that," I muttered, wishing I could take my words back.

She shook her head. "I just want you guys to be okay."

I stepped to the side, and before I could think too much about it, I hugged her close to me.

"Me too."

We exited the barn and headed toward the back porch. The yellow hue of the two-story farmhouse glowed in the late afternoon sun as Michelle opened the fence that led into the smaller yard the kids played in. There were plastic dump trucks and fire trucks littering the grass as well as a small inflatable pool spotted with grass and dirt from the kids playing in it all day. We made our way to the wrap-around porch and pushed through the back screen door.

The kids were all in the living room, playing video games and reading—avoiding emotions, just like me. This day was hard on all of us, which was why my sister had driven out. She knew I'd been hiding behind the one-year mark, knew I'd been having a shit time with processing his death, just like my children had, which had me wondering…

Leaning against the counter, I quirked a brow at my sister. "Hey… did you by chance set my alarms this morning?"

She had a cookie shoved halfway into her mouth when she looked up at me. Her brown eyes were a lighter shade than mine and always opened just a little too wide when she'd been caught doing something wrong. I knew she had done it, which somehow made me feel better about my whole theory of the ghosts and whatnot.

"Guilty, sorry…" she mumbled around the crumbs in her mouth. "I knew you'd feel better if you got the day started instead of sleeping in and feeling behind."

I let out a small chuckle. "You felt the need to set two alarms?"

"I knew you'd turn one off." She shrugged.

"That wasn't me, idiot!" Steven, my eleven-year-old, yelled at his older brother. He was standing up, game controller in his hand and a grim look on his small face. I knew what was coming next, and I needed to get ahead of it before my oldest got upset.

"You're the idiot!" Michael boomed just as I cut in with, "Kids, come in here, please."

I turned to wipe down the kitchen island with my hand to clear a few crumbs and to help clear my mind. I needed to do this, for us, for him, for me…

The game was paused with a few muffled comments tossed here and there. They all settled in on the stools in front of the marble countertop.

I took in each of my children and watched for some emotion to show up on their faces, but each one seemed to be hiding it.

Michael, my fourteen-year-old and the oldest child, had his dark hair askew. A few red pimples had popped up along his jawline, and his dark t-shirt was wrinkled and likely dirty. Steven, my second oldest, was sitting there, staring a hole into the counter; Jovi, my only girl, was circling the top of her water glass with her finger; and Henley, my five-year-old and the youngest, was chewing on the collar of his shirt.

"You guys know what today is." I didn't ask, because I knew they knew. Small nods around the island confirmed this, downcast eyes encouraging me to continue. "You all know I've been avoiding a few things, like talking about your dad or letting you guys talk about him much."

Jovi peeked up at me and nodded; she'd probably suffered the most from that. She was the one who'd put out all of her daddy's pictures when he first passed. She was the one who helped us to remember him.

"I want to change some things for us..." My voice caught. I cleared it to keep the tears at bay and refused to look at my sister, who was standing off to my side. "We need to get better. No more hiding in our rooms, eating crap dinners. No more fighting and hating each other... no more of what we've been for the past year."

I leaned forward, placing my hands flat against the countertop.

"What are some things you guys want to do that will help you start feeling better or move past this pain?" I chanced asking when really, I was terrified to hear what they might say. What if they wanted to move back to Oregon? What if they wanted to live with my sister instead of me? Lord knows they'd been living there half the time anyway.

The kids were quiet as they all contemplated my question. Finally, Steven spoke up, his blue eyes lit up with excitement. "I miss the yummy chocolate shakes he'd make," he whispered.

Everyone froze for a second until Jovi laughed and corrected him: "Malt shakes, not chocolate."

Michael sat back on his stool a bit. "That's right. Malt."

"It's different," both Steven and Michael joked in unison. We hadn't had a malt shake since we'd lost him, and hearing the smallest laugh in Michael's voice had me desperate. He hadn't laughed in so long. He was moody, angry, and mean—all the time.

My voice sounded foreign when I offered, "We should make them."

"Yeah?" Jovi asked, sitting taller. "Are you sure, Mom? You said doing things Daddy used to do makes you sad."

I blinked my dry eyes and pushed past unshed tears I refused to let fall. "I'm sure, baby. I want to do what will make us happy. I think that's what Dad would want."

"If we're being honest here…seeing his pictures around makes me sad," Michael quietly added, killing the hopeful wave we'd just started to ride.

I surveyed everyone's faces. Steven slowly nodded his head in agreement, and Henley kept chewing his shirt, changing feet to sit on to seem taller. My baby girl met my gaze with watery eyes, and my heart nearly gave up entirely. Internally, I begged for her to put up a fight, to say no. *Give me some reason to keep his pictures up, to keep him here with us.*

"I think Mike's right…I miss him so much but seeing him every day is too hard. It's like we can't move on, or if we do, then…" She trailed off.

"We're doing something wrong, or we're not honoring his memory somehow," Michael finished for her. I swallowed the pain cutting into my throat and nodded my head. This was for them. The one-year mark had to be different. We had to be different.

Before I could respond, his sapphire eyes that matched his brother's and father's flicked to mine as he added, "It's time for us to move on, Mom. We have to start living our lives again…all of us."

I felt like he'd punched me in the throat. I wanted to cough, to clear the blockage that was suddenly there, but I couldn't show them that this was killing me. Hearing that they were ready to move on was worse than hearing they were ready for his pictures to be put away.

I had one last lifeline. I looked over at Henley again and leaned forward. "Henley, baby…what do you think about this? Do you want Daddy's pictures put away?"

He shoved some of his mop of brown hair away from his face as he sniffed. Dirt smudges ran across his nose, as well as his shirt. "I get happy sometimes, and then when I see Daddy's picture, I get sad again. I want to laugh when Steven farts, but when I see the pictures of him, I think about when he'd pretend to fart louder, and it makes me want to cry. I think we should put them in a hiding spot." He shifted on his little legs on the stool.

"Okay...I'll pack them away tomorrow," I promised, feeling my gut sink.

"I'll help," Michelle offered from beside me. "Let's get those malts started." She moved to retrieve the blender and ice cream, getting the kids' spirits up like she usually did. I felt a buzzing in my ear, causing everything to lose focus. My breathing sounded too loud, so I excused myself to the bathroom.

Memories tugged and taunted me, reminding me that this pain couldn't be fixed with details. It wouldn't magically come back together like the missing pieces to a puzzle just because I'd finally decided to be the mother my kids deserved.

I needed to do more than just face what I'd been ignoring, and something told me those tiny details were going to be my undoing.

2

Layla

"MOM, WHERE ARE YOU GOING?" STEVEN ASKED AROUND A LARGE BITE of cereal. I ran my fingers over his dark brown hair and walked toward the landline. "You guys have my number, I'm going into town for a bit."

"Town?" Jovi asked with a tiny quirked brow. She looked like my mother, with her sassy tilted head and hand on her hip.

"Yes, town. Michael is watching you, so listen and don't leave the house." I slid my feet into a pair of black flip flops and grabbed my purse.

"Why is she going to the tiny town of tiny minds?" Henley whisper yelled at Jovi. He scrunched his tiny nose, making me want to ditch the town and snuggle him.

"I never said they had tiny minds," I let out a heavy sigh.

"You did, that one time." Henley tilted his head like a dog.

"Yeah, remember when we wanted to go to that big Fourth of July picnic? And you said…"

"Okay, I did, alright. But I was wrong." I waved them off, trying to ignore the blooming disappointment in my parenting skills.

"I'm leaving, be good," I said again as I opened and shut the door before anyone else could say anything. I had to do this before I backed out. I was done hiding from the people of Douglas and I was ready to start looking in the mirror again, which meant I needed to change a few things.

I PUSHED OPEN the glass door of the Ride and Dye hair salon and tried to form a smile. Loud country music blared over the sound of blow dryers and women talking. The place was full, and I tried to swallow my anxiety about being around so many people.

It had been a week since the one-year anniversary, one week since the kids had talked about the pictures and moving on, one week of me trying to be a better version of the new me and trying not to cry every five seconds. This was a start.

"Hi there, do you have an appointment?" asked a tall woman standing behind the counter with a brilliant smile. Her red curls cascaded down her back and her blue eyes were decked out with dark liner and shimmery eye shadow. She was so well put together, it was like looking at a photograph in a magazine. I wanted to take notes on her outfit, makeup, and everything she had going on.

I cleared my throat. "Yes, it's for Layla Carter." I stepped closer to the counter and tried to peek at an appointment book or whatever would have my name listed, but everything was digitized now and the woman was glancing at a screen I couldn't see.

"Yep, gotcha right here." She smiled and waved for me to follow her.

I did, clutching my purse and trying to ignore all the turned heads now looking at me as I walked to the only empty chair in the room.

"You can hang your purse there." The hairdresser pointed a mani-cured finger toward a silver hook positioned next to the big mirror I was facing. She opened a barber's cape and draped it over me, snapping it in place at the base of my neck. "So, what are we doing for you today?" she asked while scrutinizing my hair.

I flicked my eyes away from her station tag that said 'Star' and gave her a small smile.

"Um, just a trim, nothing drastic. Maybe some layers?" God, I hated this. Why was I so nervous? Conversations around me seemed to have stopped or just quieted and the one blow dryer was off now, so I just heard the country music overhead.

Star chewed a piece of gum and toyed with the ends of my hair. "When's the last time you had it cut?" She popped a bubble and I tried not to wince, but I hated gum poppers and I hated talking about the last haircut I'd had—two days before the accident. *Details.*

"About a year ago." I lifted a shoulder, nonchalant-like. She didn't respond, and it made my stomach churn with anxiety. Some people waited that long to cut their hair, right? I wasn't a caveman or Tom Hanks in *Castaway*, some societal reject. I was just busy...and tired and generally not giving a damn about my appearance.

"Hmmm." Star continued picking up the ends of my hair and dropping them. "Let's get you washed, then we'll start with a trim."

I nodded my acceptance and followed after her toward the wash-bowls, cutting right through the middle of the room. Heads turned again, and I suddenly hated that I hadn't taken the time to get to know a single person in this town over the last several months.

I leaned back and flinched as a blast of hot water hit my scalp, and then I eased into the seat as it turned comfortably warm and Star's fingers moved.

"So, you're that single mother who moved into Sara's old house, right?"

I barely opened my left eye to see her gazing down at me, still scrubbing viciously at my scalp. "Uh...I don't know who Sara is, but yes, I moved onto a ranch a few months ago. I have four kids," I replied vaguely, feeling awkward. I hated this.

"Shocked that she sold it, but I guess since her brother hasn't been back in forever, it kind of makes sense. We just all assumed she'd marry that guy she was so in love with and settle down." Star rinsed out the shampoo and started with the conditioner.

I didn't know what to say because I didn't know Sara or her brother or the guy she was in love with, so I just kept silent.

"Well I hope you're getting settled well," she said, moving on to rinse the conditioner.

I nodded. "Yeah, thank you. We are."

She put a small towel on my neck to stop the dripping and motioned for me to head back to the chair. "We have a few singles events that we do here in the summer and closer to fall. You should come. Might be fun for you to get out and see the town," Star offered while taking a wide-tooth comb to my hair.

I didn't want to be rude or tell her that the idea of going to a singles event made me feel about as excited as scheduling my next pap smear. I was overdue for that too because I'd procrastinated before Travis was even gone. I just generally liked to put things off, and now it was all catching up to me. The kids' dentist appointments, yearly checkups, immunizations, school registration, sports...it was all on my plate now, and I had to handle it all by myself.

"I'll keep that in mind." I smiled at Star in the mirror and thankfully, she dropped the subject and started gossiping with the stylist next to her for the next hour, leaving me free to relax and enjoy the idle chatter of someone else. I learned a lot about the town from sitting there. I learned that Douglas had several coffee shops but the main place to go was called Wake Up & Roast, a little bistro that served baked goods along with the best coffee from here to Casper. That made me perk up a bit. I loved coffee, and before Travis died, I had loved sneaking away to a cozy spot and working, getting lost in the buzz of the room. I started picturing myself there, sitting, headphones in, fingers punching away at the keyboard. Elation filled my chest at the prospect of getting back a part of me that was just mine, something that didn't belong to the kids or to the grief...or to Travis.

"Meina just bought it, though, so who knows if the coffee will keep being the best." Star scoffed to her neighbor and shook her head. The women laughed, and a few others clicked their tongues. "That girl is more boy crazy than a prepubescent teen."

"Well you heard who was coming back to town, didn't you?" said an elderly lady with pink curlers tightly wound into her hair, her eyes narrowed.

Star kept her hands in my hair but twisted her neck to see the woman better. "Who?"

"I heard Landon just hired Reid Harrison." The old woman brought her hand to her chin in all-knowing, 'I have secrets' kind of way.

Everyone's heads snapped in her direction, Star abandoned my wet locks, and someone gasped somewhere near the hair-drying station.

"Reid is coming back?!" Star exclaimed, bringing her hands to her hips, her mouth hanging open, that pink piece of gum just sitting there doing nothing. She must have known this person, or this guy was a celebrity of some kind.

"I heard he starts next week, teaching kids how to ride horses and work with them or something like that." The elderly woman waved her hand and returned her gaze to her mirror, looking into her reflection, likely thoroughly satisfied that she had just topped everyone's gossip for the day. If I had been a dog, my ears would have been standing straight up. *Horse lessons...*

"Well, I'll be. I had no idea that boy would ever come back. And to think, his sister just left." Star laughed and then narrowed her gaze on me. Slowly, the rest of the room did too. Was his sister the one who'd left? The one who had owned my house before me? I was too timid to ask, so I just sat there with my fat assumptions and awkward stares. Whoever he was, I hoped he kept his distance. I didn't need some nosy relative snooping around the property he felt some sense of ownership toward. My gut twisted in panic. Would he try to get his sister's place from me? Would he try to find some loophole in my paperwork and kick me out?

I couldn't afford to uproot the kids, not again.

"So, do you think he's moving back into his place then?" Star asked, back to snipping away my dead ends.

The elderly know-it-all nodded her head from her place across the room. "Oh yes, Janette set those kids up nice and proper when their daddy died. As far as I know, his place is still sitting free of a tenant and ready for him to come home."

That was good. It meant he wouldn't want my house, right? Peace settled in my stomach, allowing my mind to drift to the idea of those horse lessons that'd been mentioned. I'd had plans to look into who might be available in the area as soon as I got home, but now I knew there was a man named Landon who offered them, and a man named Reid who taught them. I was definitely going to be coming back into the salon more often, especially when I needed some information.

HENLEY CAME into my room dragging a long Transformers blanket behind him, his dusty brown hair sticking out in all different directions. He came to where I was sitting on the floor and curled into my side. "Mama, I don't want to see you cry anymore."

He'd caught me talking out loud to Travis with my wedding ring gripped between my fingers. I was debating whether or not to put it in my dresser. The selfishness rooted deep in my bones argued against it, but the arrangement I'd made with my kids to start moving on and living had me surrendering it.

I breathed and wiped at my tears. "I know, bubba. I'm sorry. Mama won't cry as much anymore, I promise." I tried to reassure my little five-year-old while I rubbed his back and moved his hair away from his brow.

"Can we go ride Thor at sunset?" he asked while pulling his blanket higher, and I smiled. It was something Henley and I had started doing recently, and I liked that he enjoyed it.

"Yes, baby. Let's do that."

Thor was a jerk and I hated him, and he probably knew it too. I didn't care. We both put on appearances for the kids, and this night was no exception. Once I put the saddle on and got him completely secure, I put Henley at the front and told him to hold on tight to the horn. He looked so cute with his messy hair sticking out under his little black helmet. I took the reins and led Thor out of the barn, past the corral, and all the way through the second pasture gate.

I gently pulled myself up and sat behind Henley then we walked around the property. I loved these times with my youngest because it was just the two of us. I also kind of loved putting on a cowboy hat and riding Thor, but I never would have admitted it out loud.

We rode closer to the fence line than we normally did, and I noticed we were riding right behind the neighbor's property, which made me think of what I'd heard in the hair salon about Reid Harrison.

Suddenly, I was very aware of the fact that my five acres of ranch awkwardly butted up right against his land. We shared a driveway and our mailboxes were side by side. I hadn't thought much about it before because the neighbor's house had been vacant since we moved in. Now there was a silver truck parked in its driveway and a shirtless man controlling a barbeque on the back porch. I couldn't see his face, but his presence made my pulse race because suddenly my little paradise was being invaded.

Reid Harrison had moved back.

The women at the salon had made it seem like he was a good guy, someone who'd grown up there…but he *could* be a bad guy, someone who might hurt my kids. I tried to swallow the fear that crept up my throat, tried to ignore the agony of having to deal with being a single mother now, and rode faster past the fence.

Henley, of course, started asking questions. "Mommy, who's that man?"

I kept riding and stayed quiet, not wanting the stranger to hear me, but I wasn't fast enough to clear him completely. I noticed him lift his head as he watched us ride away. I knew I had plans to pursue the riding lessons for the kids, but until I crossed that bridge, I was going to be like the ugly troll guarding the path between our two worlds. No crossing, no talking, no nothing. I wanted nothing to do with him or the unknowns he'd just brought into my life.

I continued riding back toward the barn then felt bad about cutting our riding session short, so I looped back around to the closer pasture and rode the perimeter of that fence. Once the sun was about to set, we rode Thor into the barn and put him away together. Henley stood on a stool as he helped me brush Thor out, at which point Jovi came out to help.

She still hadn't gotten on her horse yet, but she'd always come to brush them out with us. Michelle had started teaching me all things horse-related every single weekend she visited. Sugar Cube and Samson, our two other horses, were ready to be brushed out too, so I had Jovi get her brothers. I liked it when we were all in the barn together because it was something new for us, something not tied to their dad.

There was a thick silence between us, one that could have been cut down the middle if anyone came in with a metaphorical knife. Michael's shoulders were tense as he brushed out Sugar Cube, and he didn't speak to her the way Michelle said we should. He just used angry strokes and harsh pats to her skin. She tossed her head and shuffled in place as a result.

"Michael, what did your aunt tell you about how to act around them? They can sense your frustration." I coaxed him calmly, hoping to get maybe a huff or an exasperated sigh, just not a yell—anything but an outburst.

A loud angry thwack echoed through the barn as Michael tossed his brush forcefully into the stainless-steel bucket. I pinched my eyes closed and braced myself for the storm.

"I didn't ask for this!" He threw his arms wide, yelling at me. "I didn't ask for any of this. I shouldn't have to brush out this stupid horse every day. I have no idea how to ride it, and I have no idea how to even take care of it. What are we even doing here, Mom?" He shook his head in disappointment and ran out of the barn. Henley watched him and then looked back at me, uncertainty flickering in his little eyes.

Steven sniffed, and Jovi let out a frustrated sigh.

This was my new normal, and I hated it.

3

THE THING ABOUT BEING BACK IN THE HOUSE YOU WERE SUPPOSED TO live in is the misplaced feeling of home. It didn't feel like it. Still, I pushed past the awkwardness of the house and shuffled my couch to the side to see if it looked better.

It didn't.

Everything looked wrong. The flat-screen needed to be mounted on the wall, but I needed an extra pair of hands to help me get it centered properly. I still had to put my bookshelves together, and boxes of all my other shit were strewn all over the place. It wasn't the home I'd imagined I would once have. Although, even at twenty-five when I had last been home, I hadn't imagined much because I was on the road so often. I just wanted a place to put my boots and hang my hat, have a beer with my friends. I liked what my sister had done with her place, but she had an eye for design and knew what the hell she wanted.

I had no fucking clue.

Letting out a heavy sigh, I walked away from the damn couch, grabbed a soda from the fridge, and threw it back, trying to enjoy the cold feel of it as it coated my tongue and throat. I hated how quiet and lonely my house was. I needed a roommate or something, maybe a dog…just something to help with the silence.

I walked toward one of the windows and shoved it open, not caring that the air conditioning was blasting and all the cool air was going to escape.

Sounds of laughter and yelling filtered in from next door through my open window. I stared at my floor, listening, enjoying and hating the fact that my sister had relinquished her house to a bunch of kids. Now, I was stuck here, dealing with the sounds of some happy family living next door.

But at least it was noise against this chaotic silence. I closed my eyes and tried to picture my neighbors having fun. I'd seen a few kids hanging out, had seen the mom and her son riding the horse the other day, and from the way they looked, I knew they were one of those families that was disgustingly happy. Happiness was something I hadn't obtained in a long time, longer than I cared to think about, so I slid to the floor with my back against the wall and listened as the sounds of joy surrounded me, swallowed me up, and drowned me.

———

THE WYOMING SUN created a hazy heatwave in the outer pasture I had been staring at. My foot was lodged on the second bar of the fence as I heard, "Glad to have you back," and felt a strong clap on my shoulder. I turned to see Landon smiling at me, looking genuinely happy to see me.

I returned the smile in the same fake way I had been doing for the past month. "Good to be back." It was partly true. I missed being around horses, and honestly, I even missed my old boss. Landon had been the first guy to ever give me a job back when I was an eager teenager, hungry for money to enter as many rodeos as possible. He'd taught me a lot growing up, but being back here just felt like my nose was getting rubbed in the dirt.

Not worthy. Not whole. Not ready. Not forgiven.

"So, when do we get started with classes?" I scanned the paper attached to the clipboard I was holding and waited for Landon to clue me in. The deal had been that he'd start spreading the word that I was returning home and start some beginner classes so when I arrived, I'd have clients ready to go.

"You have about six students signed up, and three of them are siblings. They're going to need a consultation on how you want to work their appointments and if you want them to do shared time or not." Landon furrowed his white eyebrows and tucked his hands into his pockets. The man was getting up there in age, and it made me think about my dad. I wondered what he might look like if he were still alive.

I lightly slapped the clipboard and nodded my understanding. "Sounds good. When's the first consultation?" I moved around Landon and went to eye his latest breeding horse. He had the same forty acres he'd had when I was there ten years earlier. Yellow grassland rolled for as far as the eye could see, past his green pastures and grazing property. Landon Clayton was a wealthy man who just kept building his empire with breeding, boarding, training, and showing horses. He was the name on every tongue in Wyoming and most parts of Montana when people talked about where to buy a good horse or where to go to train one. His horses won titles and bred champions, or at least they had in the past. I hadn't kept up with him or his legendary equestrian empire after I traded my cowboy boots for a pair of business-appropriate loafers.

"Today if you're free," Landon said, spitting a wad of chew to the side. Spitting chew was as common as clearing your throat in this part of Wyoming, but I still hated it, mostly because my dad had died of lung disease. He'd smoked since he was a kid starting out on the rodeo circuit, and when he couldn't smoke, he chewed. The only time he didn't have some kind of tobacco in his mouth was when he slept at night.

"I'm free. The only thing I've got on the agenda is trying to settle in at the house," I said, taking my ball cap and swatting a few flies away from my face.

I left out the part where I had little time for much else since trying to forget my previous life and *her*.

"Great. Looks like you'll have an appointment in about an hour." Landon clapped my shoulder again and walked off. I watched him retreat and tipped my head to the sun.

This hadn't been in the plans.

This wasn't how it was supposed to go.

4

AVOIDANCE WAS A PETULANT GAME I WASN'T VERY GOOD AT. JUST THE same, I practiced it frequently and diligently, especially when it came to my next-door neighbor, the one I'd seen riding along the back fence of my property the previous week. It wasn't the first time I had to stop myself from thinking about her, which made me feel ten thousand times more pathetic than I already did.

The woman atop that black horse had been stunning. She had shiny blonde hair that went to her chest, and it had bounced off her back with every stride of her horse. The brown cowboy hat on top of her head had shadowed her face, but I had still been able to see that she was beautiful, and what I hadn't been able to see had left me curious for a closer glance.

Which was exactly why I'd avoided looking out my window or going outside except to walk to work this past week. I didn't need to get infatuated with some married woman. She had kids, more than one, and she was the kind of beautiful a man wouldn't leave on purpose. So, I was sure someone had locked that down.

I shook my head at how stupid I was being. Even if she was single, I wouldn't act on it, because I was a total clusterfuck and I needed to get my life together.

I laced up my tennis shoes, put on a baseball cap, grabbed a backpack for the groceries, stuffed my t-shirt in, and headed outside. If I was going to walk the twelve miles into town in the August heat, I was going shirtless.

I had the day off and needed to make this trip before the next day's clients came in. I'd met with one student the day before and things had gone well. I was a little rusty with being around horses and entirely out of practice with kids, so I needed to learn how to have patience and a little grace.

I let the screen door of my house snap behind me as I set out into the early morning sunshine. I could hear roosters crowing, letting the world know it was time to get up, and cows going on about being hungry and whatnot. I loved the ranch and all its sounds, always had. There were five or six close farms nearby, and I'd worked at each of them at one point in my life.

I heard the crunch of gravel under my shoes as I made my way toward the road, and I glanced over at my new neighbor's house. The black SUV was still there, but no other car. On the weekends, I occasionally saw a red truck, and a darker-haired woman in dark glasses would get out of it. I wondered where my neighbor's husband was.

As I was looking at the house, I saw movement on the front porch, and before I knew what was happening, a brown-haired little boy was running toward me, the same one who'd been on the horse the other day. He was a cute kid with blue eyes and a mop of dusty brown hair. He still had his little baby teeth, and as he got closer, I noticed a frog in his pocket. I stopped walking so we'd stay in view of his house.

"Hey mister neighbor, where you headed today with no shirt on?" he asked while squinting at the sun.

I laughed and looked back at his house. "I'm headed to town."

The little boy smiled and put his hands over his eyes to help block the sun. "You're gonna walk the entire way?" he asked, clearly surprised. I itched to look back at my truck but stayed focused on him instead.

"Yep," I answered, smiling down at him.

"Why?" He pulled at the frog in his pocket and I glanced at his house again, sure his mom or dad would come out any second and start yelling at me.

I also didn't want to tell this little kid about my issues with driving or why I couldn't hold a pair of keys in my hand without breaking down and needing a therapy appointment.

"It's a nice day." I shrugged, looking over his head.

"Cool. What's your name anyway?" the kid asked, still holding the frog tightly in his little hand.

"My name is Reid." I stuck my hand out for the little guy to shake, and he shook it as he said, "I'm Henley." I didn't want him to get in trouble, so I told him, "Better get back home before your mom or dad gets upset."

Henley looked back at his house and frowned. "I only have a mom. My daddy's in heaven." That brought me up short. I wanted to tell the little guy I was sorry, but I had no idea how fresh it was, so I figured it was better to leave it.

"Well better not worry your mom then."

He smiled at me and waved. "Bye Mister Reid. Have a good day and don't die from the sun on your walk."

I waved back then turned toward the road and kept on walking, trying hard not to think of the new information I'd received about his mother.

DOUGLAS WAS PRETTY MUCH EXACTLY how it had been ten years earlier, minus the few new paint jobs and smaller restaurants that had popped up here and there. A few of the playgrounds had finally updated their equipment, making the slide and chipped wood that used to adorn the spaces actually legal to play on now.

I had always loved this town. Small shops, old brick buildings, a few still had poles to tie horses up outside. That was the thing about small towns in Wyoming- everyone was country born. Even if they migrated, they caught on quick. There weren't skinny jean wearing men or women here. People wore clothes that kept them safe around horses and livestock. The smell of leather had filled my home growing up, from belts and boots to saddles. My dad had been a professional bull rider until an injury had him retiring at forty. My mother was thankful and said that injury likely saved their marriage because his frequent absence from my sister's life and mine had been a constant argument for them.

I didn't really dive too much into their marital issues. My dad had been good to me and Sarah, and here in Douglas, he had practically been royalty. If my mother had cared to keep their ranch or stay there, he still would have been, but time passed, and everyone's memory of Greg Harrison faded. Funny, it was me I wished they'd forget.

"Reid?" I heard someone call my name, causing me to turn in the middle of the sidewalk. I was just about to head to the barber to get a quick cut.

I squinted and saw a vaguely familiar figure running up to me.

"Reid Harrison, that you?" the guy asked through a huff of breath. It was Kip Burwell, one of my oldest friends.

I leaned forward without a thought and pulled him into a tight grasp. "It's been forever, man."

He leaned back with a big smile on his face. "Way too damn long. How ya been?"

Fucking horrible was right on the tip of my tongue, but I smiled and instead replied with, "Pretty good, just getting adjusted."

"I just moved back two years ago, so I get it." Kip smiled and started walking with me toward the barbershop. "You have a place around here?" he asked, his larger-than-life smile taking up his whole face. He still looked like my high school best friend, still had the same white-blond hair, blue eyes, and thick eyebrows. He just looked more grown into all those features now.

"Yeah, next to Sara's old spot." I nodded in return. I had learned that my sister had moved to Europe via text message from my cousin, Jed. That same text had told me I had new neighbors and to have fun. He'd been taking care of both our places for us while Sara and I were away.

Kip shoved his hands in his pockets and searched the ground.

"Well, shit, I hate fishin' for an invite, but I wouldn't mind catchin' up with ya, man." He laughed.

Shit.

"Yeah, of course. Come over any time. In fact, I could use some help hanging my flat-screen if you have the time."

"Yeah, I can come over this Friday." He clapped my shoulder then started walking backward. "Gotta run, see ya later man."

I smiled after him and turned toward the barbershop, which was connected to the Ride and Dye hair salon. The large glass window had an entire room full of eyes glued to it and absolutely no one working. I saw Star Shelling and gave her the side-eye as I moved past the window and toward the left side of the building. She gave me a weak wave and moved back to her station.

Fucking small towns.

THE WALK to and from town wasn't easy. I was tired—really tired. The sun had beaten down on me, and although I had soaked my shirt with water before I put it on for my journey back, I was hot. The added weight of groceries and ice on my back didn't help matters either. I got back home around dusk and was too tired to even make dinner. I put the food away and dozed off.

I didn't know how long I'd slept for, but I woke up to a dark house and the sound of thunder. It was loud and the trees were moving outside, swaying like they might fall down at any instant. The sound of doors slamming and horses whining had me sitting up and looking around in the dark. I heard it again and realized horses shouldn't be out in a storm like this, and the closest ones to me were my new neighbor's.

I stood up and looked around, not sure what to do. I was sure she had it under control, but the thunder was booming again, and the horses sounded more frantic. I went to the window and, in the dim light from the barn across the field, I could make out the black horse struggling against its reins as Henley's mom pulled for him to go into the barn. The horse kept resisting. More thunder sounded overhead, and a bolt of lightning struck somewhere in the field. *Shit.*

I threw on my work boots, shoved through my front door, and ran as fast as I could toward her house. I didn't care if she was a stranger and I should stay away—she needed help or they might both get killed. I made my way past her small yard and headed for the barn. She was still outside of it, pulling and pleading for the horse to follow her. Her hair was wild and blowing all over the place like a blonde tidal wave. She wore sleep shorts, an oversized sweatshirt, and flip-flops. *What the fuck is she doing?*

I cleared the fence and carefully headed toward the horse. I didn't even look at her as I gently pulled the reins from her hands, keeping my gaze on the big Arabian. I softly talked to him and tried to calm him, hoping another bout of thunder wouldn't scare him again. I carefully pet his neck and tried to soothe him as I also began leading him sternly so he knew I was in charge.

Henley's mom backed away toward the barn and opened the stall door for me. The horse started following me. He was still jumpy and had that crazy look in his eye, but he was following me.

"That's it, buddy. Come on in here, let's get you safe from the storm," I murmured. The horse took a few more steps until he was inside the barn. Carefully, I pulled him toward the only open stall and secured him. I quickly double-checked the stalls of the other two horses and then turned toward my neighbor.

She had her arms crossed over her chest, her face was wet from the rain, and her hair was matted to her cheeks. I wiped my hands on my jeans, suddenly nervous as I took a step toward her. Thunder boomed again, the rain pelted the roof of the barn, and a chill swept through the space between us.

"Thank you," she whispered.

I waited, biting back the thoughts I had running through my head about what in the hell she was doing with these horses.

"I'm Layla." Her soft voice broke through my reverie.

"Reid," I responded as I stared at her, still not sure what to say because she was way more beautiful up close and I hated myself for noticing.

"You must be Sara's brother, right?" She smiled, and my eyes homed in on her white teeth and how the smile lit up her face.

"Sorry, have we met? I've been gone for a while..."

She shook her head back and forth, stopping me. "No, I've just heard a bit about you from people in town," she muttered softly, biting on her lip and looking at the ground. She pulled her arms in tight around her middle and glanced over toward the black horse that had just nearly gotten away from her. "He doesn't listen to me on a good day, so I should have known it wasn't any use in a storm. I was about to just let him go before you showed up," she admitted weakly, changing the subject.

I threw my thumb toward the black beast in the stall. "This guy?"

She nodded. "Yeah, Thor. He's my son's horse and doesn't much care for me."

I put my hands in my pockets and let my eyes wander. They chose to scan Layla's bare legs, and finally, they landed on the purple flip-flops on her feet.

"He knows you don't know what you're doing," I said, gesturing toward her feet.

Her face went red as she followed my hand.

Shit. Probably shouldn't have said that.

"I mean, if you did, you'd know better than to have left him out in this storm, and your feet..." I gestured toward them again. *Why do I keep pointing at her feet?*

She cleared her throat. "Well, thanks for the help...I should be getting back." Her lips thinned and her eyes narrowed on me as she pointed her thumb over her shoulder.

"I'm not trying to be an asshole about it, it's just...*do you* know what you're doing?" I asked, still rubbing my neck. I was honestly curious. Her horses were expensive breeds, her barn looked immaculate...everything seemed to fit the picture, but she seemed like she was just playing a part.

"It's late...someone moved my shoes..." She trailed off, her gaze downcast.

Her defensive nature made me hate myself, and the reminder that her husband had died hit hard. Fucking damn, I shouldn't have been so mean.

"Look, sor—"

"Can you just go?" she asked, her inflection turning sharp and her eyes blazing.

Who was I to stand there and argue with a single mother in the middle of a lightning storm? Fucking no one.

"Yeah, sorry," I mumbled then turned around.

I almost expected her to stop me, maybe continue with the gratitude she had been leading with before I rudely stopped her, but she didn't. She watched me go with one lone tear slipping down her cheek and a look that should have killed me on the spot.

5

layla

THE STORM LASTED ALL NIGHT. IT SHOOK THE HOUSE AND MOVED THE trees and scared the children—all of them. So, I had a bed full of limbs and feet sticking out in every direction by morning. I was awake, glad to see the sun peeking through the shades. I needed to buy blackout curtains. One of these days, I'd actually remember.

Jovi's face was in my neck and Henley's feet were shoved into my ribs. Steven was over my feet, near the bottom, and Michael was snuggling Jovi. I let out the smallest sigh and prayed my bladder would just hang in there. My mind drifted to the previous night, to the kindness of my neighbor.

It had been a bad day. I'd taken a nap on the couch because I was exhausted. I had been painting Henley's room and my emotions were still pretty shattered from my big decision to move on for the sake of the kids. I'd planned to wake up and make dinner, put the horses away, and do everything else, but no one woke me. I assumed Michael had microwaved chicken strips and burritos for the kids and everyone put themselves to bed.

When I heard the first big clap of thunder, I shot up then looked at the clock and saw it was past ten. I was about to head upstairs when I heard a horse whining outside. To my horror, Thor wasn't put away and was running around the corral. I had no idea how Samson or Sugar Cube were put up or who'd put him in there instead of letting him graze in the pasture, but I thought surely Michael and Steven wouldn't leave their five-year-old brother's horse out just because he couldn't take care of it. Except they did. Just another reminder of how broken we were.

I pulled on a sweatshirt and angrily searched for my boots, remembering too late that Jovi had taken them to the front to water the yard earlier in the day. Panicked and out of options, I grabbed my flip-flops and ran outside. Of course, Thor wouldn't budge. He was scared, and he hated me more than anyone. I was terrified and was sure both of us were going to get hit by lightning. Then I saw him, my neighbor, running toward me, and I didn't even have time to feel anything but relief.

My arms were shaky when he took the reins, and I gladly moved out of the way. I'd have to take a thunder and lightning training course from Michelle the next time she came because Reid was right —I didn't know what I was doing. Sure, it hurt to hear it, but it was the truth, and I couldn't hold that against someone who clearly knew how to handle horses. Still, he didn't have to say every single thing that popped into his head.

While we stood under the lights of the barn, I noticed Reid's eyes were green, set under brown eyebrows, and framed by a firm face and a strong jaw. I wasn't buried too far under grief to notice he was handsome. I remembered how he'd looked shirtless that evening on his porch, and although the shirt he'd been wearing last night was loose-fitting, I had still been able to see the veins in his forearms.

I PUSHED my eyes closed as the feeling of guilt washed over me at noticing how attractive Reid was. I felt like I was betraying Travis, cheating on him somehow. Tears began to build at the corners of my eyes. Travis was gone, and I needed to cope and come to terms with it. I could appreciate good-looking men, even if said good-looking men were assholes and didn't deserve the admiration. It was a small step, but it was one I could take. I hated that Reid was helping me move past this tiny hurdle when I'd have preferred to just throw it at his head. I supposed it had to be someone.

From somewhere in my room, the sound of a wind chime went off. I blinked and slightly turned my head to the left. It chimed again. One of the kids rustled near my feet but stayed put. It was probably my sister texting me, but my phone was lost to the disaster that had been the night before. I hadn't plugged it in, didn't even know where it was.

I closed my eyes, desperate for just a little bit more sleep, but the chime went off again.

And again.

Three more times in succession, which had me furiously clawing my way out of the pile of limbs I was buried under.

For fuck's sake.

Small groans and a quiet yelp emanated from the pile as I pushed into someone's leg to get up and tugged on Jovi's hair. Finally free, I stood and looked around the room as more chimes went off.

Who the hell is texting me?!

I eyed the pile of clothes in my oversized chair near the window and darted toward it as more fucking chimes sounded. Someone was going to die.

I shoved two sweatshirts to the side and finally pulled the phone free. Pressing the side button, I brought the screen to life and found I had a dozen or so notifications. I swiped my thumb up and narrowed my eyes as I looked at the number.

It wasn't one I had in my phone, nor had I ever texted or called it before. I sat down and began scrolling through each text that had come through.

Hey! It's Star from the hair place
You remember me, right?
I cut your hair
Anyway, of course you remember me
I wanted to let you know I'm offering to cut kids' hair for free before school starts.

Well, the whole salon is, but since I cut your hair and I'm now your stylist, I wanted to invite you.

So, text me back and let me know when you want your kids scheduled

Did that seem too pushy?

I keep getting told I'm too pushy

Well that's what my ex says, but he's a piece of work

Anyway...sorry, yeah. Text me back

Or call the salon phone

Her antics made me smile. I had totally forgotten that the kids would need haircuts and new school clothes before the end of August. I had originally planned to just go to Casper back when I did remember things like this and planned things out. I'd been planning to do all of that stuff with Michelle, but free haircuts would save me about forty dollars plus tip, so I was absolutely going to take her up on it.

I smiled as I punched in my response.

Hey, thank you for reaching out. We can come as soon as tomorrow if that works?

She replied instantly.

Yep, that's perfect, just bring them all and we will work them all in

I smiled, thankful she'd reached out, thankful I had finally, maybe, possibly made a friend? I wasn't sure if she was one; as a thirty-four-year-old, it was more difficult now than it had been in middle school to gauge females and friendship.

Either way, it made me feel happy, like we were taking steps in the right direction.

"WE'RE HEADING out in a few minutes." I sorted a few papers in front of me while talking to Michael. He'd been a bit of jerk since breakfast, and because of what I had planned for him, I was on edge.

"Okay, have fun." He gave me a two-finger salute and sauntered toward the couch.

I turned toward and him and planted a hand on my hip, "not so fast."

He faltered mid-step, turned on his heel and gave me a quizzical look.

I stepped forward, "you've got some work to do, while we're gone."

Those serious eyes lowered to slits, "what is that supposed to mean?"

"Exactly what I said. Thor could have been seriously hurt last night." I jutted my chin out in the most serious form of authority I could muster and stepped closer.

"I was asleep, which meant you were in charge. I can't believe you didn't put him away last night."

"It's not my stupid horse or my job!" He yelled, throwing his arms wide.

Lord help me.

"It is your job!" I yelled back.

Hurt flickered in his hardened gaze as he took in my posture and raised voice. I hadn't yelled or really done in parenting in a year, so this was new for both of us.

"You were in charge, Michael. I counted on you. While we're gone, you need to bathe Thor, refresh his oats and let him out in the big pasture." I paused, while Michael registered everything.

"That all?" He quipped rudely.

"No that's not all, then you can wash out his stall."

"You've got to be joking me. I did everything else last night!" He yelled, with his face turning pink.

"And I appreciate that, except that Jovi said she made her and Henley's chicken nuggets last night. So no, you didn't. Have it done by the time we get back." I walked away from my angry son and went outside. I hated fighting with him and this new existence where he hated me and his life. I didn't know how to fix it and it terrified me.

6

Layla

PART OF BEING A GROWNUP WAS SWALLOWING YOUR PRIDE AND DOING things you didn't want to do. At least that was what I was telling myself over and over again as I turned onto the gravel road leading to Landon's ranch. Jovi, Henley, and Steven were all glued to a window, looking, watching, waiting for what was next.

None of them knew I had met their teacher the previous night, and none of them knew I currently hated him. All they knew was that I had planned for them to get some horse-riding classes set up. Today was our first consultation where we'd figure out if Reid wanted all the kids at once or if he'd prefer to work with them individually.

I put my blinker on and turned down a large asphalt driveway. Steel railing lined either side of the path, fencing in the beautiful horses who were grazing in the large pastures that preluded the estate Landon's farm sat on. *Sweet baby Jesus.* He was made of money, that much was clear. The house, if you wanted to call it that, looked like a log cabin mansion. With a dark green metal roof and a wraparound porch, it looked like it had about fifty bedrooms. A large fountain sat in front of his round driveway, and next to his house were several nice barn-like structures. All had the same look and feel as the house, just with different materials.

It was beautiful, and I found myself leaning forward, trying to take in as much of it as I could.

"Is this where our lessons are going to be?" Henley asked from the back seat. I couldn't tear my eyes away from the beautifully landscaped driveway and the path leading around each large barn and arena.

"Yes baby, this is it," I whispered, turning toward the designated area shown on the map Reid had emailed me a few days earlier. I should have known then this was going to be beyond gorgeous. Anyone who needs a map for their estate is definitely a big deal. The area the kids would be practicing in was a small round pen, and a brown horse was already tacked up inside. I didn't see Reid but knew it was the right place, so I put the car in park.

I sat back and looked over at my eleven-year-old, who had pursed lips and a deep scowl on his tiny face. He would be starting middle school, but he still looked so young, so innocent. I turned my neck and tried to gauge how Jovi was doing; she was staring at her nails, refusing to even engage with this new plan.

A knock on my driver side window had me snapping back to the front and staring down the one man I was hoping to avoid. In some strange alternate universe, I'd thought I could drop my kids at a registration booth, like daycare, and avoid this awkward interaction. I let out a slow exhalation and opened my door.

Reid was wearing a pair of dirty Wranglers that molded to his thighs like something sinful and delicious, something men shouldn't be allowed to wear. *Eat your heart out, skinny-jean-wearing men of America—country boys have you beat.*

"Layla, did you hear me?" Reid's voice drew my gaze back up to his. Had I been staring at his thighs?

My face heated, and I cleared my throat. "Um, sorry. Hi. No. What?" I muttered like an idiot and tucked hair that wasn't loose behind my ear, making me look like I was blabbering and incoherent.

What is happening?

Reid let out an innocent chuckle and ran his large hand over his chin, scraping at the day-old growth there. "Just wanted to say hey and ask if your kids were going to get out of the car or not?" He peered around me, toward the car, where my kids were still buckled in. I gave Steven a look that said *Get the hell out here*, but he just shook his head and hit the automatic locks.

Shit.

"Um, they just need a few seconds." I tried to recover, but Reid was already laughing, shaking his head.

"They don't want to do this?"

"Not exactly…" I looked back at my traitorous kids.

"Look, Layla…I want to help, but if the kids aren't interested, it's not going to work. Maybe if you give them another year or try doing personal lessons with the horses you have at home…?" He grabbed his neck and tugged.

My heart sank, and I began grasping at thin, breakable straws, totally desperate and infinitely confused.

"They want to be here, trust me." I stepped closer to the car, trying to open it. I thankfully had the keys and hit unlock, grabbing the handle just as Steven hit lock again.

Dammit.

My eyes went huge as I glared at my son, who was giving me an evil smirk, one that made him look like he was starring in some horror movie. Reid chuckled again, and I snapped—from the weight of the last week, from being social at the salon and facing all those new people, from looking like an idiot and being embarrassed in front of this man not even a full twenty-four hours earlier. I snapped from all of it.

"Look." I stepped forward, forcing Reid to take a step back. "My kids need this. They need the horses for therapy, but they haven't been around them enough to actually want to ride them. They can't get therapy and heal from losing their dad if they don't get on the horses, and as you so kindly pointed out last night, I don't know what the fuck I'm doing!" My voice was paper-thin after screaming all that at him. He was looking around, turning red. A few workers had walked from the barn toward where we were standing, and the kids suddenly exited the vehicle.

My eyes were watering, and my hands were shaking. I was so angry I literally couldn't see straight. Why was everyone so willing to give up on us? Why was it so easy for the rest of the world to just close the book on my family? I thought of the judge who'd failed us. I thought of how I'd had to come up with the money for the funeral because the life insurance company wouldn't release the funds. I hated how pathetic it made me feel.

I felt like I was clawing my way out from a six-foot-deep grave, trying to make people hear me.

"Uh-oh...Mommy used her mad voice," Henley quietly whispered from his spot near the car.

Reid had his hands raised like he was trying to talk someone down from a narrow ledge. That'd be me, the out-of-control mom who'd just screamed at the innocent bystander. Shame swam through me, fresh and potent.

I blinked and turned toward my kids. "Come on, back in the car. This wasn't a good idea, and we need to go." The kids listened, piling back in as Reid stalked closer to us.

"Hang on a sec. Please. Just…" he tried to cut in, but I stopped him.

"No, it's fine. You're right. We'll just try something else." I shut the back-passenger door and climbed into the driver seat, but before I could close my door, Reid's hand stopped it.

"Look, I'm sorry. Please…can we just start over? From yesterday, today…all of it?" The kind of green like when the sun hits the top of a tall evergreen reflected in his desperate eyes. His dark brown hair was soft, feathery, and fell across his forehead, hitting just at the eyebrows. He was handsome, and it made the fire in my veins burn hotter, angrier.

I tugged on my door as hard as I could and Reid's hand slipped free just in time, but his eyes went wide just the same. I backed out of the pristine property and drove home broken, hurting, and alone.

Just like I'd been for the past year.

"Dammit, fucking, shit," I cursed as the stepstool I was standing on toppled over, nearly causing my ankle to roll. I lay on my carpet, trying not to cry. I could do this. I could measure my window for blackout shades without asking for help and without fucking crying.

I needed them, so badly. The sun was breaking into my room every single morning, interrupting my precious sleep, and lately, I'd been getting none at all, so at six AM, I was desperate for it.

"Mom, you okay?" Michael walked into my bedroom, surveying me on the floor with a quizzical lift of his brow.

"Yeah, I'm fine." I groaned as I sat up and rubbed my butt. "What can I help you with, son?"

"Nothing, it's just our neighbor is on the phone. He wanted to talk to you." Michael held the cordless phone toward me without covering the speaker. I violently waved my hands, trying to convey that he should say I wasn't available and didn't want to talk. Everyone knows this gesture. Everyone who ever used a cordless phone growing up knows if your parent waves at you silently like that, you better damn well stay quiet and walk out of the room.

Everyone except my son, apparently.

He leaned his head to the side and loudly asked, "What?"

I made an awkward facial expression, putting my finger to my mouth for him to be quiet. Then I slid it across my throat and pointed it at him to threaten his life if he said anything else.

"Mom, what in the world are you doing?" he asked again, somehow louder this time. *Damn these kids and their lack of cordless phone use!* I decided I would be taking his cell phone and forcing him to learn this shit.

Or maybe my son was still rebelling from having to spend the day working and being around Thor. This was some kind of bullshit payback.

I finally gave up, snagged the phone from him, and waved him out.

I wasn't proud of what I was about to do, but I wasn't mature enough to deal with Reid. So, I put the phone to my ear, tightly closed my eyes, cleared my throat, made sure my voice matched the same pitch as my son's, and said, "She's not here right now," then hung up.

It was childish, but so was the way he'd acted. He was stupid, and I had things to do. I eyed my tall windows and glared at the stepstool. *I can do this.*

7

Reid

"HAVE YOU EVER EVEN DONE THIS BEFORE?" KIP ASKED AS WE LIFTED the sixty-five-inch flat-screen together.

I laughed and let out a little scoff. "Of course, I have."

I hadn't actually ever mounted and set up my own flat-screen. In college, we hadn't had one, and when I was on my own, I'd just used my laptop for everything because I didn't have much time for relaxing and watching anything. That or I'd go over to a friend's house. When I had lived with *her*, we'd paid someone to set everything up for us.

Kip angled the television toward the wall and peeked behind it to ensure we were lining it up properly. "I don't know, this seems off."

Shit.

He was probably right, but I was determined to get this thing hung up. I'd even duct-tape it to the wall if I had to. I needed a distraction from everything that had happened with Layla the night before and earlier in the afternoon.

The sound of metal sliding against metal filled the small, cramped space behind the television, and I could feel relief swim through me. "There, see?" I stood back and beamed at my friend. "It's perfect." I walked toward the kitchen, clapping him on the back as I passed. I pulled open the door of my refrigerator and snagged two glass bottles of soda. "Thanks for coming over to help me, man." I handed one over then veered for the couch.

Kip followed and landed in the chair next to the sofa. I saw him eyeing the bottle with a small lift of his brow, but he didn't say anything about it not being a beer.

"No problem. I'm glad we ran into each other the other day, man." He tilted his head back, taking a swig.

The need to make some kind of attempt at friendship had me asking, "So what have you been up to since high school?"

Kip tipped his drink back. "Well, I've been doing a ton of construction. Did some online courses for business, was an apprentice for welding and whatnot…I guess a little bit of everything."

I smirked and tossed a small baggie of screws we hadn't used to the side. "No wife, kids…dog?"

Kip laughed, running a hand down his chin. "Nah. Guess it never really worked with anyone, but I'm not against trying. Just haven't found the right person yet. What about you? You show up here, ten years later, looking like an abandoned puppy—what's your story?"

I smirked, trying to make light of his question, but it struck a chord with me.

"You know how it goes…tried my hand at the big business thing, tried my hand at a serious relationship, and it all blew up pretty spectacularly, so I thought I'd try coming back, get a new perspective," I admitted weakly. I may have kept a few details out of my explanation, but I was surprised by my honesty.

"I'm sorry, man. That sucks." Kip winced, tipping his bottle back again. The silence hung for a few seconds before he sat up to reengage. "So, were you going to tell me the deal with that phone call?" He smiled at me over the rim of his bottle. He was referring to the phone call I'd made to Layla, trying to apologize. Kip had laughed like hell when I told him how she pretended to be her son, only to hang up on me.

"She's my neighbor. I met her for the first time last night, and we had a shit start to things." I let out a heavy sigh, tipping my bottle back. I stared at my blank wall, trying to ignore the shit-eating grin on my friend's face.

"And?" He leaned forward, the bottle resting in just one hand. He sported a pair of worn jeans and a threadbare shirt, a change from when I'd known him in high school. Nearly every single day he had donned tight Wranglers and a collared shirt that was always tucked in, and on his head would be a big cowboy hat. Even between classes, he'd carry the hat and wear it on breaks. We were all cowboys, essentially, even the asshole football players to a degree, but if you went and made a big show of it, they'd let you know and make you feel it with one of their testosterone-induced methods.

"*And* nothing. Her kids were supposed to start lessons today out at Landon's, but I put my foot in my mouth with that too and now she's pissed at me...hates me...I don't know." I shrugged, trying to let it go.

Kip smiled, and I could see how much he'd changed. Nearly an entire lifetime had passed between when I'd left and now. I had left for college, returning off and on while my parents still lived there, but when Dad died, everything changed. I hadn't set foot back in this town since I was twenty-five. It had been ten years, even with my sister living there. I'd meet her at Mom's in Crescent, or she'd come visit me, but I just couldn't come back after Dad passed. It hurt too much.

"Well, why does it bother you so much if you just met her?" Kip asked with a tilt to his head and a stupid grin on his face.

I liked that we could just fall back into an easy friendship after all this time. I hadn't kept in touch with anyone after I left. I had social media to a degree, used the marketplace thing every now and then, but *she* had essentially done all our social media for the both of us, so I never looked up old friends, or even family, for that matter.

"I don't know...it bugs me, I guess. She's a single mom, lost her husband, and she has a bunch of kids. I don't like being an asshole to someone who's already havin' a hard time with things." I stared ahead and scrunched my nose as I thought over what had transpired between Layla and me.

"Then you should try again, but maybe make it to where she

doesn't have the chance to hang up on you," Kip offered, moving to stand. He walked back toward my dining room and surveyed the mess. "Let's get these bookshelves set up while I'm here, so if you end up having any company, it doesn't look like you're a squatter."

I laughed and stood. "I don't plan on having any company any time soon."

"You probably said the same thing before you asked my sorry ass over here." Kip laughed, set his bottle down, and moved toward the flat box on the floor that held my unassembled bookshelves. I heaved a sigh and headed toward the table where my tools were. He was right; I'd had no plans to let anyone into my house—or my life—but there he was, and I was already mentally throwing around ideas for how I could open the door for my neighbor to be a part of it too.

I MESSED with the collar on my shirt six times before changing my mind and just taking it off and pulling on a loose t-shirt. I didn't need to look fancy or nice; there was no need to dress up. At six, I walked across my yard, the late afternoon sun touching everything nearby, and headed toward my sister's house—except it wasn't her home anymore, and I needed to get used to that. I thought about my sister and wondered why I still hadn't heard anything from her. It bothered me that she hadn't reached out, but after the fight we'd had, I supposed I wasn't surprised. I just thought after everything, she'd call.

The large wraparound porch was full of toys and dirt pies. I smiled at the evidence of life being lived over there. Sarah would have loved it. I took a steadying breath and knocked on the white door, praying Layla would answer it and not slam it in my face. I owed her an apology...I owed all of them one. The comedy from her fake voice and hang-up still hung in my throat with a chuckle dying to be let loose. Now at her door, I swallowed that laugh and sobered with the realization that she might slam this door in my face as soon as she saw me. I really didn't want her to reject me. My stomach twisted uncomfortably as I thought back to what had brought me back home to

Wyoming, what I was running from, why I shouldn't have been getting close to anyone with kids… This was all a fucking bad idea.

The door opened and standing there in just some shorts and a backward baseball cap was Henley. I grinned and held out my hand. "Hey, buddy."

He smiled and pulled the door open farther, revealing the entryway. Instead of horse paintings and tackle like my sister used to keep, there were jackets, about a thousand pairs of shoes, and a few hats. It was mildly organized, but there were dirt prints everywhere.

"Hey, Mr. Reid…you want to come in and talk to my mama?" Henley tipped his head back and squinted at me.

"Yeah, is she here?"

He nodded, his floppy hair moving back and forth. "She's here… tryin' to barbeque burgers with no tank stuff."

He opened the door wider for me to walk in, but I felt awkward about just barging into her house.

"It's okay, Mama says we can let in people we trust, and you're s'posed to be our horse teacher, which means we can trust ya, right?" Henley argued, lifting his tiny shoulder, making all kinds of logical sense.

I chuckled and followed him through the house but still made sure he knew, "Buddy, that only works if your mom is home. If she's not, it doesn't matter who's at the door—you can't let them in your house."

The living room was exactly as I remembered, except now there was hardwood through the entire space and a large island separating the rooms. There was a huge, light-colored, wraparound couch with several accent pillows neatly organized along each section. A large-screen TV and smaller accent chairs framed the rest of the living room. The place was nicely decorated, and it felt full and warm, happy. I saw a few other children milling about, but once they spotted me, they all stopped moving.

There was a boy a bit older than Henley who had dark brown hair and was wearing a Batman shirt. He was the one who'd kept hitting the lock button in the car yesterday. Another boy, much taller, was in the kitchen, and he didn't look very happy to see me while he munched on a piece of cheese. A small girl, a few years older than Henley, made her way over from the laundry room, and she looked just like her mother.

"Come on, you son of a bitch! How on earth am I supposed to cook these burgers without propane?" Layla threw something down on the porch, and I heard her yelling through the screen door. She didn't know I was there, so I took a second to watch her through the open door.

Her light hair was tucked back into a loose braid, and she wore a baggy, gray, off-the-shoulder shirt with a pair of shorts that showed off those damn legs again. Her bare feet padded along the porch as she made her way inside, holding a tray of red, uncooked burgers.

Her face was pulled tight, each muscle twitching with frustration and her thin eyebrows drawn in tight. For some reason, that look hit me like an arrow to the chest. She wore grief like a heavy coat soaked in water. It was so similar to the tense feelings I carried around on my shoulders. I wanted to remove the burden, to take the coat off and help her breathe again.

When she saw me, she froze in place. Anger twisted her lips to the side and had her brown eyes narrowing on me.

I cleared my throat and held up the flowers I'd brought. "I come in peace." It was the only thing I could think to say. I knew she hated me, but at the moment, I really didn't want her to.

I wanted to see her smile. I wanted to see her laugh and see some of that weight lift from her shoulders.

She took one hesitant step forward and then another.

"I wanted to apologize to you and to the kids." I rushed the words out, not sure if she was going to let me speak or not. The kids were all bug-eyed, staring at me in awe. Layla's eyes transitioned to something normal, and an exasperated breath was released from her lungs. She walked toward the island and set the patties down, wiped her hands, and turned toward me.

"Fine, go ahead...say you're sorry. Not sure it will do you much good." She sighed and kicked one leg over another.

I eyed the pan of burgers and smiled. "What if I offered to cook those for you?"

She eyed them and me, bouncing back and forth between the two. "What do you mean?"

"I have propane and a barbeque that works. You all are welcome to come over and eat there, with me. Let me apologize properly and feed you." I swallowed, oddly hoping she accepted but also silently praying she didn't. She was so fucking pretty. I hated that my body was so alert to her.

She looked at her kids, blinked, looked at the floor, and let out a heavy sigh. "I'm only saying yes because we're starving, and I have no more dinner ideas or time to figure something out."

"I'll take it." I smiled and headed toward the pan of patties so she couldn't back out.

———

"So, you guys move here recently then?" I asked with my back to Layla. She was sipping on a soda while sitting in a wicker chair and watching her kids play horseshoes. I tried to ignore how each time she pressed her pink lips to the rim of the bottle, I felt the need to clear my throat and adjust my pants.

"Umm, yeah, I guess it's been about six months now."

"Hmm, interesting," I replied while flipping the burgers over. The sound of sizzling grease and laughter surrounded us as the kids played beyond the porch.

I waited to see if Layla would engage with me, and I guess her curiosity won out because she perked up and asked, "Why is that interesting?"

I turned for a second and gave her a side smile. "Just trying to figure out the timeline for when my sister moved. She didn't say anything about packing up and leaving the only home she's ever wanted, so I'm just surprised is all." I moved to the side to grab the cheese slices and carefully laid one on each patty.

"You haven't heard from her then?" Layla asked, concern in her tone.

"Not yet, and I've been back for a bit." I shut the lid of the barbeque and turned toward her.

Her lips thinned, and her pointer finger danced on the arm of her chair. "What about before you moved back?"

I blinked, looked up at the sky, and thought about it, but thankfully I didn't have to answer as I was saved by a fight breaking out between Steven and Michael. They began shoving each other, yelling loudly.

Layla stood to stop them, but I interrupted by yelling, "Food's done. Everyone come and get it!"

"No way!" Henley said in awe while moving his legs under his butt to sit taller.

I smiled while snagging a kettle chip. "Yes, sir. I won quite a few buckles in my time."

"Could you teach me?" Henley shouted, excitement bursting from him.

Layla sputtered as she took a sip of water and started coughing. I leaned over and gently patted her back to help clear her airways, but as soon as I touched her, I thought of hugging her. I thought of what it would feel like to wrap my arms around her shoulders, what it would be like to have her head tucked under my chin and her small hands go around my waist... *What the hell is wrong with me?*

I sat up and cleared my throat. "Little man, I'd be happy to show you some horse tricks, but the rodeo circuit will have to wait until you're a bit older," I explained, hoping to save Layla's nerves but also show her I wasn't a moron when it came to kids, show her I could be trusted. *Why the hell does that matter?*

All night Henley had been peppering me with questions about growing up in Wyoming. Rodeo seemed to be the most common topic that came up, and it enthralled him and Steven.

I'd apologized to everyone, although the kids hadn't seemed to know what I'd done wrong. I offered to work with them and their horses, separate from Landon's ranch, for free.

Layla argued, demanding I get paid, but I just shook my head and said I'd reserve time every day to come over and work with them. I won her over when I explained that it'd build more of a connection between the kids and their horses if we did it there instead of at Landon's.

Michael seemed uninterested and kept to himself. Jovi asked a few questions about horse training and whether or not girls were allowed to compete in the rodeo. When I talked about barrel racing and rodeo queens and how I'd dated one back in my day, Jovi lit up like a damn Christmas tree.

"Could you show me how to rodeo with Thor?" Henley begged.

"Yeah, and Samson too?" Steven added. These kids were funny. They made the heaviness in my chest feel lighter.

I glanced over at Layla, silently asking for permission to train her boys. She flicked her brown eyes to mine then to her sons' and deflected.

"Boys, let's take it a day at a time. I'm sure Mr. Reid has work and other things to do, so let's be respectful of his time. In fact, it's getting late, so we should probably head back home." She moved to stand up and started gathering the plates that were scattered around the table.

"Don't worry about those. I can get them," I said, standing and grabbing a few plates myself.

"I don't mind. In fact, we should wash these real quick," she said, looking over at the kids, encouraging them to offer to clean up too.

"I'll wrap up the food." Steven headed toward the kitchen.

"I'll grab the fridge stuff and put it away." Jovi snagged the ketchup and mayo from the table.

"No, please—I insist. You provided amazing burgers, and I can't let you clean these. Get the kids to bed and I'll see ya around," I said, hoping she'd let it go. The later it got, the harder it was for me not to feel like this was normal.

"Okay, if you're sure." She smiled while pulling on Henley's hand to help him down and push him toward his shoes.

I watched her movements, and for the smallest second, there was a sign of indecisiveness that flashed across her face. It was so fast I almost missed it. Her lips thinned, those eyes narrowed on mine, and then it was gone.

"It's completely fine. Thank you again for the company and the dinner. It can get lonely out here." I dipped my head and headed toward the kitchen.

Jovi walked out and headed for her shoes. Michael opened the front door and was swallowed by the night as he grabbed Jovi's hand and stepped outside.

I followed them as they all followed Michael's lead.

Layla and I hung back a few feet, walking side by side as the warm breeze brushed through the trees and rustled our hair.

"I really am sorry, Layla. I was an asshole for saying anything about the horses and for suggesting you wait with lessons. I hope you can forgive me..." I stammered, nervous as hell that she'd shut me down.

We continued to stroll toward her house as the kids crested her porch and went inside the house.

I swallowed, hoping to draw on some courage, and continued. "If you need anything...anything at all, please reach out and ask. In fact..." I stopped in my tracks, pausing our conversation and forcing her to stop with me.

It was dark out, but the light from her porch and mine casted enough shadow that she could see my movements. I searched her features for any hints of forgiveness, but she just kept that perfectly straight poker face in place, brown eyes engaged, pink lips thinned, arms tight across her chest. I dug my hand into the pocket of my jeans, hoping for some phantom bravery as I handed her a piece of paper.

"Here's my number, just in case you have a horse emergency or something."

I carefully watched her as she looked at my outstretched hand and the small white piece of paper pinched between my fingers. I swallowed the lump of nerves that had gathered in my throat and stretched my hand out to offer the olive branch. Her warm fingers grazed mine as she accepted the scrap of paper.

Her eyes focused on her fingers as she muttered a tiny, "Thank you, Reid."

Her lips pushed together, not smiling but not frowning either. She gave me a slight nod and then flicked her gaze to her door.

She turned away from me and headed inside, leaving me staring after her, wondering what on earth I'd just offered and how big of a mistake it might have been.

8

Layla

"I don't want a buzz cut, Mom," Steven argued from his seat in the salon.

Star clicked her tongue as she ran her fingers through his hair. "No one said anything 'bout a buzz cut, kid."

I watched my son in the mirror and tried to gauge his frustration. "Why do you think that's what you're getting?" I asked, curious why that was his first response when he got set up in Star's chair. Henley had gone, and Jovi too, so it was just him and Michael left, but my oldest argued that he had his own money and would go next door to the barbershop. Apparently, only women went to salons, in his opinion. For the moment, I ignored it, because the last thing I wanted was a public argument with my teenage son.

Steven shrugged his small shoulders, lowered his gaze, and said, "Dad always said if someone roped you into a free haircut, run away because they're just going to buzz cut it." His blue eyes slowly drifted up to mine in the mirror. I was quick to adjust my face, putting on a smile instead of a depressed scowl. Of course Travis had told him that, because he was joking. Travis only ever joked, and Lord knew how many other lies his kids were carrying with them because of it. Just one more reminder that life isn't fair. No one is supposed to die before they watch their kids grow up and have the opportunity to clear up all the half-truths they fed them in their youth.

Thankfully, Star covered for me. "Steven, baby, I would never ruin this gorgeous head of hair with a buzz cut. I was thinking we shave the sides a bit and keep it longer on top." She started spritzing his hair with her water bottle.

He quirked an eyebrow as he asked, "Kind of like Hawk in the new Avengers movie?"

She laughed again, her red hair falling off her shoulder with the movement. "Exactly like him."

He smiled his acceptance and she got to work. It was a slow day at Ride and Dye, and I couldn't have been more grateful for it. Henley and Jovi took my phone to watch Netflix while huddled on a bench near the entrance, leaving me sitting near Steven while he got his cut.

"So, how's it going with your new neighbor?" Star asked quietly while she pulled out her tools. Black cords and clipper accessories were tossed on the counter as she eyed the sizes of each one then tilted Steven's head a bit.

"It's fine." I shrugged, feeling awkward about the topic of Reid. I didn't know why, except that I had accepted his number and that made me feel strange.

I couldn't figure out if it was because we'd had a social meal without Travis, or if I'd just enjoyed the company of another man and felt like I had basically spit on my husband's grave by doing it. Either way, I felt off, and my brain and heart told me the only way to rectify it would be to stay away from Reid.

Star peeked at me from over her shoulder. "Fine?" Her tone implied she knew there was more to it than that.

I shrugged again, like an idiot. "Yeah…I mean we had a rocky start, but he's starting to teach the kids and that's fine."

My face flushed with how clumsily my words were coming out. I felt like a fawn getting used to its new pair of legs.

Star moved around the chair to start buzzing the other side of Steven's hair. "When's the last time you got out and had some fun?" Her subject change made me feel even worse, as though my awkwardness was so obvious it was practically a large red arrow saying *This is way worse than the topic of a man—help her!*

"Um, I don't really get out much," I mumbled, feeling heat creep up my neck. *Details.*

Star turned off the clippers and straightened, eyeing me again and then moving to the top of Steven's hair.

"Hmmm, might have to fix that." She didn't look at me as she said it, just kept going with my son's haircut. For whatever reason, it made me feel like sagging in my chair with relief. She'd had the opportunity to flick a judgmental glance at me and write me off, but instead, she decided to reach out and offer me a hand up.

I nodded my agreement because deep down I knew I needed it. I wanted it. I hated how broken I felt, and I'd have given nearly anything to feel whole again, even if that meant I had to push myself into uncomfortable social situations.

THE KIDS all had beautiful hair. Michael had gotten a simple, classy trim at the barbershop, making him look like an extra in some fifties film. His brown hair was slicked over, with just a little taken off on each side and his neck lined up nicely. Steven had the best hair out of everyone, and the second Michael saw it, I noticed a small twitch in his lips. He kept looking at it until he finally said, "Didn't know she could do styles like that or I would have stayed."

I smiled and laughed to myself, because what he'd done was misogynistic, and I hoped he'd learned his lesson. We were settling in for the evening when I heard a knock on my door. My guard was down, and I was unprepared for the sight of who was on my doorstep.

Reid, wearing a tight navy-blue t-shirt and worn jeans with a baseball hat snug on his head, had me backpedaling and feeling like a fool. I had set my sights on ignoring the man, but as he stood there with one hand in his pocket and a gorgeous grin on his face, I found myself stammering awkwardly while I tried to figure out exactly what excuse I had in my arsenal to get some distance from him.

"Reid is here!" Henley beamed, running up and pushing me to the side. Steven ran up behind him, both kids looking so eager to see him.

"Jovi, Reid is here! Time for lessons!" Steven yelled behind us, and the instant sounds of thumps down the stairs had me opening the door wider. They were excited, happy even, for the first time in a year. They had smiles on their faces and a genuine excitement about something. Reid walked in and followed the kids through the back door, where they began their lessons.

I stood against a fence post in jeans, boots, and a cowboy hat as I watched him talk to the kids about the basics of horse care.

"We learned this already from our Aunt Shellie," Henley said, blinking.

Reid smiled down at him and patted Samson's side. "That may be true, but we're going to be learning how to talk, communicate, and bond. So, we need to touch base on the basics. You need to know how to brush them, not because you have to, but because it benefits them. Think of them as your friend, your partner, someone you want to see healthy and strong. It will change your mindset."

The kids agreed and went through some basic care functions with each horse. It was slow going, but they each seemed to have smiles glued to their faces once they were done. Jovi's disappeared quickly, but it had been there just the same.

"That went well," I said kindly to Reid as he rolled the rope around his arm, getting it secured to be put away.

He looked up at me and smiled. "Yeah…you've got some good kids, Layla." He walked into the barn and I followed, trying my hand at adulting and discussing schedules with him.

Hands shoved into my back pockets, I watched as he settled Samson back into his stall and refilled his oats. It was oddly peaceful to watch him care for them. He looked happy, content, like caring for horses was his natural state of being.

"So, about the schedule for the kids," I started, but Reid cut me off by changing the subject.

"What about you?" He tilted his head up, his baseball cap covering his hair, except for just a few pieces that had fallen free from under the rim. His firm jaw was set, and those green eyes were blazing with curiosity.

I shut my mouth and took a step backward. "What?"

"What about your lessons? *Your* therapy?" He turned toward Thor's stall and clicked it open. "Come on, let's get you tacked up. I want to show you a few things," Reid suggested.

I looked around, not sure I'd heard him correctly. "Um…no. I don't really have any plans to ride, except with Henley."

Reid laughed. "That'll never work. These kids are taking their cues from you, on how to move on, how to smile, laugh…they'll look to you on how to ride and care for the horses too."

Shit. He was right.

I brought my hands out from my pockets and reached forward to pet Thor's side. "Does it have to be this one?"

Reid smiled and nodded his head. "Definitely this one."

REID SKIPPED MOST of the basic care with me because I'd been present when he explained it to the kids, and now he was currently atop Sugar Cube and I was on Thor. We were riding side by side in the back pasture. The crickets were humming, invading the summer air, along with the slight breeze that had picked up. Reid led the way through the fence that separated our properties and moved us toward a narrow trail.

"You sure the kids are okay with you being gone?" he asked from his position slightly ahead of me.

"Yeah, Michael can do the bedtime routine and I have my cell on me, so we're okay," I assured him, although I was anxious to get back, anxious for my stomach to stop flipping and dipping at being close to Reid. I had no idea why it kept doing that, but every time he cracked a smile or his gaze cut my way, my insides swarmed.

"So, you pretty well settled into the town and everything? You mentioned you'd heard I was moving back from the local gossip train, right?" He looked over his shoulder and lifted a dark eyebrow.

I smiled, enjoying how peaceful it was to ride Thor and how easy it was to talk to Reid. "Yeah, at the hair salon. My stylist, Star, seemed really interested in your return," I joked as I felt my mind slowly drifting toward murky waters...waters infested with questions like whether he had a girlfriend.

"Sounds like Star. She always was getting excited about things." He clicked his tongue, maneuvering the horse into a wider opening. "Dang, we better start heading back—the sun is already getting pretty low." He narrowed his gaze on the pink and gold skyline.

"They made it seem like you'd been gone for a while," I continued, following after him. The path widened, allowing us to ride side by side, and I realized too slowly that I enjoyed being next to him while I rode. I liked seeing his forearms flex when he grabbed the reins, and I liked seeing his body shift with every movement of the horse.

I hated that I noticed. I hated that I enjoyed it. I hated that I was there.

"Yeah, I moved back from Seattle..." He shrugged.

"Seattle? That's a pretty big change," I noted, leading Thor toward my property.

"Yeah, you could say that, but it was time for one." He sighed and tipped his head toward the darkening sky.

I could sense that he wanted to change the subject, so I did.

"I don't really care because it's none of my business, but for the sake of our shared driveway..." I stammered, feeling bolder as the sun dipped farther into the night.

Reid looked over at me and waited for me to finish. "Go on, shared driveway..." he urged with a smile. He slowly turned his hat backward, causing some of his hair to bunch through the gap. He looked cute, and this attraction and my question were entirely too much.

"It's just that...um, are you one of those guys who has a lot of female company that'll be coming and going? Not that it's any of my business at all...but Henley asks so many questions and it'd just be easier to tell him you have a girlfriend if that's what it is...you know what I mean?" I watched the path in front of me and ignored how warm my face had become.

He let out a hearty laugh, causing Sugar Cube to sidestep to the left, which forced Reid's leg to brush against mine. Thor had nowhere to go, so I just endured it and the closeness of his body.

"For the record, no, I'm not one of those guys, never have been... and I don't have a girlfriend. I'm too busy crushing on women who are unavailable and out of my league." He kept his head low, not looking at me...which I preferred because his words were moving slowly over me, like a ray of sunshine breaking free of a vast cloud.

Maybe he was talking about someone else. He likely was, but like a girl in grade school, I was mulling over what the odds were that it was me he was referring to.

I trotted ahead of Reid as my barn came into view. I needed distance from him, needed space and time, more than just a driveway between us. Attraction is just superficial. That's what I mentally told myself, but it still made me sick that I felt it toward anyone but Travis, that I couldn't even be faithful long enough to mourn him past a year before eyeing a new man.

Travis deserved better.

9

Reid

"No, just the coffee is fine." I smiled and put down five dollars on the bakery counter, hoping Meina would just take it and let me go.

"Reid, whatever you want is on the house, honey. Best you remember that." Meina winked at me then bent over the glass case that held an assortment of baked goods. She let her low-cut shirt do the work it had been made to do: show off the curve of her breasts. Meina and I went way back, back to high school and, more specifically, the back seat of my father's truck our junior year. We only made out that one time, but after that, Meina was hard to get rid of.

She once snuck into the boy's locker room to surprise me. She told other girls we were dating when we weren't -so none of them would ever talk to me. Figures she'd bought the only bakery in town that doubled as the best place to get coffee.

"Thanks, Meina, but I'd like to pay for it and anything else I buy in here." I gave her a wink and walked away from my five dollars. She could keep the change if it meant she would get the hint.

"Reid Harrison, is that you?"

"Yes, sir. Good to see you, Mr. Thompson." I shook the older man's hand and smiled at him. He was a friend of my family, and the fact that he still lived in town made me nervous. I didn't want anyone to hear about what had happened.

"What brings you to town?" Thompson asked, tipping his hat back a bit, revealing his thinned gray hair.

I smiled, relaxing at the notion that he might be ignorant of what had brought me home. "I moved back a few weeks ago and am just settling in, working over at Landon's place."

"That right? Well, I have work for ya, if you're interested," Thompson offered, clapping me on the shoulder. Of course he had work for me and offered, even knowing I already had a job with Landon.

"I could always use the extra work." I smiled. "What exactly do you need help with?"

Thompson rubbed his wrinkled forehead. "Hauling hay and driving a few horses out to auction. Landon always sweeps up the younger kids who need temporary jobs, but if you know of any who might want in, let them know too."

I let out a little laugh. "It's nearly fall now, so all the easy hires are back in school."

"Right, right...well just the same." He adjusted his hat and walked toward the coffee counter. "Let me know what you decide," he added from his place in line then waved goodbye. I had no intention of driving his horses to auction and hauling hay wouldn't pay me what the backache would be worth, so I just smiled and stepped outside.

Cringing, I briskly headed toward the grocery store. September had graced us with its temperamental presence, and I was getting frustrated with its mood swings. Wyoming had harsh winters and blazing hot summers. In between, our days swung like a pendulum between hot as hell and frigid as fuck.

I shoved my free hand into my pocket and tried to shake off the chills that ran down my arms. My flannel wasn't doing much to help push past the cold air, but movement usually helped, that and hot coffee. I had a few more errands to run before I headed back home. I usually tried to save up all my shopping for one day since it was such a long walk there and back.

Thompson bringing up kids who might be able to work had me thinking back on a topic I'd tried to avoid for the last three weeks. That was how long it had been since I'd really seen Layla with any success. Sure, I'd seen her when I went over for riding lessons, but she was withdrawn and distant. She smiled, watching as we worked and encouraging her kids, and then thanked me, but she'd always go back inside with them, ensuring that we didn't have any more personal trail time together. Then she had canceled the last three appointments, and I had no idea why.

I'd seen her try to put together a backyard playground set by herself, struggling with instructions and the larger pieces that were too heavy to stand on their own. I was so tempted to walk over and help, but her silent walls had been erected and I refused to be that asshole who tried to knock them down. I'd obviously overstepped when we'd gone riding and I'd admitted to being attracted to her. I had hoped she wouldn't pick up on the fact that I was talking about her. Stupid move on my part.

She didn't need to get tangled up in my mess or get hurt anyway, so this was better. Layla didn't seem like the type who wanted temporary amusement, and if I was honest, she was dream girl material, so even if she did proposition me for no-strings-attached fun, I'd likely decline.

"Hey, look, it's Mr. Reid," a soft voice called from behind a rack of bread. The grocery store wasn't large, with about five aisles in total. I turned toward the sound and peeked over to see a little brunette, slightly-less-mop-like head of hair tucked under a baseball hat.

"Hey Henley, how's it going bud?" I carefully asked as I cleared the aisle and met him and his mom in theirs. Layla was wearing a pair of jeans that hugged every inch of her lean legs and a white tank top under a black and red flannel shirt. Her blonde hair was curled and thrown on top of her head in some interesting style, making her look all beautiful and dreamy.

"Layla." I nodded toward her and smiled, trying my hardest not to act affected that she hadn't called me or texted me one time since I gave her my number, trying to act like it didn't dig at me that she was obviously avoiding me.

"Hey…" she whispered as she dug her clear nails into the front pocket of her jeans. Her face flushed just a little, but that tiny bit of pink gave me hope. Something about me *did* affect her, and fuck me if it didn't feel like a challenge.

"What are you guys up to?" I asked, putting my hand on Henley's hat and moving it around his scalp, making him laugh and take it off.

"Nothin', just getting some food before we starve." Henley answered, shrugging his small shoulders like it didn't matter much.

I squatted down until I was eye level with him. "Didn't you start school?"

He smiled at me. "Yep, but they only let me go for morning time."

I stood back up and watched Layla, who started eyeing the shelves next to me, trying to avoid my gaze.

"Cool," I responded, my eyes still on her.

"You walking again?" Henley pulled on the straps of my backpack.

I looked down at him again and nodded. "Yep, there and back."

Henley tipped his head back and squinted at his mother. "Can we give him a ride? We're going to the same place."

Heat filled my face. I didn't want to bum rides off the woman like I was some teenager, especially because I was fantasizing about said woman at night.

Layla smiled at me, likely swept up with the cuteness of her kid. "You need a ride?"

God, I wanted to push her back against the bread rack and taste her pink lips. They were plump and perfect and saying things that weren't dirty at all, but my depraved and very deprived mind was twisting each syllable around, securing them for later use.

I swallowed and adjusted my backpack to get my mind somewhere else. "I don't want to impose. You guys have other errands after this?"

"No, Mom already went to the haircutting place where they put that stuff on her face so she doesn't have a man mustache," Henley said while swinging a bag of bread. My eyes immediately jumped to

Layla's mouth, and sure enough, that red I'd noticed was somewhat attributable to her waxing appointment.

"Henley, those are things we don't share with people," Layla whisper-yelled at her son while carefully bringing her hand to her mouth to cover the evidence.

I let out a laugh and, on instinct, grabbed her hand to stop her from hiding her face. Once my skin brushed against hers, it was like time stopped. I'd just fucked up and breached a wall I wasn't supposed to scale. She'd be sending her sharpshooters out to kill me any second.

She stared with wide eyes at my hand. A second later, I dropped it like it was on fire. I blinked and grabbed my neck. "You guys go ahead. I'll head back later—"

"No, please...it's fine. We can give you a ride," Layla countered while gripping her basket a bit tighter.

I resisted the urge to say no. I really didn't want to walk back, and I really wanted to spend time with her, so I nodded.

"Yeah, okay...thank you."

"I'll lead the way," Henley declared while pointing his thumbs at his chest.

LAYLA GRIPPED the black leather steering wheel with one hand. Her black and red flannel opened enough to show off her tight tank top underneath, and it took all my willpower not to stare.

"So..." I cleared my throat, hoping to end the awkward lull in conversation and looking for a distraction from her chest.

Layla peeked over at me quickly and smiled then dragged her gaze back to the road.

"Haven't seen you around much lately," I muttered, realizing too late that it made me sound desperate and creepy.

Thankfully she laughed, her shoulders shaking with the movement.

"School started, so things have been hectic. This is my first school year doing everything on my own, so things are..." She trailed off.

Shit. I had just put my huge foot in my mouth by forgetting she was doing this alone and so recently after losing her husband.

"I'm sorry, I didn't realize," I replied, voice barely above a whisper, not wanting to clue Henley in on what we were talking about.

"It's okay, you didn't know." She shook her head, just barely, and kept her eyes on the road.

I watched her and lifted my arm to grip the hand bar above my head. "I didn't realize it had happened so recently…" I trailed off, trying to wrap my brain around the fact that it had been less time since her husband's death than I realized.

She shook her head, letting a few of those golden strands brush her neck. "Sorry, I should have clarified. Last year, they all home-schooled with an online teacher…it's been about a year since he passed," she spoke softly, sounding too broken to be sitting upright.

My chest ached. Damn this day. I was failing horribly at this.

"Still, wish I would have known…I could have helped out a bit, maybe cared for the horses or something, took something off your plate."

She turned her head, just slightly, and adjusted her hands on the wheel. "You would have done that?" Her tone was curious, not skeptical.

I swallowed the thick lump of uselessness I'd felt over the past two years and nodded. "That and anything else you need help with. It's not easy being a single mom, I imagine…you need to get help where you can."

She flicked those chocolate eyes to mine again and blushed. "That means a lot, Reid…thank you. I might just take you up on that some-time because Thor hates me even more now that the kids are gone all day."

I laughed and relaxed as the sight of our shared road came into view.

"Use that phone number I gave you. Day or night." I turned my head to stare at her as I not so subtly added, "For anything, Layla."

She adjusted her body in the seat, glanced at me, and gave me a weak smile. Her rigid posture conveyed that she was uncomfortable.

Fuck.

Why wouldn't she be? I'd just practically hit on her right after she got done telling me her husband died recently. She wasn't ready to be flirted with or won over, and honestly, neither was I.

I turned my head back toward the window and decided right then and there to back the hell off. I'd help if she wanted it, but I had no business getting lost in those brown eyes that made my gut twist. I had no business wishing I could run my fingers through that golden hair or slide my hands up those tanned, toned thighs. I had no business doing anything with her.

"I'M TELLING YOU, man, just come check it out," Kip argued through my phone's speaker as I folded a pair of jeans and put them away in my dresser. I was having a shit evening, my demons trying to track me down and drown me. I hated how I'd left things with Layla and hated even more that she was over there at her house, with her kids, living a life I could only ever dream of. Fear pulled me down the ugly road I'd been traveling for the past year and a half, the one where I was convinced my entire life would be like this.

"I don't know...I didn't exactly want to get back into the whole social scene yet." I closed my eyes at my lame excuse. I didn't have a decent reason to turn him down; I was just enjoying this pity party I'd been throwing for myself and was having a hard time leaving it.

"It's practically the weekend. Just come for an hour. I'll pick you up in twenty, and I swear I'll drive you back if you want to leave," Kip offered, toeing the awkward line of me not driving. He didn't know why I refused to do it, just knew that I wouldn't. I forced my eyes shut. If I was going out, I wanted my own wheels, my own escape if I needed it, but the act of driving was in itself a form of being trapped.

"Nah, I can meet you," I forced out, trying to hide how close I was to hyperventilating. I fucking needed to start sorting my shit out. It was way past time for me to put this behind me. It was different this time. I was different.

"Sounds good. See you in a bit." Kip hung up. I stared down at the carpet by my feet and tried to rationalize what I was about to do and why I was about to do it.

Fuck.

I needed to just do this.

I ignored how my chest burned as I tugged on my boots, how the anxiety nearly broke through my chest as I pulled on my flannel shirt and grabbed my keys.

Without thinking, I walked outside, stormed toward my truck, and opened the door. My movements were jerky but I needed this. I had to do it. I shoved the key into the ignition and flipped it over, the sound of the engine coming to life filling the empty air of my cab. I blinked once, breathed through my nose, and put my foot on the brake as I shifted the gear into reverse.

I gently pulled away from my house and drove past Layla's, wishing I was there right now instead of here, alone in my truck, with these demons that clung to me everywhere I seemed to go.

I put my blinker on and turned down the back road that went west for exactly one mile before it merged with the main highway that would take me back into town. Just as the highway came into view, a pair of headlights caught me, and that was all it took.

To transport me back to *her*. To that night. To what I lost. To why I was here.

I slammed on the brakes, shoved the gear into park, and got out of the truck. I leaned over and struggled with heavy breaths. They were stuck inside my chest and refused to come out.

Fuck this hurt.

I couldn't do it.

Tears sprang to life in my eyes, reminding me of all the reasons I'd stayed off the road, why I wasn't fit for this, why I couldn't go enjoy a night on the town.

I tugged my cell free and shot a text to Kip: **Sorry, man. Can't make it.**

10

Layla

THE DRY HEAT OF SUMMER HAD TURNED INTO THE COOL BREEZE OF FALL, and Wyoming was proving to be just as gorgeous in both. I found myself anticipating winter in a giddy way. We hadn't gotten much snow being so close to Portland, so we would always have to drive an hour or so just to see it. Not here though.

"So, what are you going to do with your free night?" My sister twisted the blue lid on her water bottle as she surveyed me. She was taking the kids to a movie and dinner in Casper. I normally would have gone, but I had writing to do and needed a little time to myself.

"I have bubble bath plans and at least three medical reports to type up." I sighed and started wiping down the kitchen counter. I wished I were writing for fun, but I had been contracted to help with medical reports and editing. I had taken so much time off that I was oddly excited at the idea of getting back to it.

"Well, maybe you could also check out the town tonight? I heard there's a festival of some kind going on down there." Michelle tugged the fridge open, thinking I wouldn't notice her little hint. The kids had told her about Reid. Henley had overshared, as usual, and made Reid seem to be some hero. He also made it seem like we were seeing him much more frequently than we had been. He normally came to do lessons with the kids three times a week, and if I saw him while they were riding, we were friendly, but otherwise, I didn't really engage with him.

It had been over a week since I'd given him a ride home from the store, and I hadn't seen him again. Lessons had been put on hold as I wrangled getting the kids back into school. There were so many forms that kept coming home, so many things I wasn't prepared for. The kids were behind on immunizations, so I had to make an emergency appointment to ensure Henley and Jovi were all caught up, and I had to get Michael a physical so he could try out for track.

There was an orientation for each child's class, which was fucking horrific and exhausting. I'd made it to one only to find out I was late to the other one, which was across town. Henley rode a shuttle from the middle school to his kindergarten, which I was so thankful for, but for things like this, it was hard. I felt like I was drowning, and I had no idea how to come up for air.

The lessons had fallen to the back of the pile of things I needed to get done, but unfortunately, I noticed the kid's attitudes suffering from it.

"Yeah, maybe." I shrugged. I had zero plans to head into town, but I wasn't in the mood to hear about why it was important for me to start socializing. Star had texted, asking if I wanted to go out the other night, but I hadn't been able to do it. I'd noticed Reid's headlights leaving his house that same night, and since Douglas was so small, I figured it was a blessing in disguise that I had decided to stay in.

Michelle narrowed her gaze at me for a few more seconds before she finally gave up. "I'll bring them back tomorrow morning. The movie we're seeing doesn't start until seven, and I don't feel like driving back tonight."

"Sounds fun. Love you." I kissed my sister's cheek, more than ready to have the house to myself. Honestly, I had been holding in tears and emotions since the kids asked that we start being happy. Afraid they'd call me out, I hadn't been showing any signs of sadness. I wanted to play videos of my dead husband and even talk out loud to him and tell him how much I missed him. I didn't want to be judged by my kids for being sad and grief-stricken.

"Bye Mom, love you," the kids all sang in unison as they piled into Michelle's truck.

I waved and blew them air kisses then relished the silence that followed. I climbed the stairs and started my bath, cued up my favorite sad-song playlist, and then ran downstairs to grab my favorite bottle of wine.

I soaked for an entire hour in lavender and some kind of rose petal concoction that made me smell like a flower patch. I felt relaxed and ready to binge-watch something sappy and sad. The work I had planned to do would get pushed to another day. Grief sometimes acted like a highlighter for what needed extra attention. In my life, it emphasized the fact that I didn't take very much time for myself. So, I decided tonight would be dedicated to self-care.

I was gracefully walking around the back of the couch, wearing just my long sleep shirt and underwear. I'd shaved my legs and even painted my toes. It felt good to feel human and like a woman again. I started up Netflix and turned toward the kitchen, ready to pop my pizza in the oven, but then I stopped mid-step and let out a bloodcurdling scream.

I awkwardly scrambled on top of the island and started panting like a madwoman. Thank God it was a huge surface, big enough for eight stools to tuck underneath. I crawled on all fours as I eyed the predator on my kitchen floor.

Curled up in a thick coil was a green and yellow snake. I had never encountered a snake in my entire life, not in California, not in Oregon. I knew they were there, but I had never seen one. So, I had no idea what I was supposed to do. I spotted the home phone lying off the charging cradle and frantically pressed the number two button to speed-dial my sister. She was a vet, so she'd know what I should do. But, as the phone rang and rang, I realized it was past seven and her movie had started.

"Shit," I whispered, eyeing the tormentor on the floor. There was no way I would even run upstairs or outside; if I let it out of my sight, I wouldn't know where it had slithered off to. Hesitantly, I held my thumb down on the newest speed dial number I had entered into our home phone weeks ago. It rang three times before Reid's husky voice answered.

"Hello?"

"Reid? Um...are you busy?" I asked, trying to clear the fear from my throat. I wanted to cry and panic and scream at him to come over right away, but I had to chill out.

"Layla? You okay?" Reid sounded so worried that it made my stomach flip. Somewhere, subconsciously, I liked having someone worry about me.

"There's a snake on my floor and I'm kind of freaking out. Can you help me?"

Silence met me. I pulled the phone away from my ear and looked to see if it was still connected; it was but there was no one on the other end. A few seconds later the front door burst open and Reid materialized in my entryway. He wore a black t-shirt that made him look menacing and rugged, especially with his slightly dirty jeans and work boots, but it was the look on his face that paralyzed me. He was worried, genuinely worried about me.

"Are the kids okay? Where is everyone?" Reid looked around the living room as he slowly stalked forward.

"They're gone, with my sister. It's just me." I looked down at the coiled mass of green and added, "And the snake."

Reid's gaze dropped to the pile in front of the island and his eyebrows shot up. The look of concern was replaced with amusement. He chuckled, getting even closer to the pile on the floor.

"Wait! Shouldn't you have like a stick or a gun or something?" I panicked, trying to stop him with my hands out in front of me, not touching him but close to him just the same. He looked up at me and laughed, moving his hand toward me, like he was trying to calm me down.

Weirdly, I really wanted to feel his warm touch at the moment, so I met his outstretched hand and pulled it into mine. He didn't look at me as he held it, just eyed the snake and crept closer. Once he got close enough, he stopped and looked at me, taking his gaze off the serpent. I gulped and slightly panicked, imagining it attacking him at any moment.

"I need my hand," he whispered, leaning just a little bit toward me, and if I hadn't been a grieving widow…I might have let that dark gaze of his drag me into a kiss. Instead, I dropped his hand like it was the snake on the floor. I scooted away from the edge and pulled my sleep shirt down, realizing too late that I wasn't decent.

Reid lowered himself to a crouch and carefully picked up the snake, its long body drooping down, limp like it was dead but letting out a low hiss. "Careful, it might bite you," I whispered, watching the interaction like a hawk.

Reid chuckled again. "This guy won't bite. It's a rubber boa." Thankfully, he didn't wait for me to understand what in the heck a rubber boa was; he just walked outside and let the thing go. I silently prayed it would never ever make its way inside my house again. Reid came back a second later and washed his hands. I should have gotten down, but I still felt so freaked out over the encounter that I stayed put.

"So, they're not poisonous?" I asked, trying to fill the awkward silence in the air.

Reid looked up at me as he dried his hands and smiled. "Nah, they're harmless to us. They just look scary." He held his hand out for me to take, I took it and then scooted to the edge of the counter. Reid placed his hands on my hips and lifted me, setting me on the floor, and my sleep shirt rode up above my waist with the movement.

He didn't let go right away, and for whatever insane reason, I didn't pull away either. Maybe it was because I hadn't been held in any capacity in so long, or maybe it was because instead of getting lost in his gaze, I felt found. Whatever it was, it had me standing there with my shirt bunched at my waist and my regard for my cotton thong underwear being on display flying out the window. He swallowed, causing that thick Adam's apple to bob, and finally released me. Reality sank in like a painful sliver. I shoved my nightshirt down and crossed my arms, slowly moving away from Reid.

He walked away from me, toward the couch, and plopped down.

This wasn't a good idea.

"So, you have a big evening planned by yourself?" Reid leisurely asked, flipping through different Netflix options.

I tucked my hair behind my ears and moved closer to him. "Something like that. I wanted to binge-watch a few shows and just be sad tonight," I replied honestly.

Reid glanced over briefly and nodded his head. "Well, I'll leave you to it then." He started to stand, and something in my gut twisted uncomfortably.

"Um...would you...?" I stammered and looked away, not wanting to ask him to stay but not wanting him to leave.

"Would I what?" Reid softly encouraged while standing up and heading toward the door.

"Would you maybe want to hang out here with me for a little bit? I was going to make a pizza..." I twisted my fingers and hoped he would decline and put me out of my misery. I was freaked out and didn't want to be alone, but I also liked being around him and I hated myself for it.

"I would maybe want to do that, as long you're okay with having me here. I get that sometimes it's nice to have the freedom to be yourself without anyone around." His gaze lowered to my legs. He was giving me an out. I wanted to take it and thank him, but I was selfish and shook my head instead.

"I'll go throw on some sweats so it's not weird. I'd like it if you stayed...but again, only if you didn't have plans."

A small smile crept up the side of his face and those white teeth peeked through; he looked like he was about to laugh. His eyes flicked to my legs once more before he cleared his throat and looked at the TV.

I turned toward the stairs and tried to prepare myself to sit in the company of another man for the evening.

11

THOSE LEGS WERE GOING TO KILL ME. THE SIGHT OF LAYLA IN BLACK thong underwear was also going to kill me, but both thankfully and regrettably, she'd put on sweats and, from the looks of it, a bra. I rubbed my hand down my face as the credits rolled toward the bottom of the screen and a new movie suggestion popped up. Layla was asleep next to me on her couch, wrapped in a blanket. Part of her hair had fallen across her face and the shoulder to her shirt had fallen, revealing her smooth skin.

I needed to go because I couldn't stop picturing how those legs had looked when I walked in or the way she'd looked on that counter. My mind kept playing images of her laid down on her back, those legs...

"Are you still watching?" Layla's soft voice interrupted where my thoughts were headed.

"No, it's over...I can turn it off and head home." I leaned forward and foraged around in the cushions for the remote. Layla leaned up too and stretched. I tried to look away, but my mind was still on the image of her on that counter, so I watched. Her thin gray shirt pulled snuggly against her chest, showing off the perfect curve of her breasts. I grabbed one of the couch pillows and pulled it into my lap while stretching my arm to the side so it didn't look weird.

"You don't have to go. It's still early…wanna watch something else?" Layla offered, snagging the remote and moving through new movie options. I wanted to say yes, but I also didn't want any more temptation. We hadn't talked through the first movie, just ate our pizza, drank our sodas, laughed at the appropriate places, and then just relaxed. It was the most enjoyable experience I'd ever had where I was just kicking it with a woman.

"Aren't you tired? You did fall asleep through the last half of the movie," I lightly joked, even jabbing her in the side with my elbow.

"That's because it was boring. Let's watch something funny." She elbowed me back, and it made me feel like a middle-schooler again. "And snacks—let's eat snacks." She shot up from the couch and wandered toward the kitchen. She seemed looser, more open and less awkward around me. In turn, I felt myself loosening up more as well.

"So, what should I pick?" I yelled over my shoulder toward the kitchen.

"Um…you decide," she said, licking something from her fingers. I scrolled through until I found an older movie with Jim Carrey. Layla made her way back to the couch with a large bowl of popcorn and a box of Milk Duds. *Fun with Dick and Jane?* I love this movie!" She beamed, snuggling back into her spot next to me. She felt closer this time.

I snagged a piece of candy and tossed some popcorn in my mouth as I pressed play.

Layla turned toward me and let out a heavy sigh. "Do you think I'm an idiot for being afraid of the snake?"

I looked over at her and smiled. "No. Why would you think that?"

"Because I feel stupid and now, I've messed up your evening, asking you to stay here with me." She tugged on the pillow, hiding her crimson face.

I wanted to pull her entire body into my lap and prove just how much I didn't mind staying with her, but I didn't want to get kicked out. "Trust me, I'd much rather be here than the Douglas Dine and Date." I gave her a side smile, and she perked up then laughed.

"Wait, you were going to that tonight?" Her smile was infectious.

"Yeah, I was bored...was going to get a ride from a friend of mine and try it out." I shrugged and cleared my throat, hoping like hell that she wouldn't ask who the friend was. I didn't want to admit that I had actually caved and told Meina from the coffee shop she could pick me up and have dinner with me. I had texted her that I couldn't make it the second Layla asked if I would stay.

"Did this friend happen to be of the female variety?" Layla joked while pouring a few Milk Duds from the box into her palm. My face actually flushed red. Why did I care if she asked about my dating life? Why did I care if she had an opinion on it either way?

"Kind of," I gritted out, wishing I could just dissolve into the blankets.

Layla gave me a quick smile that disappeared swiftly. "You should have said something...I feel even worse now."

"Don't." I laughed and let out a heavy sigh. "Seriously, it was a low moment for me when I agreed to go. I just get kind of lonely out here...ya know?" I looked over at her and nudged her arm.

She pulled the blanket up to her chin and slowly nodded. "You can always come over here if you're looking for company."

I watched her as a flush slowly worked its way from her neck to her cheeks.

"Well, it feels like every time I try to push that or anything, you pull back. I respect that, so I don't want to wear out the little welcome I do have."

I realized too late that the way my words came out was rude. I brought my hand to my eyes and rubbed, trying to figure out how to fix it, but before I could, Layla let out a small sigh.

"I didn't realize I had offended you...I'm sorry," she said softly, and if I wasn't mistaken, she sounded a little choked up.

I turned toward her and wanted to pull her hand into my lap so badly. "No, you didn't. I swear...I'm just trying to respect your boundaries and be helpful but not pushy," I tried to explain.

She turned her head to the side a bit and drew her thin eyebrows together.

"Respect my boundaries and not push?" She said each word like she was examining them for half-truths.

"Yeah..." I coughed, shifting uncomfortably, and I was thankful for the low lighting to cover my own red coloring. "I mean, it's not like I haven't noticed how attractive you are, Layla...and that person I mentioned when we were trail riding..." I lagged, pulling on my neck and sitting forward, feeling incredibly awkward.

Layla didn't say anything, which nearly made it worse.

"But I know you're not looking for anyone to make a move on noticing how beautiful you are. Maybe you won't ever be, but I'd still like to help you if I can. I just don't know how not to come across as a creep while trying to win your trust."

Layla cleared her throat. "I don't think you're a creep. I'm sorry I was so standoffish to you. I just..." She stopped and sat up taller, dropping the blanket.

I waited for her to continue while watching the soft glow from the TV highlight her light hair and tan skin.

"It's just that I have to protect the kids and myself from any more heartbreak. And no, I'm not ready for dates or being asked out or any of that..." She moved her gaze to the floor. "I still love him and miss him and...don't want to betray him," she admitted quietly, slowly lifting her gaze up, meeting mine with tears in her eyes. My heart broke at the sight of how much pain crossed her face. It was something I was unfortunately familiar with.

I sat forward and pulled her into a hug.

It was one of the most fractured moments of my life, feeling her heartbreak and the hot stream of tears hit my neck. She sniffed and then let out a sob, and I slowly rocked her. We stayed like that for a while.

I finally pulled back a bit. "Could you use a friend? Because I could. I promise not to ask or expect anything more from you."

Her soft brown eyes searched mine and softened. She gave me a small nod then tucked herself under my chin for another hug. "I could use a friend," she admitted, continuing to cry into my shoulder. Half the movie had gone by when she finally turned to watch what was left, and then she fell asleep in my arms. I turned the TV off, pulled the blanket over us, and closed my eyes, feeling a new purpose to my life, feeling like I finally had a reason to wake up in the morning.

I was going to help Layla heal.

12

Layla

I STARED DOWN AT MY CELL PHONE AND LET OUT A SIGH. I DIDN'T WANT to talk to my mother, but she had called three times since yesterday and it had me wondering if something might be wrong. She could have just left me a voicemail so I'd know one way or the other, but that wasn't her style. I held my finger down on her number for a second and placed the phone to my ear.

A few rings in, my mother exclaimed, "It's about time!"

Oh, for the love.

"Hi, Mom. Sorry, just been really busy." I sipped from my straw and relished the cold Diet Coke that slid down my throat. It was either this or alcohol, and my kids were due back soon.

"Well, I only called to let you know I have some of your mail."

I tipped my head back and rested it against the couch. My mail got forwarded from my old residence, but sometimes a few pieces landed with my mother from the few weeks we'd lived with her before we moved.

"Okay. Do you mind sending it, or does it even seem important?" I asked.

She scoffed, obviously still irritated with me. "It's from that woman..."

I sat up and narrowed my eyes on my blank television screen, clearing my throat. "Another one?"

"Seems like it. Why do you encourage this?" my mother scolded.

"I like writing to her. I can't explain it…and I don't feel like I need to." I then launched in on her. "So, does that mean you read it then?" I asked, accusation coloring my tone.

"It came to my house, so of course I read it. You need to put a stop to this before it gets leaked to the wrong person."

I placed a hand over my eyes and drew in a steadying breath. "Please just send it to me, Mom, and any other mail I get. I have to go." I hung up, beyond frustrated with her and the emotions this topic brought up. I was back in that place where I was trying to avoid details, the ones that colored my husband's accident with broad strokes of anger and judgment.

She judged me for not going to the trial, and for not taking the kids with me. For the judge and jury to see what was left behind. My mother accused me of letting the other person involved in the accident get off without so much as a slap on the wrist. Like it was my fault.

I tried to explain that hate isn't a disease; it's an addiction. Once the heart gets a dose, it will always crave more. I didn't need a face or a name to put to my rage, didn't need to encourage the demons that tried to drag me down to that pit of bitterness.

I was plenty bitter on my own.

The crunch of gravel drew my focus to the front door. I opened it and stepped out to see Henley running toward me, holding out a huge cowboy hat. "Mom, guess what?"

I bent low to meet him and scooped him into my arms. "What's that?"

"Auntie Shell bought me a cowboy outfit so I can rodeo like Reid." Henley pulled the kid-sized but still rather large cowboy hat down onto his mop of hair.

I looked up to see my other three children crawling out of my sister's rig. Michelle had her hair in a low bun and her thick glasses on her face with her nose scrunched up.

"Sorry, hope it's okay. He wouldn't stop talking about this Reid person." She placed her hands on her hips and eyed me distrustfully. I'd known this was going to be something we had to talk about eventually, but I didn't feel like explaining that Reid was just a friend. She'd believe me until she saw what he looked like; then she'd call bullshit or press for me to try to make my heart beat again.

"Yeah, it's fine. Reid is the neighbor I told you about and their riding teacher. He told the kids a little about growing up here in Wyoming and the whole rodeo thing came up." I waved my hand around, trying to skip past the important details I knew she'd be after soon enough. "Hey, baby." I wrangled my oldest son into a firm hug, but he grunted and moved past me. He was practically a moody zombie these days, more so since the new school year had started. Michelle watched as the kids all unloaded their overnight bags into the house, but before she followed after them, she turned her head toward the house next door.

"So, when was this whole rodeo conversation?" Michelle pushed her too-heavy glasses up her nose and narrowed her brown eyes on me. I swallowed and cleared my throat.

"A few weeks back over dinner. He kind of invited himself to make us burgers to try to apologize for being an ass."

Michelle kept watching Reid's house as though he'd emerge any second. She was bullish enough to stomp over there and force her way into his house just to be sure he didn't have a meth lab in his basement or something.

"I see," she muttered quietly, likely drawing too many assumptions from me not telling her about him. This was new for us. It was strange. I'd always told her everything, especially about boys or men as we got older...but there was something about Reid that had me wanting to lock him away inside my chest and throw away the key so no one knew about our friendship. I didn't want to jinx it, I suppose, or something close to that...I just wasn't ready to explore it all. All I knew was I felt miffed at the idea of explaining it.

"How were the kids?" I tried to derail her from being my snoopy, overprotective sister.

She turned her head toward me. "Good. They always are. We want to go hiking next weekend if that's okay. There's a huge waterfall area that's pretty popular, but it closes early in the season due to snow."

I wrinkled my nose and took a few steps toward the front door, hoping to herd her toward it with me. "It's only September...why would you be worried about snow this early?"

My sister laughed and stayed rooted in her spot, watching Reid's house like some kind of human-sized hawk. "It can snow as early as October, sis." She turned that incredulous glare on me like I was igno- rant and unprepared. Because I was. October? We'd moved here at the tail end of March, so we had missed the majority of winter.

I looked around the property and tried to calm down. In Oregon, it was rainy, and if it did snow, it never stuck. I knew how to drive in it, thanks to Mount Hood being so close. It was always a fun winter destination for us, but tending a property in the snow? No way. I winced as I thought over what that meant for the horses.

"Shell, you have to give me a snow preparation course for the horses. I have no idea what I'm doing."

Michelle's face softened, and she finally turned her gaze from Reid's place. "Calm down. I'll help you, okay?"

Finally, she walked with me to the door and helped put me at ease by suggesting I watch some winter care tip videos on YouTube.

"Knock, knock," I said to warn my fourteen-year-old that I was entering his room, and he stopped strumming his electric guitar then swiveled toward me in his office chair. I made myself comfortable on his bed. "You have fun this weekend?" I watched as he looked down at his guitar and nodded.

Moody zombie.

"Well...what happened? You haven't spoken a word since you got back." I gestured at him with my hand as I leaned back on my arm.

"It's nothing, just forget it." He scoffed, standing and swinging his guitar away from his body.

"It doesn't sound like nothing. What happened?" I didn't move, hoping my relaxed posture would encourage him to calm down...like he was an animal. I'd learned too much from those YouTube videos.

"It's this shitty town and these shitty cowboys." My son's face scrunched up into an ugly snarl.

Inside my head, I was screaming, *LANGUAGE*, but I was learning to let them feel what they felt and not get upset about it.

"Did something happen in Casper?" I gently asked, sitting up slightly to watch his pacing.

"No, it was at school on Friday." He ran his hand through his hair, clearly upset.

I waited, hoping he'd continue.

Finally, he let out a heavy breath and sat down on his swivel chair. "I was talking to this girl...she's in my English class. This stupid cowboy saw us and pushed me against the locker. I pushed him back, and he got in my face and told me to watch myself."

Michael clenched his jaw, and the muscles in it jumped a few times as I waited for him to continue. He pulled up the sleeves of his long flannel and showed me his wrists.

I gasped and moved forward. "What the hell?"

"The jerk and his friends found me after school, knocked me to the ground, and told me to watch my back then tied my hands behind my back with a rope."

My eyes watered as I watched anger and pain lace my son's face. Instead of showing him how much I was feeling all of it with him, I swallowed the emotions and asked, "How did you get out of it?"

He shook his head back and forth and let out a sigh. "Some kid found me and cut the ties, helped me, so silver lining, I guess. Looks like I'm not the only one here who hates cowboys."

My heart blanched at his 'silver lining' comment. It was what Travis had always asked the kids to think about when they faced something hard or unfair. He wanted them to find the silver lining in the situation and not be so focused on the bad that they couldn't see the good.

"What are you going to do if you see them again?" I whispered to my very angry son.

I was worried he might do something stupid like take a knife to school.

"Nothing. If I see them, I will ignore them...don't worry, Mom." He turned toward his desk.

My face was red as anger and hurt simmered in my veins. I hated that my son was treated like that by stupid kids here, and I hated that he felt so out of control. In turn, it made me feel like we were falling, and I couldn't see the bottom. I wanted to take my son's heart out of his chest and carry it within my own, just to protect it.

I stood up and held his face in my hands. "You are stronger than you know, baby boy. I love you, but if anything—*anything* else happens, you need to tell me." I gave him a death glare, hoping he'd know how serious I was.

He gave me a half-smile. "Don't worry, I doubt they'll do anything else. They're all about the show."

I hoped he was right.

13

Layla

THE SUN WAS STUCK BEHIND A SLEW OF ANGRY CLOUDS, CASTING A DARK shadow over my yard. I was prepared with a pair of jeans and boots, even a sweater in case it rained, because today I was finishing the damn swing set I'd set out to assemble weeks ago. It had been my stupid sister's idea; she'd seen it all put together in a big-box store over in Casper and bought it for us. So kind of her, except she was nowhere to be seen when it came to helping put this beast together.

"Okay, I can do this." I let out a heavy sigh as I bent down and snagged the instructions. The sound of distant thunder rumbled across the nearby pasture, but I ignored it because, like I said, today was the day this thing was going up. I focused on section one, studying the picture of tiny parts that needed to be included in this particular step, and then surveyed the items on the blanket to my right. There weren't any screws, or washers, or anything else I'd actually need according to the instructions.

I let out a groan and got to my feet. This entire situation of being alone was so insanely shitty. Travis had always dealt with this stuff in the past. The basketball hoop that needed set up, our kids' playset, the treehouse, the cars, clogged toilets—he'd done everything. I was kicking myself for not sticking to him like glue, absorbing all the tricks and tips. The propane incident from a few weeks ago had been mortifying, and I was so grateful that Reid hadn't said something snarky about me not knowing what the hell I was doing. I didn't know there were different types of barbeques, and I didn't know the one we'd bought required propane.

Setting my hands on my hips, I stood and looked over toward my neighbor's house. Reid's truck was parked out front like usual, but I had no idea if that meant he was home or not. We'd agreed to be friends so, not letting my mind overthink all the intricacies of what that meant, I decided to just force my feet to move.

I crushed the dead grass between my property and his, watching the horizon deepen with a dark blue, covering the hills with what looked like white lightning or rain. Gravel crunched under my boots as I cut to his driveway and made my way up his steps. I swiftly knocked three times and waited.

"Hey." Reid swung the door open and greeted me with a smile.

"Hey, you busy?" I smiled, hopeful for his help.

He stepped through his screen and tugged a baseball hat over his dark hair. "Not at all. You finally going to ask for some help with that play structure?" He laughed, shoving me in the arm with his elbow.

I leaned to the side and laughed. "Yes, please."

We traveled back to the blanket of parts and instructions. After he surveyed the white paper for a minute or two, he folded it and placed it in his back pocket.

"First things first, we need to go get the right tools to set this up. I have a drill, but not the right kind of screws or anything else you'll need." Reid flicked his green eyes over the lumber at our feet then tipped his head back to survey the sky. "You got any tarps?"

I drew my eyebrows together in confusion. "Um…I think so. I can check the shed. Why?"

"Because it's going to rain, and you need to cover all this." He met my gaze and turned to head toward the shed.

My heart sank. I just wanted to get this thing built. "So much for my plan to get it done today." I sighed and followed him.

"Don't worry, I'll help you once the weather clears up a bit." He smiled at me over his shoulder and continued forward toward the shed. Once we both cleared the backyard, I saw an old Mustang with blue chipped paint pull up next to my SUV.

"Who's that?" I asked from where I stood behind Reid.

He laughed and turned halfway toward me. "How am I supposed to know?"

He ducked into the tool shed, but I continued watching the stranger in front of my house. Seconds later, a loud squeak emanated from the door that swung open, revealing Star. Her red hair was tamed into straight, shiny strands hanging down her back.

I smiled and walked forward to greet her. "Hey!"

"Hey, girl. You ready?" She beamed, her blue eyes dancing with excitement. Her jeans were tight, paired with high-heeled boots and a tight halter top. My brain was gathering all the information, but I was too slow.

"What?"

"I texted you earlier, said I was taking you out tonight," she explained, placing her hands on her hips.

I was truly maintaining the world's best poker face because I had no idea what she was talking about. "I didn't get your text."

"It says read on my end, and that's enough for me. We're going. I straightened my hair, which was a bitch to perfect, but girl, I did, and it's not getting wasted on some misunderstanding."

I let out a soft sigh as the revelation dawned on me that Jovi had probably clicked on the text while she was watching a show on my phone but never said anything to me about it.

"I'd love to go out, but I'm not dressed for it, and I have no one to watch the kids." I swept my hand down my body to emphasize that I was definitely not dressed for drinks and dancing.

"I can watch them," Reid piped up from behind me, wrangling a large blue tarp in his arms.

"Hey Reid, how's Kip doin'?" Star asked, narrowing her focus on him like a hungry bird.

I didn't know who Kip was, but Reid smiled and said, "You should ask him yourself."

Star blushed and turned her focus back on me. "There, now go inside and get ready. I'm going to go see what your house looks like and go through your fridge, because I'm kind of hungry," she informed me while walking toward my front door.

I stood frozen, not really sure what had just happened.

"Is it okay if I watch them? Does that bother you?" Reid asked softly from beside me.

I immediately shook my head, because of course it didn't bother me. I trusted him, otherwise, I wouldn't have let him around my kids at all.

"No, not at all. Thank you for offering. I'm just trying to wrap my head around the idea of going out with Star." I moved toward the porch, knowing he'd follow.

"I'm guessing it's going to be a bit more than you're ready for, but I also think it might be important to get out." He lightly laughed as we entered the house. The kids were counting in unison near the kitchen, where Star stood tossing grapes into her mouth.

Lord, have mercy.

Reid clapped me on the back, smiling at the spectacle she was putting on. "Definitely more than you're ready for."

14

Reid

"WHAT ARE WE DOING OUT HERE AGAIN?" STEVEN ASKED SKEPTICALLY while tossing his large comforter on the bale of hay. He was wearing a thick sweater, like everyone else, trying to ward off the cold. I situated the thermos of hot chocolate and plastic bin of cookies so the kids could reach them.

"We're bonding," I answered happily as I ensured that Henley and Jovi were set up against one of the bales of hay with a blanket.

Michael scoffed, "This horse stuff is their thing, can I go back inside?"

"Nope. You're out here with us because it's fun and I like you being around." I handed him the thermos and a paper cup.

He let out a heavy sigh and plopped down next to Steven. The horses shuffled in their stalls, Thor stuck his head over the wall, ruffling Henley's hair with his nose. I relaxed against the barn wall and watched as each kid filled their cups and snuggled in. The barn was crisp and chilled from the cold night and from the earlier rainfall.

"How do we bond?" Henley asked, reaching up to rub Thor's nose.

I gestured toward what he was doing, "Just like that."

"This seems silly," Jovi said while watching her brother.

"Horses are companion animals. They bond with whoever it is that cares for them and rides them; there's a deep connection that you can make if you care enough to make it."

"So, we have to sleep in the barn every night?" Henley asked, sounding confused.

I laughed, "No, bud. This is just something you can do once in a while to help your horses know that you care about them. Especially if your horse ever gets sick or gets hurt."

"Won't they be at the doctor if they get sick?" Henley tilted his head while he sipped from his cup.

"Nope, a doctor comes to you," I answered and exited the small space we were crowded in. It was an empty stall with large bales of hay lining the walls, big enough for birthing and doctor visits. I walked around the wall and opened Thor's stall and led him back into the space with us.

"Did you know that there are legends about horses?" I asked while I patted Thor's side. Henley automatically stood and walked over to him, mirroring my movements. Jovi joined a second later as I dove into the story.

"Many cultures treat horses with great respect because they're lucky creatures. Horses were known to bring glory to armies going to war. Long ago, they used to place spears on the ground and they'd have horses step over which one would tell them what direction to go or what path to take."

Thor shifted forward and headed toward Michael, softly nuzzling his hand. Michael startled and sat up straight.

"Whoa...why did it just do that?" Michael whispered, as though he would spook the animal.

"He can sense something in you...maybe pain...anger. Maybe he can understand it." I continued to pat Thor down.

"They know that stuff?" Jovi whispered, watching in awe as the horse dipped his head toward Michael and nudged him with his nose.

"They do. They're much more aware of what's happening than people think. That's why they're such great therapy buddies."

Michael stood and stalked toward the exit.

"I don't need therapy. None of us do," he muttered sternly before slamming the side door shut.

"Mommy says he needs a whole lot of Jesus, but I think Jesus is getting tired of his attitude," Henley commented while reaching for the cookies.

"So...if we're feeling sad," Steven started, moving to stand near Thor.

I waited, hoping he'd be interested and help heal the sting of rejection I was feeling from Michael. I wasn't used to kids or teenagers being disinterested in horses.

Steven placed his hand in between Thor's ears and gently rubbed, "They'll sense it?" He lifted his eyes to mine and waited.

"Yes...they sense everything and if you let them, they'll try to comfort you." I felt relief swim through me as I watched the three of them pet Thor and smile at each other as a comfortable silence surrounded us.

I twisted my head back toward the exit, wishing I could figure out a way to get into Michael's head. He didn't want to do the classes or learn about riding because he was older. So, it limited me with how I could extend these lessons to him. I was already starting off on the wrong foot if he assumed I just wanted to fix him.

If only he knew how much I could relate.

15

layla

"I HONESTLY CAN'T BELIEVE YOU DID THAT TO ME," STAR COMPLAINED for the hundredth time.

I put my finger up to shush her and pulled off my boots. The living room was dark, save for the television and side lamp that were still on. I walked farther in and noticed Reid snoozing with his head tilted back against the couch and some car show playing on Netflix.

"I was supposed to flirt, dance—hell, maybe even kiss a guy." Star threw her hands up and walked toward my fridge like she'd been there a thousand times. The volume of her voice was sure to wake Reid, and possibly the kids.

I winced and shushed her again, louder this time.

"Geez, sorry." She rolled her eyes and pulled out a glass from the cupboard.

"Hey, you're back. You guys have fun?" Reid stirred on the couch and tilted his head even farther back so he could see me better.

Seeing him so relaxed like that with his green eyes searching mine made my stomach do a little flip. Frustrated by the sensation, I gave him a small nod and moved to join Star.

She poured me a glass of milk like she'd done for herself and turned the plastic container of chocolate chip cookies toward me.

"I'm willing to share, even if you did kiss-block me tonight." Star raised her thin eyebrow and took a chunk out of her cookie.

I scoffed. "First of all, they're my cookies. Second of all, kiss-block?"

Reid made his way over and leaned across me to reach for a cookie, which was normal, totally normal, but the stupid gymnastic routine that was happening in my stomach was not normal. I inhaled his delicious scent of something spicy, clean, and sweet and tried to ignore how much it made me want to lick the column of his throat.

"Yes, kiss-block. That's all I planned to do tonight." Star's blue eyes jumped from Reid to me and back to her cookie. "I am a lady, after all. Gotta save the goods for someone who is, in fact, actually good."

"Atta girl. Just keep holding out for Kip," Reid joked, which had Star tossing a cookie at his face.

He caught it in midair and let out a low chuckle.

"What's it going to take for you to be comfortable goin' out to bars with me?" Star set her hands on her hips and stared me down. I hated that she was so annoyed by tonight. I mean, I was too, but I couldn't force it.

"What happened?" Reid softly asked, moving closer to my side. His tone betrayed the concern he had for me and my stomach responded with more flips and dips. *Damn him.*

I let out a heavy sigh. "I tried to go out with her to the bar, I really did."

Star cut in. "She stepped in for two seconds and saw how many people there were."

"There were way more guys than girls, and within the two seconds I was there, three of them sized me up. It was too much," I explained.

Reid flicked his gaze to Star, who was still staring at me, and then cut back to me. "I don't think you should rush that sort of thing."

Star laughed with a small mixture of annoyance. "Of course you'd think that."

"Why do you say that?" I asked, confused by the cocky grin she was aiming at Reid.

He continued to chew his cookie, ignoring the accusation.

"Nothing, never mind... So, what will it take, Layla?" She focused on me again.

Panic bubbled in my chest. I wanted friends, wanted to go hang out, but the idea of her leaving me to go make out with strangers and getting hit on by men—it made me freeze up. I couldn't force it. I wasn't ready.

I lifted a shoulder and tipped my milk back. "I don't know..."

"What if you went with more than just Star?" Reid asked, leaning over me again for another cookie. I was two seconds away from handing him the entire bin so I didn't have to keep smelling him and feeling his strong chest brush against my arm.

"Yes, that's a great idea!" Star beamed, drawing her hands together like she was praying. "We'll go in a big group."

"A group?" I drew my eyebrows together in question as I considered it, thinking that might actually work. I wouldn't feel so out of place or pressured to talk to people.

"Yeah. Me, Kip, you, Star, and maybe even ask your sister if you want," Reid suggested with a smile. It sounded perfect, but...

"What about the kids? Who would watch them?"

"Oh honey, Michael is more than old enough to watch these kids." Star waved me off and snagged another cookie.

"But," Reid cut in, focusing his gaze on Star, "if you're uncomfortable with that, I could ask around about a babysitter. There are bound to be a few eager teens tryin' to make some extra cash."

"Yeah, exactly—*teens*," Star said pointedly. "Michael would never let another person close to his age babysit him or his siblings. Just offer him some money and he'll take it seriously." She shrugged her shoulders like she was an expert.

"You don't even know my kids—how do you know that will work?" I joked, moving to put the milk away. It was close to eleven at night, and I was more than ready for bed. We hadn't gone to the bar, but we had gone to dinner and a movie.

"Because he's a teenage boy, and they all pretty much work the same. My brother is fifteen, so I understand at least somewhat."

Admitting defeat, I shrugged. "Okay, I'll go in a group. Set it up and I'll go."

"Excellent." Star clapped her hands together. "Guess I'll be needing Kip's number then." She winked at Reid.

He laughed and nodded. "Guess you will."

We closed up the cookies, and Reid headed toward the door for his shoes. I followed after him as Star made her way toward the bathroom.

"So, thanks for tonight," I weakly muttered, suddenly feeling awkward. Those earlier flips and dips were throwing me off and making me feel like I was abusing our friendship somehow.

"Anytime. Plus, you know I like your kids. They were great." Reid turned away from the door and smiled at me. His dark hair was messed up in the back where he'd fallen asleep against the couch, and his sleepy eyes were saying things to me that his mouth wasn't. They were drinking me in, smiling all on their own, and making more emotions surge inside me, making me even more confused than before.

I didn't respond to him, because in the darkness of my foyer and with the heat of his gaze, I was falling into something dangerous with him, something off-limits…something I desperately didn't want to want.

"Night, Layla," Reid whispered, shuffling a foot closer to me. My brain was trying to tell me he should be moving toward the door, not toward me, but I think it was my damn lady parts that were controlling the show because they were mesmerized, enthralled at the idea of him moving closer to us.

"Night," I muttered back just as his long arms came around me in a hug.

Warm, firm…that spicy-clean scent overwhelming me, drowning me, tempting my tongue to trace his throat—holy damn, was I that out of practice with the opposite sex that a mere hug could cause me to orgasm?

After a few agonizing seconds, he stepped back, released me, and opened the door.

The cold air hit my face about as delicately as a bucket of water. *What the hell am I doing?*

I turned around and came face to face with my friend grinning from ear to ear.

"That was hot." Her eyebrows danced up and down suggestively, but before I could say anything in reply, she added, "Can I crash on your couch?"

I wanted to lash out at her, defend what I'd just felt, except no one knew what I felt. How could a hug be hot? I had questions, but I feared discussing them might make her think I cared about Reid more than a friend should. So, I ignored her and just muttered my agreement regarding the couch.

"Knock yourself out."

16

Reid

WORKING WITH KIDS WAS SEEMINGLY EASY. RIDING HORSES WAS EASY; IN fact, it was like breathing, and currently, I needed the simplicity of it. The only exceptions to this were Layla's kids—specifically, her daughter, Jovi.

Henley ate up all the lessons with a big grin and an excited attitude. Steven was a good mixture of both, where his excitement would leak through but he'd put a damper on it with a glare or stalking off quietly. Jovi, however, was a little enigma I couldn't figure out. My mind was still mulling over our lesson the day before.

She was standing, her head tucked close to Samson's, and she had that thin-lipped, anger-laced expression on her face, the one that was nearly impossible to penetrate. If she only knew that every emotion she warred with was openly displayed across that little face of hers. It made me hurt, made me ache in ways I'd never experienced before.

I walked to Samson's side and patted the white fur along his back, letting his tail swish back and forth. He canted his head toward Jovi, and I knew he could feel what I did. They were like tiny waves of energy emanating from her small body, begging for someone to fix her, begging for someone to reach into that little chest of hers and heal that broken heart.

I lowered my head and softly spoke to her, hoping she'd hear me.

"Remember what I said in the barn the other night?"

She kept her face tucked in toward Samson. I waited a second before I gave up and tried a different tactic.

"When the hurt gets too big and there's no one who will understand, I tell them." I tilted my head toward Samson and ran my hand along his mane. "They listen better than anyone, and my soul always feels lighter when I'm done." I continued to gently pat the soft coat of the horse. "It's what I did when I lost my dad."

Her brown eyes drifted to mine then slowly moved beyond me, a glossy sheen consuming them. She didn't speak, didn't do anything, but after I'd walked away, I noticed she was turned in closer to Samson and whispering something in his ear with a stream of tears falling down her face.

In a way, their training from home was a blessing. If they were working with Landon's horses, they'd have to disconnect after each session and the therapy might be strained because of it. This way, Jovi could curl up outside Samson's stall and stay there, talk to him all night if she felt like it. I knew that was how I had felt, back when my world felt too big for me to live in it.

I was on my way to Landon's, but I wanted to check on Layla's playset beforehand. Because it was getting dark so early, I wouldn't be able to do it when I got back home. I jogged through the tall grass and cut across the side of the house to enter the smaller yard. Just as I opened the gate, I saw Steven sitting on the steps of the back porch with his head lowered and his soccer ball under his arm.

Concerned, I bypassed the half-assembled play structure and slowly sank down into the seat next to him. "What's up, bud?" I hesitantly asked, hoping I wasn't overstepping my boundaries.

He lifted his left shoulder, let it fall, and kept his palm under his chin. His eyes were still downcast, scouring the dirt at his feet.

"Oh, I know what this is." I snapped my fingers like I'd figured out the solution already.

Steven snapped his head up. "What?"

I gave him a small smile and shoved him in the shoulder. "This is about a girl, isn't it?" I knew it wasn't, but I also knew it'd make him start talking just to shut me up.

"No way!" He sat up, more alert. "I don't even like any girls." He kicked the dirt pile he'd been making with his shoes. "I want to make the soccer team, but Coach said I'd need to step it up next practice or I won't make it." Steven hunched his shoulders inward, looking defeated.

I sat back and held my hands up. "Why aren't you practicing, then?"

Steven looked over and glared like I was a moron. "Because I have no one to practice with."

I looked around the empty yard and quirked a brow. "Where's that older brother of yours?"

Steven let out a heavy sigh. "He's in his room, moping like usual. And don't suggest that I ask him because he hates me."

I leaned closer to him and put my arm around his shoulders. "Bud, that's not true."

Steven scoffed. "Yeah, it is. Ever since Dad died, he's hated everyone, but especially me."

His pained tone made me want to open my veins and give something I didn't even have to offer, something like hope or a fresh start. I shook him a bit, trying to lighten his load. "Buddy, there are a million things you can do by yourself to train. You don't need a partner. Come on, I'll show you."

We got up and walked toward the side of the house. I gestured toward the soccer ball and Steven tossed it into my hands. I'd never been very good at sports if a horse wasn't involved, but my sister, Sarah, had been pretty decent back in the day. I went through a few drills with him, showing him how to use the house as a defensive object, bouncing the ball off the wall and meeting it midair with a kick. Occasionally he'd use his head too, and he'd laugh when he'd nail the house with a hard thud.

We were two fools kicking a ball against the side of the house and missing most the time, but Steven was laughing, and his smile made the fact that I was an hour late to work completely worth it. It didn't hurt that I caught Layla watching us from her top window, a fat smile on her face as she watched her son smile.

I was starting to realize she was doing all she could just to get their little hearts to heal, but she was neglecting her own.

It made me want to fix her, but after the other night—the night she came home with Star and they talked about how Layla wasn't ready to go to bars—I knew I wanted to use the kind of tools that weren't found in the friend zone. My heart rate sped up and that useless organ in my chest thrashed around at the image of Layla dancing with men in a bar.

I knew I wasn't going to do this friendship thing right, but it didn't change the fact that I still wanted to fix her. Shit, I wanted to fix all of them.

"OKAY, are you sure you're going to be fine?" Layla drilled Michael with a stern glare while she shoved an earring into her ear.

Michael rolled his eyes because Layla had asked the same question about ten times in the last half-hour. "Yes, we're fine. We're doing pizza for dinner and a PG-rated movie so it's okay for Henley and Jov. I have emergency numbers. The horses have already been cared for and put away. We're fine." He exaggerated the last word and turned his mother's shoulders toward the door.

I was waiting near it, already ready to go. Michelle was meeting us at the bar, as were Star and Kip because of their work schedules. Star had arranged for us all to go on a bit of a party crawl since so many locals hosted get-togethers at their houses on Friday nights and Douglas didn't have that many bars. High school football had started, as had college and the NFL, so essentially it was like a town crawl where one would go to watch a game and drink some beer. Although the high school was pretty strict about that sort of thing, it didn't stop people from doing it.

"You ready?" I asked Layla, trying to make sure she was actually prepared for leaving her kids. She had this dazed look in her eye like she was confused or things were just getting away from her. She dug through her purse as she muttered something, but I couldn't make it out. I tried to act entirely unaffected by the fact that she looked drop-dead gorgeous tonight, because friends don't really notice that kind of thing. They also don't comment on it, so I hadn't, but I wanted to. I really, really wanted to.

"Mom, what if Michael tells me to go to bed for no reason tonight?" Steven swung around the staircase like he was worried he'd miss us. His soft brown hair was disheveled and matted on one side as if he'd been lying down for a while.

Layla gave up on whatever she was looking for in her purse and homed in on her son. "He won't."

"But what if he does?" Steven crossed his arms and tilted his head, ready to argue with her.

Layla let out a heavy sigh and yelled, "Michael, no one goes to bed early. Get along."

Steven, seemingly satisfied with that, ran off, leaving us alone in the foyer. Before anyone else could interrupt, I opened the door and stepped out. She followed, still looking unsure of herself. She'd already agreed to drive us without even asking me if I wanted to, which was nice because it was one less excuse I had to make.

"Let's get out of here, I guess," she said, climbing into her SUV. I smiled to myself and did the same on the passenger side.

MEN NOTICED LAYLA, which was no surprise since she was wearing jeans she'd likely need to be cut out of and a black tank top that looked nearly as tight. She wore a teal necklace that hung down near her breasts and a pair of tan cowboy boots, not to mention that hair of hers was cascading down her back in perfect loose curls. I didn't like to get crass, but fuck me, she was looking very fuckable, and I was getting really tired of the way the men around me noticed.

Kip and Star had hit it off and hadn't stopped dancing with each new song that came on. We were currently at the local bar, where we were going to end our evening. The few parties we'd gone to had been duds, with not much happening but talk about politics or people making out against walls. So, we'd headed here and decided to just call it a night after this. Layla hadn't really loosened up yet, keeping to herself and clinging to the strap of her purse like it was the only thing keeping her feet on the ground as she stuck close to her sister.

Michelle was currently dancing with some dark-haired cowboy who was spinning her around the dance floor. Two men had asked Layla to dance, and she'd politely turned them each down. I was sipping my root beer, watching, just trying to be a supportive friend.

"Seems like this place keeps getting fuller by the second," Layla shouted near my ear, sipping from a dark bottle of beer. She'd been nursing the same one for the last forty-five minutes.

"Yeah, tends to, I suppose, with it getting later." I shrugged, not hating how close this conversation was taking me to her ear. The bar top was busy, and people were milling about around us, shoving in and out of spots to catch the bartender. Each time someone squeezed in next to her, it pushed her closer to me. When one guy did it while smiling at her, she turned around to face me completely and seemed to finally give up.

"Will you dance with me? I need to get away from this bar and I have no idea where else to go without looking stupid," she yelled in my ear over the music, grasping my arm. I schooled my features, trying not to react because a friend wouldn't react to dancing with a friend.

I nodded, grabbed her hand, and led her to the floor. The lights were low, the space crowded and emotions charged. The song had turned from something fast-paced to a slow and sensual tune, a man talking about a woman he wanted to make his own but who belonged to someone else. I hated how close the lyrics were landing to my own emotions and what I felt with Layla. The man who owned her heart might have been dead, but he still held it.

Layla felt stiff as my arm moved around her waist and my other went up to grab her hand. It felt as though she might not move at all, until I whispered in her ear, "Just move with me. Pretend we aren't even dancing, just movin' around the floor."

I could feel her nod against my chin and shuffle her feet. I felt like we were back in middle school, barely moving, barely touching, but I'd take things as slow as she needed.

Halfway through the song, she loosened up and wrapped both her arms around my neck, bringing us closer. When I looked down at her, I saw that her eyes were closed, but a tiny smile was gracing her beautiful lips. Something swelled inside me seeing her like that, so unguarded and raw. She was perfect.

I pulled her closer, adjusting my hands on her waist, being greedy with how her watermelon smell invaded my senses. We existed in some strange moment suspended in time where I could feel each heartbeat and hear every small exhalation of breath stolen from the reality we were tied to.

"You guys are too cute," Star screeched from beside us, breaking the moment. Layla's eyes flew open and her body tensed. Star tossed her head back and Kip whispered something in her ear; they were both drunk and being obnoxious.

Layla let go of me and stepped back. "I think I'm ready to go home now."

She grabbed her elbow and looked around, which caused Michelle to come over and take her away toward the bathrooms.

All I wanted was for her to have a fun night out, forget her heartbreak for a bit. Star noticed what was going on and stumbled off toward the bathrooms, leaving Kip and me on the floor watching them go.

17

layla

"YOU ARE OVERREACTING," STAR BLURTED OUT AS SHE FIXED HER HAIR IN the mirror.

With her eyebrows raised, Michelle gave me a look that said, *Your friends are interesting.* I wanted to shove her arm and say, *At least I have friends.*

"I'm not. I just…I feel a little overwhelmed by this place and the people. You wanted me to go out and I did," I stated firmly, splashing some water on my face.

"I thought you wanted to push past this, start to heal," Michelle said softly, turning me toward her.

"I do. Obviously I want to start to heal, Shell." I glared at her, but her responding look was just of confusion, a cold reminder that none of them knew what it was like to lose a husband. No one knew what it was like to dance with someone you were fighting an attraction to and to feel something click into place that shouldn't be there. No one knew what that kind of guilt felt like.

"Look, I just don't see the point. You guys are all dancing and having fun, but this isn't fun to me. I don't want to do this," I argued, ready to leave. I had my own damn car and didn't need anyone's permission to go.

"Okay, I hear you. We're sorry," Star said, flicking her eyes to Michelle and back to me. "Let's try something else."

I contemplated saying no, pushing past them, and driving like a bat out of hell toward my house. I had a pair of pajamas waiting for me, along with a Netflix movie and half a tub of chocolate ice cream. Instead, I relented and asked what Star had in mind.

"You'll see." She wiggled her eyebrows up and down, plastering a smile on her face.

THE SOUND of pins being smashed and people screaming in joy echoed throughout the room. My clown shoes looked ridiculous with my outfit, but Michelle and Star didn't look much better. Ryan had joined us; he and Michelle had hit it off, and when she'd told him she was leaving, he had asked if he could come with. He seemed nice enough, but I was too preoccupied with the fact that Star cared enough about my discomfort to change our venue to focus on him.

"Strike, mother-duckers!" Kip spun on his heels like a professional dancer, snapping his fingers together. I laughed, feeling like some hardened rock had broken open in my chest. It felt good...free. I sipped my beer and smiled as Kip argued with Reid over scores. Star was up next, rocking her red and blue shoes with her miniskirt and tank as she strutted over to our designated lane with her green bowling ball.

"Don't mess up," Kip yelled with his hands cupped around his mouth. Star looked over her shoulder and gave him a wink before drawing her arm back then swinging it forward and letting her ball fly free down the lane. It landed square in the middle of the white pins with a crash, causing her to squeal.

Michelle leaned in toward Ryan as they whispered back and forth to each other, smiling and flirting. The earlier freedom I'd felt was now replaced with envy—horrific, ugly envy.

I watched as Michelle's cheeks flushed red when Ryan whispered something in her ear and played with her hair. She was tucked into his shoulder, and they both ignored the game that was going on, oblivious to anything but each other.

"You going to stare at them all night?" Reid whispered in my ear, breaking me out of my reverie.

Shame stung me somewhere square in the chest. I cleared my throat and took my turn, ignoring Reid and the fact that he'd called me out. I eyed my neon green ball, stuck my two fingers in, and grasped the third with my thumb, pulling it free. I stalked to the white line separating the floor from the lane and eyed the pins at the end. Country music was playing above me, and swarms of people occupied the rest of the lanes and stations. I realized too late that I had no idea what I was doing. I hadn't gone bowling since I was in high school.

Travis had taken the kids a few times, but every time he'd gone, it was with his buddies and Jovi would stay with me. It just wasn't something we enjoyed doing as a family, for whatever reason. Or was it that I hadn't enjoyed it? Maybe I'd ruined it for everyone? Maybe Travis had been dying to play every weekend but I was a stick in the mud and never wanted to? I didn't realize I had essentially frozen until I felt someone's hand on my lower back.

"You okay?" Reid's voice fluttered across my neck as he leaned in close.

"I don't even know what I'm doing, or how to do this…" I kept my gaze forward, terrified to see him notice my callowness.

I held my breath as the lights above dimmed, blurred, and lost focus. Emotion strained against my chest, tight and eager to explode.

A second later, I felt a warm hand cover mine, gripping the bowling ball with me. His other went to my waist to steady me.

"See those white triangles on the floor?" he asked, so close to my ear it nearly felt like it was just the two of us in the room. I nodded, lowering my gaze to the shapes making a line on the slick wood at my feet.

"Line your ball up with the middle one, like this." He kept his hand on mine, bringing it up until it was level with my chin. "You got your eyes focused on that middle one?" he asked, still standing at my back, his voice raspy in my ear.

I nodded.

"Good. Now bring your hand back, but keep your eye on that line." He shifted his body so he could help me shift the ball backward. "Now, keep your eyes focused." His grip on my waist tightened. "Now throw it forward and let go right when it crosses the line at your feet." He pushed my arm forward. I released just like he said, and the ball spun down the lane with speed, not as much as the others, but enough to get all the way down the lane until it hit just left of the center pin, knocking down several.

"There ya go!" Reid clapped from behind me. I spun around with a huge smile glued to my face and threw my arms around him. He grabbed me and spun me in a circle while our friends clapped from behind.

"A split is plenty to be proud of," Kip muttered, sipping on his beer. I didn't even know what a split was, but I was damn thankful Reid had helped me.

The rest of the night went on with more laughter than I'd had in a year. Michelle and Ryan left a little while later, and I was thankful to see her in some kind of romantic situation, though it was new for us. She hadn't been with anyone I knew of for longer than me, but then again, maybe I had just been so involved in my own life that I hadn't noticed. When I'd lived in Oregon, before Travis died, she and I only spoke once a week if that. I was busy, and when we did talk, it was just the basics before one of the kids pulled me away.

"So, you want to talk about what happened tonight?" Reid asked from the seat next to me. The street lights cast a temporary glow as we traveled through the town. I'd had too many beers, so Reid was driving, looking somewhat rigid and intense as he did so, but he was doing it. I was a little too buzzed, so maybe his rigid posture was in my head.

"The not knowing how to bowl thing?" I asked with my head against the window.

He cracked a smile, a beautiful one I shouldn't have liked. "No, you watching your sister and Ryan like that."

I felt my face flush with embarrassment. "Oh…that." I looked down to where my hands rested in my lap.

"Yeah, that. You looked…" He trailed off.

"Jealous?" I finished, looking over at him, wishing I could read his expression. Because who on earth got jealous over their sister flirting with a guy?

Reid glanced over at me briefly. "Yeah, you looked like you wished you were her."

I shook my head. "It's kind of confusing…a little stupid."

"Try me." Reid peered over at me again, those yellow lights popping in to break up the darkness every few feet or so.

I let out a heavy sigh. "She just looked so happy. To be flirted with like that, those fresh relationship butterflies…having that connection with another person, where they get to touch you and have that closeness…" I trailed off, lifting my hands briefly, like they could help explain somehow.

"Does it bother you to see that after…?" Reid inquired softly.

I scrunched my eyebrows together as I thought it over. "No, it's more like I'm afraid I'll never have it again."

Silence flourished between us as my strange truth hung there, waiting for him to do something with it. Although, I supposed there was nothing he could do. He couldn't change my fear or fix it; he could merely listen. What I hadn't shared was that I hated myself for ever wanting it again. I felt like I was pushing against the very human nature that grew in my veins.

Once he flipped the blinker for our shared road, he let out a strained-sounding sigh and replied with, "You'll have it again, Layla. I promise you, you will."

His eyes met mine, somehow offering me this promise that surely wasn't his to give, but my heart reached out and took it anyway.

"Okay," I whispered back.

18

Reid

"REID, HOW YOU DOIN' THIS MORNIN', SON?" LANDON ASKED, CLAPPING me on the back as I started for the stall in front of me.

I turned and smiled at my old friend. "Feeling good," I answered honestly, pushing my gratitude past the ugly sting of shame. Humility was like a slow-moving tidal wave that snuck in and obliterated anything not tied down. Coming back to this life felt like I was swallowing knives, and I hated the metallic taste of blood it left behind.

"It'll be good to see you working with them again." Landon's white eyebrows lifted in excitement. I tried to mirror the sentiment. I'd been working with my students but had yet to break any colts or do any one-on-one training with them.

"Yeah, it's been some time though, so it's probably a good thing I'm starting out with the young ones," I joked, grabbing for the halter on the thoroughbred colt stomping in the stall in front of me. Landon had me working with kids when they signed up, but while they were in school, I was helping to break in some of his colts.

"It'll be like medicine to the soul. Fresh air, the company of a horse —nothing else a man needs besides a good meal." My boss squeezed my shoulder with a vicelike grip. *How the hell is he still that strong?*

I tried not to wince and forced a smile. I appreciated his sentiment and that he'd left out the need for domestication in it. I hated how often my mind thought about Layla and our conversation the other night, how she'd admitted to wanting a relationship again. I hated how often I thought of what it would be like to be hers, to be theirs… how domestication would feel with her and how good it would be. I hated where my thoughts constantly went where Layla was concerned. It was like I had no self-control whatsoever. We were friends and I'd done nothing but think non-friendly thoughts about her.

I carefully led the foal through the barn and headed toward the round pen where we started working through some drills to prepare him for riding. I was rusty, so I took it slow. I let him run around, getting used to my presence for a good five minutes before I started moving him around the pen so he'd get comfortable shifting directions and realize who was in charge.

I blinked at the autumn sun that was already high in the sky, baking everything without shade. I had on a baseball hat but missed the security a cowboy hat offered my neck and face. Already back in my element, I was mentally ticking off items I'd need to wear next time. The old, ratty tennis shoes on my feet weren't cutting it either, and if anyone looked at me, they'd shake their heads and laugh at the 'newbie.' They'd have no clue I wasn't anywhere close to being new. I was just out of practice, out of sync with this world of grass and dirt. I'd just need to find a way to get to a larger department store to stock up. I'd need to head to Casper, which meant I needed to find a ride.

Or just adult-the-fuck-up and drive myself.

I hadn't processed driving Layla home the other night, because I didn't want to muddle the memory, and besides, she had needed me to. It was more like a safety precaution, and it hadn't been as difficult with her next to me.

I gripped the bundle of rope in my glove and clicked my tongue at the colt to encourage him to change direction. His dark, glossy body turned as he canted his head to the side and back. Now I just had to wait as he continued to run around the pen, getting used to the basic command. Breaking colts took patience, and although waiting wasn't something I normally struggled with, I hated being left alone in my own head. Lately, it'd been like a prison in there, replaying images of things I'd have preferred to shut out. I'd been dreaming lately, too, making the nights drag on and early mornings nearly unbearable. I needed to start getting past this shit. In the past, I had loved being left alone with a colt for an afternoon. No one to come and bug me, unless they were just watching for tips.

This had been how'd I found peace, and now it was just a form of punishment.

After about an hour, I took the colt back to the barn to get refreshed and take a break from the hot sun. Just as I was walking out of the side barn entrance and toward the hay shed, I heard a few boys yelling from the road. At first, it sounded like a group of teens laughing and joking, just having a fun time, but as I brought up a bale of hay and tossed it into the trailer, I heard something else too.

"Stop it! I will fucking kill you!" someone shouted above the joking and laughter. The urgency of the kid's tone stopped me short and I quickly turned on my heel toward the road. This ranch was off the main highway, all dirt and gravel, but there was a bus stop about a quarter of a mile up. I shielded my eyes from the sun and tried to see what was going on with the group of teenagers when I heard someone scream, "Please...I didn't do anything to you guys. Stop!" Whoever it was sounded scared—really fucking scared.

I took off, bolting for the road, pushing my legs hard as I ran down Landon's long dirt drive. Thankful that his tall, iron gates were currently open, I kept running through until I came up behind a group of at least five teenage boys. They were huddled around someone on the ground, laughing, kicking dirt, and shoving each other.

With speed I already had built up, I burst into their group and shoved them apart to see who was on the ground in the middle. There was a boy face down in the dirt, hogtied with his wrists tied to his ankles with a thick, knotted rope. The boy who was securing the knot slowly looked up, stilling his hands, and moved to stand.

As soon as he was up, I shoved him hard. *Who the fuck hogties another person?* This shit was used for cattle, and even then, the knots weren't anywhere as tight as the one these idiots had used.

"The fuck you think you're doing?" I spat at the kids, who were all suddenly quiet. I lowered myself to the kid in the dirt and pulled out my pocket knife to cut the rope.

"We were just hazin' the new kid," one of the boys said with a slight twang that was distinctly not from Wyoming.

I looked up at the kids' faces. "You're all in trouble. Do you even understand what kind of shit this is? This bullying stuff is illegal now, in case you missed the memo." I grabbed the kid on the ground and pulled him up.

The group of boys all looked down at the ground and refused to meet his stare or mine.

Landon drove up in his Ford F-150 and got out of the driver's side with a hard slam. "Jason? What in the world is going on here?" he asked the kid who'd tied the knots.

I turned toward my boss and lifted a hand to showcase the poor kid who'd been shoved in the dirt, the one who, now that I was looking, I could see clearly.

Layla's son, Michael, stared at the ground, kicking his foot, and if I wasn't mistaken, he was blushing.

Fuck me.

Of course he was blushing, because this shit was embarrassing as hell. Seeing that it was him they were messing with brought out some foreign emotion in me, something wild, dangerous, and insane. My breathing turned ragged as I eyed those kids again. They'd hurt someone I wanted to protect, someone important to me, because however it had happened, Layla and her kids *were* important to me.

"Jason, you know what your mother said about messing around with other kids. I suggest you boys get movin' because I plan on calling each of your parents to tell them exactly what happened here." Landon's voice cut through the afternoon heat as he placed his hands on his hips and narrowed his gaze. The boys all mumbled an apology and started walking off.

I gripped Michael's shoulder and steered him away from the

departing group and toward my boss. "You hurt?" I asked, quietly so only the two of us would hear. Michael didn't respond, just lifted his shoulder and let it drop.

Right. He didn't want to talk about this, and I didn't blame him.

"Landon, you mind driving us back to his house? I live next to them and can maybe help with explaining what happened to his mother." I didn't remove my hand from the kid's shoulder. I knew he might have preferred that I did, but I also knew that in this moment, he needed to know he wasn't alone, needed to know there were people in his corner.

"Of course. Here, just take it and bring it back tomorrow morning," Landon said, eyeing the boy and giving me a wink. He probably knew I needed a second to talk to the kid without anyone around. Pride was an ugly wall that wasn't easy to tear down, and in this case, actions would speak much louder than words would.

I grabbed the keys, feeling an itch in my consciousness at how the silver felt in my bare palm. I inhaled through my nose and closed my eyes, allowing the concern for Michael to fill the hole that usually opened inside of me when I thought of driving again.

"Hop in. Let's get you home," I called over the hood to Michael, who was standing and staring off into nothing. A second later, he was piling into the large, black beast of a truck and buckling in. I rolled the windows down and slowly headed toward our street. "So, you want to talk about what happened back there?" I softly asked, keeping my eyes on the road.

I was met with silence, which I had figured would happen.

"You know, I used to get beat up when I was in high school. Football players liked to make my life miserable because I spent my time around horses and cattle, not pigskin and cheerleaders," I said to the dash, allowing the silence to sit between us and refusing to allow it to become awkward. I caught Michael lifting his head and looking in my direction.

"They ever hogtie you like that?" His voice was small and broken, and it made something inside of me crack. I had never been in the position to give someone advice or encouragement, not to this degree. I felt like an imposter but kept going for his sake.

"Nah. It would have been me doing the hogtying...but anyone who's ever used a rope and has a soul would never do that to another person. The football guys just liked to punch me in the gut, right after I ate lunch, so I'd throw up. They did it every day for two months before I couldn't take it anymore."

Michael's entire body was facing me now. "What did you do to make them stop?"

The hope leaking from his voice just made me want to go find those asshole kids and punch them each in the face for hurting him. "I disassembled their trucks while they were at practice. Took off their tires, left them jacked up on blocks. I also took their mufflers and poured sand into their radiators. It wasn't nice, but neither was the fact that they'd made my life a living hell. I worried they'd come after me for retribution, but they never did. Guess I got my point across." I finished and smiled over at Michael, who was grinning from ear to ear.

"That's not a bad idea," he mused, relaxing into the seat a bit. It was quiet for a few moments before he spoke up, soft and unsure. "Could you...uh..." he stammered and looked around the cab. "Could you teach me how to work with horses and ropes like they do?"

I looked over at him and signaled for my turn onto our private drive. "Yeah, I could teach you."

I pulled into the spot next to Layla's black SUV, trying to calm down at the idea of seeing her. My stomach always tied itself into some crazy kind of knot when I was about to see her. My palms sweated, and my throat dried up. Michael thankfully didn't notice, but he stalled just the same with his hand on the door.

He turned toward me. "Thank you...by the way. I don't know what else they had planned, but you stopped them. That was pretty cool of you."

He opened the door and hopped out before I could respond.

"Place looks pretty nice, man," Kip noted while walking around my dining room. He surveyed the walls and the pictures of my family I'd finally put up.

"Yeah?" Thanks," I replied, my tone unintentionally clipped.

"What's up with you?" My friend turned toward me, drawing his eyebrows together. His baseball hat covered his face, and with the shadows in my dark house, it was hard to make out his expression, but the eyebrows I saw. I could tell he noticed my shitty mood.

"Nothing...I just have some stuff on my mind," I replied coolly, like it was nothing. I even inspected my laptop in earnest while Kip spectated from his spot across the room.

"What kind of stuff?"

I let out a sigh, because the emotions weighing on my chest were heavy. Heavy as fuck and I would have loved to unload them on someone, but they were too messy, too complicated. He'd just say, *Sorry man, that sucks*, then drive home and watch some reruns of football. He couldn't help, and he couldn't relate—not to what I'd been through or what I'd done.

There was no way, and the emotions I had for Layla that increased with every day that passed were just making it all worse.

"I think I just want to turn in early," I muttered, slamming my laptop shut. We were supposed to watch some UFC fight together, but I'd just put it all on ice because I was a messed-up asshole.

"Whatever you need to do, man." Kip sighed, standing from the chair. He gave me one more look before he headed to my front door and slammed it behind him.

I hung my head and went upstairs to shower.

19

layla

I WAS PEEKING THROUGH THE SHADES ON THE FAR SIDE OF THE LIVING room, the ones that faced my neighbor's house. It was dusk, and he'd already gone back home after dropping Michael off. I was still reeling from what he'd done for my son and what exactly it did to my heart. My baby boy, who wasn't exactly a baby anymore, had been bullied, and in such a way that he had rope burns on his wrists again, along with a tiny bruise near his eyebrow where they'd shoved his face into the dirt.

I was shaking from how livid I was. I'd maintained a calm demeanor in front of Reid, but I was splitting apart on the inside. There's a crazy, out-of-control place inside of every mother that roars to life when her kids are threatened. I wanted names, dates of birth, addresses—but Michael, who was in a surprisingly good mood after everything, had told me to let it go.

Let it go.

As if that were even possible.

Now, after a few hours of simmering and cooling down, the dust had settled, and all that was left was gratitude. I hadn't even thanked Reid when he'd brought Michael home, so focused on why my son looked like he'd just been beaten up and dragged through the dirt. I hadn't focused on Reid's handsome, tanned face or the fact that he'd also looked like he'd gone a few rounds with a dirt patch. He had been sweaty with dirt lines that trailed on the side of his neck, and his old baseball hat had covered his mussed hair.

Now I was peeking through my shades like a peeping Tom, hoping to catch a glimpse of movement from his house so I could go and thank him. I'd seen that Kip had been over there earlier, but I didn't see his truck anymore. Sure, I could have texted or called Reid, but none of that seemed to fit right with how I was feeling inside. My fatherless son had had someone stand up for him, had had someone catch him when he fell and encourage him to get back up again. My broody, angry son had finally cracked a smile at dinner and even joked with his younger brother about some television show they both wanted to watch—together. Lately, he was so hot and cold with Steven, I wasn't sure where they were at in their relationship. It had been a good night, and I had Reid to thank for it.

Pulling my fingers free from the wooden blinds, I cleared my throat and shuffled back toward the couch. I could either forget saying thank you and not make a big deal of it, let our lives continue going in this slightly strained platonic existence, or I could be brave and go to my neighbor's house and thank him. I shut my eyes tight as stomps and yelling echoed from upstairs. It was bedtime, which meant the older kids were all supposed to take showers and get into pajamas. It meant I had exactly thirty minutes before I was due back for turning out lights and tucking everyone in.

With a heavy sigh, I ventured toward my front door, slipped my cowboy boots on, snagged a thin wrap from the coat rack, and headed outside. I was met with the sounds of loud chirping from the beetles and grasshoppers, creating a symphony of sorts. A few bullfrogs were croaking from a pond nearby, the stars were starting to peek through the velvet sky, and a crisp, cold wind ruffled my hair, reminding me that winter was on its way. I tightened the wrap around my shoulders and regretted not changing into jeans. Instead, I still wore my frayed jean shorts that probably showed too much leg. They were my house shorts, and now, halfway between my house and Reid's, I was wishing I'd taken better inventory of my clothes.

If I went back now, I'd never go over there, because going over to say thank you after my kids had gone to bed sent an entirely different message. I thought so at least, though I was so far removed from the dating game that I had no idea what messages were sent to single men. Was Reid even single? Was he one to pick up on messages? He had to be single if he'd considered asking me out, right? And he had been planning to go to that Dine and Date thing...so he had to be. Memories of our night together flashed through my head, and as platonic as things had felt all those nights ago, suddenly they were linked with a batch of heat that simmered near the surface of my skin. My eyes roamed the dirt and gravel between our homes as though they could help me sort through the conflicting feelings I was struggling with in my gut.

Before I knew it, I was at Reid's steps and taking them up, one by one. His light green door was shut, concealing the man who'd rescued not only me more than once but who was now rescuing my son. The man needed to be thanked, and that was just the end of it.

I rapped my knuckles on his door and waited. My arms were crossed tight across my chest to hopefully conceal how frequently I was inhaling, and my posture was rigid. I tried to relax, but a second later the door swung open, revealing a wet Reid.

Water droplets sat on his bare chest and neck, on his hair and even the tip of his nose. I could physically feel my eyes go big as they raked over his defined abs and hard pecs. He had a magnificent chest, one I thought should be touched and often.

"Did someone throw a bucket of water on you on your way to open the door?" I joked while biting my lip. Reid's face went from blank to amused, and if I wasn't mistaken, his eyes narrowed in on where my teeth chewed my lip.

"Sorry, had just stepped out of the shower when I heard you knocking." Reid brushed a hand over his face to wipe away some of the water. Thank the good Lord it was slightly dark, because if he'd just stepped out of the shower and only had time to grab those shorts, he probably wasn't wearing any…

My eyes went down on their own, and I hated myself for it.

"Do you have time to come inside, or what can I do for you?" Reid moved his shoulder from the doorjamb, creating room for me to walk past. I smiled at him, embarrassed that my thoughts had gone rogue and even wandered down his frame at all. I tried to focus. I was there to say thank you; no need to go inside.

"Actually, I just came by to say thank you. What you did for Michael…it was beyond anything I could have asked you to do." I wanted to say more, but my words were coming out awkward and my tongue felt thick in my mouth, as though nothing I said would be able to truly express how grateful I was.

Reid waved me off, grabbing his neck a second later. "I was in the right spot at the right time. Thankful I was, too, because those kids weren't exactly going easy on him."

I swallowed and blinked away images of my son being thrown to the ground and hogtied by a group of degenerate boys. "Yeah, wish I could follow up with their parents, but Michael doesn't want me to."

"I think he's got other plans," Reid said with a smile so wide it nearly took away what little air was left in my lungs. I hated that smile, I hated how handsome he was, and I hated how much my stomach fluttered in response to seeing all those pearly whites.

I cleared my throat and nervously tucked a piece of hair behind my ear. "Do I even want to know what they are?" I tried to joke, feeling my stomach go tight.

"Don't worry, it's not anything violent or illegal." He laughed, moving just a fraction of an inch closer.

"Well, thanks again, and for the snake, the playset…for bowling, and for just being helpful. It means a lot to us." An awkward silence hung between us. I was looking at Reid's bare toes, and he had one foot kicked over the other, angling his body in the doorway, still leaving room for me to pass if I wanted to. I wasn't looking *at* him, though, not at his face, and the longer I waited, the more I knew he wanted me to.

Up my eyes went from strong calves to narrow hips, to a full six-pack with ridges and lines I had never seen on a human up close before, up to those solid pecs and burly biceps, further north to that firm jaw and full lips, until finally I landed on those mossy eyes, which were narrowed on me under a set of dark eyebrows. I took in a quick, sharp breath. The air between us was suddenly charged and in desperate need of a caution sign so no one would dare engage the empty space it filled.

"Means a lot to 'us' or to you?" Reid asked, voice low, raspy, and menacing, like he needed my clarification as badly as he needed his next breath.

I blinked and prayed my voice would make it past my lips. "Both."

He took a step forward, engaging that empty, charged space. I wanted to retreat but stood my ground. Suddenly, he was toe to toe with me and just inches from my face. In the dark, his features were hidden but alive, like the shadows gave him another personality. There was nothing but darkness and decisions between us, my heart thrashing around in my chest at what might happen if the wrong ones were made.

"Layla," Reid whispered, bringing his hand up to the shell of my ear. I closed my eyes tight as though I could just wait him out and he'd disappear. That same hand traveled to my waist and pulled me slightly closer to him until he was kissing my forehead. An imprint from his lips seared the space below my hairline. I didn't open my eyes; I just waited. A second later, I felt the air swish between us and heard a whispered, "You're welcome." Then I opened my eyes to see the door closed and Reid gone.

My eyes watered as I walked home. Something tugged at me to turn and see if he was watching me go, but I couldn't...or wouldn't. I painfully forced my face forward and my feet in the direction of my house.

Something had just happened between Reid and me, and if I had been the only one who knew, it would have been perfectly fine—but I wasn't. I knew Reid had felt it too, which was infinitely worse because if he'd felt it, that meant he could recreate it. My stomach dipped at the thought of having his lips on me, and my heart took a shallow lurch into murky water. Where the hell was I going with this? My husband's casket had only been shut for a little over a year, and here I was lusting after another man. Shame simmered inside me, and self-hate reared its ugly head. I submitted, lowering my carnal desires to the honor and memory of a man I had loved for half my life. I owed my thoughts, my lust, and my dreams to him and only him.

THE NEXT MORNING, I was up before anyone else. I made a huge stack of pancakes and bacon, trying to purge the feeling of uselessness I carried in my soul. The kids all came down in their usual sleepy state, and the lights in the room were low, not too bright but enough to see. They had to be at school in an hour, but I needed just a moment with them, to remind them that I was there, the mother they'd once known, the one who held them when they were hurt, kissed owies, bandaged bears, and sang them songs.

She was still there. She hadn't left them.

So, I was there, smiling like an idiot as my kids filed in around the breakfast nook. "This looks good. Thanks, Mom," Michael said in a raspy voice, still sounding all kinds of exhausted. I pushed the plate toward him and poured him some orange juice.

"Are we in trouble?" Henley squeaked from his spot, where he was dragging a fork toward his plate.

"Why would we be in trouble?" Jovi asked with a lift of her tiny eyebrow. She looked so much like me, but I noticed she was changing too. It was all getting away from me.

"Did we leave the horses out again?" Steven asked, grabbing for the juice.

"Wouldn't we be getting some kind of gross breakfast if that were the case?" Jovi stated with a tiny shake of her head. Poor thing stuck with a bunch of brothers.

"You're not in trouble. I'm just trying to get some of my old self back. I used to get up and make you kids breakfast every morning...

do you remember that?" I asked, turning toward the sink, praying my emotions would stay tucked in today.

"We 'member," Henley muttered around a huge bite of pancake.

"Mom, can I try out for the soccer team?" Steven quietly asked. He kept his gaze down on his plate, and if I wasn't mistaken, I noticed a small blush creep up his neck.

I laid the dishtowel down. "Of course, honey. Do you need a ride, or a form filled out?" I wasn't sure what I was asking. I thought Michael wanted to do track, but I wasn't sure if he still did. Jovi wasn't interested in doing much of anything but brushing out Samson and doing her horse lessons. Henley was just happy learning some things and being around the house, so I figured the schedule should fit.

"I missed fall signups, but I was thinking for spring..." Steven said, taking a quick sip of his orange juice, leaving behind a yellow mustache.

"Why did you miss them?" I asked, confused. Had I missed a signup paper?

"I wasn't ready...but Reid has been helping me, and I think I will be by spring." He sat up taller, explaining with confidence. My heart nearly burst. Two of my children, he'd managed to help heal. I wasn't going to be able to take much more.

"Well then of course honey." I smiled, trying to evade the feelings worming their way through me. If my heart had been an apple, it would have been full of holes from those metaphorical bugs.

"Do you think Reid is cute, Mama?" Jovi asked with a tiny smirk on her face. Everyone froze, watching me. I felt like I was in front of the firing squad.

I cleared my throat. "What?"

"I think he likes you," she went on, her little face blushing.

"That's not something I want to think about, honey," I muttered honestly.

"Why not?" Michael asked with a confused look on his face. I watched him then looked at the rest of my flock, feeling my heart sink.

Had they already forgotten their father? The man I'd vowed to love for the rest of my life? They hadn't been there for those vows, though, hadn't witnessed anything but Travis and me living those words out. Still, I wanted to sink to the floor and cry, but as I watched the curious eyes watch me for signs of weakness, I shoved the emotions aside.

"It's just that Reid and I are friends...so don't get any ideas about us ever being more than that, please." I moved away from them and started washing dishes. The silence at my back made my hackles rise and angry goosebumps break out on my skin.

My mind drifted like a loose piece of wood in the ocean, useless and lost. It went back to the accident, unchecked rage simmering inside me like a pressure cooker. This wouldn't have even been a topic of conversation if not for that night.

A heaviness settled into my chest as I let my mind wander to the places I'd refused to allow it to go over the past year. I opened a door I'd sworn would remain shut, and now ugliness was running rampant in my heart as hate tried to take root.

I didn't want to, but I knew deep down I needed to face this part of my life. It grew alongside my veins like a cancer, there all along despite my best efforts.

I was angry.

So angry at myself, at Travis...at *him*. I needed to start sorting through this mess because if I didn't, it was going to consume me.

20

"WE NEED TO GET THESE STALLS WINTERIZED BEFORE THE END OF THE week. James will be updating the charts for increased food rations. Be sure to follow the updated list," Landon yelled so his staff could hear well enough. I resisted an eye roll, as I knew everyone was. These horses were spoiled to the millionth degree. As much as the entire estate cost, I could slightly understand, but horses didn't need all this fancy shit for winter. They needed water, a shed, and extra food, maybe a warm blanket for when it got bad, but that was pretty much it.

It was October now and the weather had turned from the cozy kind of cold you could fix with a light sweater to the clear-your-throat, uncomfortable kind of cold you needed layers for.

I turned to look at the road and then glanced at my watch. It was half-past three and I knew Michael should have been walking down the driveway any second. We'd fallen into a comfortable rhythm for two weeks since his incident with the bullies. I had talked to Landon about hiring him, and he was elated at the prospect of extra help. Michael was eager not to walk home with a bunch of assholes who hated him, and I enjoyed getting to be around the kid; he was funny and a quick learner. I had started driving my pickup again, only to and from work, but since I was taking Michael home, I needed it.

"Okay, that's it. Everyone back to work." Landon clapped his hands, ending our little staff meeting. Everyone dispersed, heading in different directions, and Landon walked toward me, narrowing his watery blue eyes.

"Where's your sidekick?"

"He should be here any minute...thanks again for giving him this job." I readjusted the cowboy hat on my head, uncomfortable with how proud I felt about Michael working there, prideful and protective.

"Don't mention it. He's a hard worker—reminds me of you." Landon laughed and shifted his weight to his other foot. "How's his mama doing?"

I looked up, startled at him mentioning Layla. My face must have given me away because a sly grin broke out on Landon's face just as we heard Michael's voice.

"Hey, I'm going to need a snack if you expect me to work. I feel like I haven't eaten in years." He walked up, backpack slung over his shoulder, a black windbreaker fastened across his chest, and a sloppy grin on his face. I smiled at the kid and motioned toward the work truck we all drove around the estate. "Food's in there, bud."

Michael headed toward the blue, chipped Chevy and opened the door, from which a loud squeak emanated. Landon stayed put, staring me down. Once Michael was out of earshot, he said, "Just be careful. After what you've been through, you don't need more heartbreak."

"How did you...?"

"Your mom told me about what happened," He grabbed my shoulder tight. "You should have said something, son."

"Yeah...I just..." I trailed off, not sure what to even say.

"I've known you your whole life, and I'm sorry to hear about what happened, which is why I hate the idea of you putting yourself in that position again." His stern glare felt like it was pinning me in place.

I nodded, feeling my heart squeeze tight at both the notion of letting someone in and the idea of getting involved with Layla. We'd had a few awkwardly silent days after the night on my porch then had fallen into a relaxed routine. I'd go over to drop Michael and would say hello to Layla with a grin. She'd smile, wave, and scamper off upstairs until I walked outside with the kids to start their lessons. She'd come out about halfway through to check in then she'd go back inside. She never stayed to talk or chance riding with me again.

Our lessons were getting harder to squeeze in during the week because of how early the sun was setting now. Some days when I'd drop Michael, I'd just stay to play video games with the kids or I'd help Jovi with her homework, maybe color in one of her coloring books. Those moments with her were my favorite. She'd be hunched over the kitchen island with a school book in front of her and I'd be coloring a picture of a horse in a coloring book she'd said she was too old for. Every time I'd color a picture and leave a note, she'd reply with her own. It became like a game.

Yesterday when I'd walked in, she'd slowly slid her coloring book to me and I'd flipped to where we had left off. There on the page was a brown horse with a purple mane and blue eyes. At the bottom was a scrawled note: *Do you think heaven has holidays?*

I spent fifteen minutes slowly coloring in a mustang on the following page and wrote at the bottom: *Of course! Can you imagine heaven at Christmas time? That place the Grinch comes from has nothin' on Christmas in heaven.*

I slid the coloring book toward her and walked away. She often reminded me of a skittish colt, so I treated her as such, never rushing or charging, otherwise, she'd be scared off. I'd walked over to start a game with Henley and Steven when, out of the corner of my eye, I saw her open the page and smile. That smile had stayed with me all day like a lucky token tucked away in my heart.

Landon clapped my back, bringing me back to the moment. I gave a wave to Michael, who was stuffing a sandwich into his mouth and heading toward the round pen. I didn't need to be thinking of getting hurt or losing pieces of my heart. I didn't exactly have one to risk anymore anyway.

"HEY, REID?" Michael asked from the passenger seat of the truck. I looked over, missing the breeze that used to flow through our conversations from the open windows. Crisp as it had been two weeks earlier, it was nothing compared to the cold front that had come in.

"What's up?" I readjusted my grip on the steering wheel.

Michael shifted in his seat. "Um...I heard there was this dance thing happening down at the town hall this weekend."

I smiled and leaned over to shove at his shoulder. "You want me to take you or something?"

He laughed and ran his hand through his hair. "No...I was wondering if you would...um, if you would take my mom?" His voice cracked on the last word.

I kept my eyes on the road and swallowed the sudden surge of nerves and anxiety that was attached to the idea of dancing with Layla.

"I'm not sure she'd want that, bud," I stammered. The pinch in my chest grew whenever I pictured her surprised eyes from that night. I knew she'd slightly been pushing me away, not as conversational as normal. So, the idea of doing anything else to push her away didn't sit well with me. Thankfully, the turn for our drive was coming up and I wouldn't have to be in the truck much longer.

Michael kept his gaze out the window as I put the vehicle into park. Before I could open my door, his arm reached across the bench and stopped me.

"She's being strange...like she's overdoing things, trying to be who she was before our dad died. It's nice and all, but she's in pain and she's ignoring Star and my Aunt Shellie..." He swallowed and looked down, lowered his hand and waited.

My gut tightened from the pain in his tone.

"I'm just worried about her. I think she needs to get away from the house for a night." Michael's face relaxed, and a second later he opened his door to get out. I sat for a few seconds to get my thoughts under control.

Of course I wanted to take Layla to the dance. I wanted nothing more than to have her in my arms all fucking night, but after the porch incident, she'd backed off. Without so much as a single word, she was telling me to slow the hell down. So, I had. I refused to push her or do anything that made her remotely uncomfortable, but then again, I had told her I could just be her friend, one who wouldn't try to kiss her or make her feel like she needed to move past her grief.

I followed Michael up the steps to his house and readied myself for the same scenario I had been accustomed to for the past two weeks, except this day was different.

I walked through the doorway and found Layla standing there, waiting with a smile.

21

Layla

JOVI HAD TOLD ME A JOKE, ONE THAT WASN'T VERY FUNNY, BUT JUST THE same, it made me smile. I might have smiled just because she'd made the effort to be funny, something new. I noticed, regardless of Jovi's attempt at humor, my smile had been showing up more over the last few weeks. As I looked at the clock and saw that it was close to five, I smiled for an entirely different reason. I didn't even have time to wrestle with the guilt that normally accompanied the thought of Reid showing up at our home. The door swung open, revealing my fourteen-year-old and behind him, my next-door neighbor.

I inhaled a sharp breath at seeing him walk into my house, gently shutting the door and toeing off his work boots. Just like all the other times, it turned my insides to liquid, melted me from the inside out. Because for two weeks, while I'd been dead set on honoring my late husband's memory, Reid had been coming in and getting to know my kids. He'd been playing games with them, laughing, joking, and even helping with homework, all while I hid away. I didn't invite him to stay for dinner on those longer nights when he'd smell what was in the crockpot or see me fussing away at the stove, my back turned to him and his efforts to be a friend. I just acted like he wasn't there, and yet, day after day, he was still showing up.

On weekends, he'd walk over and help the kids tack up the horses then show them how to ride and do tricks he'd done in the rodeo. The kids were enthralled and hadn't stopped talking about how much they liked having him around, how much of a nice guy he was, how he made this place better. That line had come from Henley, and it'd nearly ripped my heart out.

Better—Reid made us better. So, today, I was done hiding and done being a jerk. I was ready to face Reid in all his handsome glory and invite him to stay for dinner.

He walked in and kept his eyes targeted on the flat-screen where Henley and Jovi were racing. Jovi had her tongue pinned between her lips, looking focused, and Henley was going the wrong direction again.

Reid messed with his hair. "Bud, what'd I say about the controls? Remember how we stay going the right direction?" he asked my son, who looked up at him, abandoning the screen and the fact that his car had just gone off a cliff then said, "I 'member, but I like going away from Jovi. She's boring and once she wins, she won't play with me anymore."

Reid laughed and messed with Henley's hair again then ever so slowly drew his gaze to mine. I had no idea what he'd find there, maybe hope or hurt...confusion or contentment. Whatever it was, it had him walking closer to me. I straightened my spine, done cowering from this man and the way my stomach flipped at his nearness. I was attracted to Reid. It was a fact, not an opinion or possibility; it wasn't something to consider or suppress. It was just a fact, like the sun being hot or the ocean being big.

My eyes raked over the hard lines of Reid's shoulders and the place where his t-shirt bunched at his biceps, and then they dipped lower to his narrow hips and the way the denim clung to his legs. I swallowed the extra saliva that had awkwardly filled my mouth at the sight of him.

"Hey...haven't talked to you in a bit," Reid said, voice gravelly as he stood in front of me, toe to toe, eye to eye, heart to heart.

I swallowed again.

"Yeah, sorry about that." A lie was on the tip of my tongue. *Work's busy, things are crazy*...I had a myriad of things I could spout off about, but I didn't because Reid wouldn't believe it anyway. He knew I had been hiding from him for two weeks, since the night he kissed my forehead and made something shift between us, like forcing a stubborn wooden peg into a space that had grown too tight.

Reid shrugged, keeping his eyes on me. "You have plans tomorrow night?"

My heart skipped, dipped, and fell into a dull thud. Boldness was inside of me somewhere; it was jaded, rusty as hell, but it was there, so I grabbed for it.

I pushed hair behind my ear as I considered how to answer. I didn't have plans, and Michelle wanted to take the kids to an observatory one last time before winter came, so I'd be alone.

I cleared my throat and pushed out a, "No." Reid watched me as a slow smirk made its way to his clever mouth. I wanted to know what secret thing he was thinking and why it made him laugh, but I was too scared it had something to do with me.

"Well, there's this town hall thing happening. Hayrides, hot chocolate, hot cider, dancing...a fall-themed thing...and I was wondering if you wanted to go?" He brought his hand to the back of his neck and carefully waited for my response. Before I could say anything, he quickly added, "As a friend...like we agreed a while back."

Right. Friendship.

I gave him a watery smile and nodded my head in agreement. A night out with my friend might do me some good.

I WAS STANDING in front of my bathroom mirror, naked. It was something I did every so often because my body was like a timeline. Stretch marks that were light and faded ran along the soft space of my stomach, a stomach that used to be much firmer. A long, pink mark along the space under my belly button where my emergency c-section scar rested, from when I nearly lost my daughter to preeclampsia. A small black tattoo sat at my hip bone from when I was in college and had the entire world at my feet.

This body was one my husband had known intimately. He'd helped hold me in brokenness and create the stretch marks from carrying his children. He had loved my body and showed me frequently, even through weight gain and loss...an avid admirer. The idea of another man one day touching me or seeing me like this...was just too much. I couldn't do it.

I couldn't imagine allowing another man into my world, not like that. I wished I were the kind of woman to throw caution to the wind and just throw myself into a meaningless fling—except Reid meant more to me than a meaningless anything, and I just didn't have the genetic makeup for random romps.

Slowly, I readied myself for the dance I was headed to with Reid. The kids had been picked up early by my sister, so I'd had the entire day to paint my toes, scrub my skin, apply a face mask, and for the love of God, use a set of tweezers on my eyebrows. I'd shaved my legs and soaked in a bath, curled my hair and applied eyeliner and a berry lipstick, and thrown on a navy dress that went to my knees but had no sleeves. I paired it with a thin, tan belt and pulled on a matching pair of tan cowboy boots.

I looked like I was ready for a date. My heart nearly shred in half at the sight of it. I looked beautiful but felt ugly. I was a tattered mess of shame and lust. I wanted Reid to like what he saw, and I wanted him to want me.

A knock on the door echoed from downstairs. I turned from the mirror and tried to forget the sting of betrayal that burned under my skin.

My husband was dead, and I wanted tonight's friendly date to be much more than friendly. I put a smile on my face and walked downstairs, hating myself each step of the way.

22

I HAD CALLED LENNY, A SEVENTEEN-YEAR-OLD SENIOR WHO WORKED AT Landon's farm and was trying to earn some extra cash. He wanted to do an Uber service in Casper and the bigger towns on the weekends because he knew there just wasn't enough to do in Douglas to make anything. I hired him for the night so Layla could let go and so I didn't have to lie about why I wasn't driving.

I knocked on Layla's door to let her know the silver minivan had pulled up and was ready to take us into town. She opened the door wearing a dress that made her tan legs look long and toned, especially with those cowboy boots. Her honey hair was curled and bounced down her chest, hanging just above her breasts. I swallowed and had to search to find words for a second...*You look beautiful...I want to kiss you...*

"Hey...you look nice." I sounded like someone had just punched me in the stomach. *Nice* was such an understatement, a belittling travesty in comparison to how beautiful she was tonight, but I didn't want to push her, scare her off. I didn't want to lose the kids because I screwed this up.

Lose the kids?

Holy shit, where'd that thought come from?

"Thank you, so do you. I've never seen you wear cowboy boots or a buckle that big." She wandered toward the silver van with a small purse in her hand and a sheepish grin on her face. Her gaze was glued to my buckle.

I cleared my throat and, more importantly, my mind, of where I imagined her thoughts going then pointed toward the van waiting for us. "Thank you...figured I'd get all cowboy for this thing, give you the full Wyoming experience."

Layla stopped and looked up at me, her raised eyebrow and smirk meaning she was thinking something dirty or there was more to what I had said. She was right, but I wasn't telling her that.

"Okay, not the full Wyoming experience...but if you're interested..." I winked and relished the blush that crept up her neck. She turned as the van doors began to slide open on their own.

Lenny was in the driver's seat with his head turned toward us. "Please fasten your seatbelts and enjoy a complimentary mint that I have added to your cupholders."

Layla climbed in first and claimed the bucket seat behind him. I felt stupid for making her climb all the way over, bent and clamoring in while wearing a dress. Surely Lenny got a nice glance down the front of it too. Once I climbed in, I saw Lenny snap his head forward and a deep red coloring his cheeks. Yep, he'd fucking looked at her boobs.

I buckled up and watched as Layla suppressed a grin, looking around the van and grabbing for a mint. Lenny crawled along the road at a snail's pace while the soundtrack to *Lord of the Rings* played in the background. I leaned forward and tried to talk to him, and he looked up in his rear-view mirror and gaped. He looked an awful lot like Napoleon Dynamite with his tight head of blond curls, long face, and glasses.

"Sir, please lean back. This is the *employee only* area," Lenny reprimanded me in the mirror.

"Lenny, I'm not 'sir'...I'm Reid and we're still on a back road. Can you go any faster?"

"If you have a comment or concern, feel free to rate me on the app.

As far as the rules of the road, it's legally ten miles per hour on these back roads." Lenny gripped his steering wheel, concentrating with laser-like focus.

I fought a groan. I'd had no idea this kid would take the whole Uber business so seriously. I leaned back and fished in my cupholder for a mint then looked over at Layla, who was holding her hand up to her mouth and shaking.

She was laughing. At the sight of her slender body shaking like a leaf and a few awkward, suffocated snorts through her nose, I started laughing too. Lenny turned the music up, the crescendo of violins and angry trumpets echoing through the car, and Layla lost it. She threw her head back, and the sight of her laughing like that...the sound alone was fucking magical. I wanted to hit pause and save it forever, play it back and listen to it on nights when she'd go back to freezing up and pushing me out. I wasn't stupid—I knew those days weren't gone. She was in love with her dead husband and I couldn't fault her for it.

Thirty minutes later, we arrived in front of the town hall. Layla got out on her side of the van, but only after the doors had opened fully and Lenny deemed it safe to exit the vehicle. She giggled again and thanked the boy. I explained to Lenny that I'd be requesting a ride back from him in a few hours or so, just in case he decided to go home and get caught up in a game of D&D or something, and then I followed after Layla. The hall wasn't very big, maybe two thousand square feet in total. It had two large, wooden doors leading inside, and tonight, little white Christmas lights ran along the frame of each one and out along the gutters.

Layla looked over at me and smiled. "You ready for this?"

I met her smile and held out my arm for her to take, and she shocked me to hell when she grabbed my hand instead and pulled me toward the entrance. I gripped her fingers in mine and held on tight, enough for her to know I had no intention of letting go any time soon.

I led the way into the dim room, which was lit by more white Christmas lights and dangling glass bulbs that stretched along the length of the low ceiling. Tall tables lit with candles and flowers dotted the cozy space, standing every few feet or so. Festive country music flowed through the hall as bodies crammed around tables, others spread out on the dance floor and scrunched together at the makeshift bar. The town hall was used as the boys and girls club during the summer, so there was a large bay window that had a cafeteria feel to it. There were two servers behind it, shuffling back and forth and leaning forward to catch orders. There were a few hay bales that had been brought in to sit on, a photo booth was set up along one of the far walls, and there was a long table full of desserts being patrolled by a woman who'd likely baked them all.

It felt like a school dance, which made me chuckle as I pulled Layla farther into the pandemonium. She followed bravely and looked around curiously. I wasn't sure how often she got out and mingled with the people of the town, but I was glad she didn't seem shy or scared of all the attention that landed on us. We stood behind a few other patrons donning cowboy attire and waited in line. I leaned toward Layla, needing to be close in order for her to hear, and I brushed my lips against the shell of her ear.

"You hungry or want a drink?" I couldn't help myself—I looked down to see if that had any effect on her and felt rewarded by the small trail of goosebumps that covered her arm. I resisted the urge to run my finger along the pebbled skin.

She inhaled a sharp breath and shook her head then leaned in close to my ear and said, "I'll take whiskey if they have it…or wine."

I looked down at her and smiled. Whiskey or wine…seemed like a big jump, but I pressed forward and ordered her a glass of wine and a root beer for myself. Once I returned and handed over her drink, she narrowed her eyes on mine.

"What is that?" Her brown eyes flicked to the dark liquid and up to my eyes. In this lighting, her features were softer than normal; it made her seem more approachable, more pliable for seduction. I wet my lips and watched as her eyes snapped there and back down to her drink.

"I don't drink," I said to her, brushing her ear again with my wet lips. She shuddered but didn't retreat.

"Not ever?" she said to the shell of my ear. This was the most torturous form of foreplay I had ever endured.

I shook my head. "Used to, but I don't anymore."

She nodded and pursed her lips, letting her eyes move to the dance floor. I took her wine glass and set it on a tall table to our right then grabbed her hand and pulled her to the floor. I was going to hold Layla in my arms, and I knew if I wasn't careful, she'd make her way into my heart.

I'D DANCED with Layla before, but having her there with me in that room made me think about the last time I'd danced with someone else, the last time I'd held someone else. It was two years earlier, and I'd been living in Seattle and dating my girlfriend, Jen. It was a late work night, and she was waiting up for me in the dark. Black streaks of mascara ran down her face, and a cold, ruined meal sat abandoned on the table, complete with wine and a candle burned nearly all the way down. Wax had dribbled over the tiny holder and run along the smooth wooden surface. It was our one-year anniversary and I'd forgotten. I remembered scooping her up in my arms, turning on some music, and slow-dancing in the dark.

"Reid, did you hear what I said?" Layla lightly angled my head toward her with her delicate fingers.

I looked down and focused. "Sorry...no. What?" I hated myself for thinking of Jen, not after I promised myself I wouldn't.

"I said we should eat something soon, to soak up some of the alcohol...I'm tipsier than I thought I'd be." Her rosy cheeks rose with the small smile she surrendered.

I laughed and grasped her hand, pulling her toward the food line.

She leaned toward me, clinging to my arm as people made room for us and whispered amongst themselves. "So, how come you don't drink anymore?" Layla hiccupped, which had me laughing.

"It's just a personal decision..." I trailed off, letting my words drag. I knew she'd take it as a rejection that I didn't want to talk about it, but this wasn't the place, not surrounded by the people I grew up with. If they had dug hard enough, they likely knew about what had brought me back. Unfortunately, I knew far too well that this town's curiosity often got the better of it.

"How old are you?" Layla suddenly asked, peering up at me with her brows wrinkled in confusion.

I laughed and moved up a space in line. "I'm thirty-five. How old are you?" I nudged her shoulder.

She lowered her head and laughed then brought her gaze back up. "I'm thirty-four. Good to know you aren't some twenty-five-year-old or something. Wouldn't want to corrupt you." She giggled some more.

I raised an eyebrow and leaned in close. "How exactly would you corrupt me?" It was meant to be funny, and honestly, I was slightly taking advantage of her loose tongue.

She was saved by it being our turn to order. "What can I get ya?" said an overhurried woman with a hairnet snug over her curlers. She was likely in her seventies and already ready for bed. I looked down at Layla, who was scanning the three choices that were available: hot dogs, chili, or chowder.

"I'll take a hotdog with mustard. No ketchup please." Layla put the plastic menu down, wrapped her hand around my bicep, and shuffled to the side to let the next person in line up.

"Hot dog for me as well, but go ahead and give me the works," I told the woman, moving to the side with Layla. "No ketchup?" I asked, narrowing my eyes on her.

"Yeah, weird quirk. I hate ketchup. Ever since I was little it's reminded me of blood, and I just can't stomach it. My husb—" She stopped midsentence and looked down.

I hooked my finger under her chin and lifted her gaze to mine to encourage her to continue. I wanted her to know she could talk about him with me.

She gave me a delicate smile and cleared her throat. "My husband used to play pranks on me with the stuff, knowing I hated it. He'd pretend to get hurt or act like one of the kids was hurt. He always got a good kick out of it."

"Sounds like he had a great sense of humor." I smiled and jostled her a bit. The woman with the hairnet handed our hot dogs over with napkins and two bags of plain potato chips.

"He really did," Layla said on a sigh as we headed toward a table. "So, what did you use to do for work, before you moved back?" Layla took a bite of her hot dog and chewed, watching me carefully.

"I worked as an analyst for Microsoft in Bellevue, Washington." I took a large bite of my food to force her to talk instead of me.

"You went from bull-riding and horse-wrangling to a desk job? That sounds horrible." She leaned forward and let out a laugh.

I chuckled and wiped my mouth. "It was, but at the time, I wanted the big city life. I liked Seattle." I shrugged and snagged a chip.

"Portland was our big city. It was usually as far as we would go, but there were three occasions when we traveled further north and spent the day in Seattle. Pike Place was pretty fun. The kids loved the fish-throwing." Under the twinkling Christmas lights, her eyes glowed and her blonde hair looked angelic.

It made my stomach flip, and everything south came to life with need and desire like I'd never felt before.

"Crazy how close we were…wonder if we ever crossed paths and didn't know it," she whispered while staring down at her empty wrapper. I had wondered the same thing but hadn't wanted to say it. I didn't want to make it seem like I was saying we were meant to be here with each other tonight, because I already knew she'd say it wasn't true. She was supposed to be with her husband and stay happily married forever while I was supposed to end up broken, shattered, and disgraced.

"We should go dance again," Layla suggested then slid off her chair.

23

Layla

REID GRASPED MY LOWER BACK WITH HIS STRONG HANDS, AND I WRAPPED my arms around his neck. I looked up and felt my world crack as the soft lighting gave off a glow, making this moment feel like a dream. I blinked and looked around the room instead. I hated how erratic I was being, how one moment I wanted Reid to want me and the next I didn't want him to even look at me. More than one time tonight, I had run my fingers along my bare left ring finger. More than once I'd looked around the room as if any second Travis would walk in, grab my hand, and take me away, to safety...to before.

I was struggling, and the lust for Reid that burned through me was like a liquid fire, singeing all the memories and important ideals I was clinging to, the reasons why I had planned to die a lonely spinster, still clinging to the love of my life who was gone.

My eyes focused and I realized people were watching us. The barista from the good coffee shop in town was wearing a tiny denim miniskirt and staring daggers at me. Older women standing near the baked goods kept whispering to each other while they watched Reid dance with me. I'd nearly forgotten he grew up here, that these people knew him more than I did. I knew Reid had a past he didn't like to talk about, but I wasn't one to pry, especially when I had an entire vault lying in my heart with no key.

Reid leaned in to whisper, stopping our dance. "Let's go see what they have going on outside."

I hadn't even heard the song change. I nodded and grabbed his hand, following him outside. I liked the feel of his hand. It was firm and warm, entirely different than how Travis' had felt. It was like a string holding me to land when reality threatened to tear me away.

"Looks like they're doing hayrides—you in?" He cocked an eyebrow in question.

I smiled and nodded, trying to shake off the depressing thoughts tracking me like thirsty bloodhounds. We stepped in line behind the three others already there. My arms pebbled against the crisp October night. I hadn't thought to bring a jacket or sweater, and neither had Reid from the looks of it. He noticed my hands shifting up and down my arms, trying to warm them.

"Shit, here." He stepped behind me and took over, rubbing them faster and pulling me into his chest. I was instantly warm from the contact and from the desire welling inside me. I felt like a sixteen-year-old girl again, on a date with the hot guy from school.

"Can't believe Star and Kip missed this tonight," he joked, his laugh ruffling my hair.

I let out a small scoff. "I know. She texted me that they're on an official date. Fancy dinner and everything." I lifted my chin to see over my shoulder, and he looked down. With him at my back and his arms on me, I could have been wrong, but I swore he was about to lean in and kiss me.

"Reid the Speed!" A loud man came up and clapped Reid on the shoulders, breaking our moment. Reid shifted with a sudden look of annoyance passing over his features. It was quick—a furrow of his brow, a tiny curl of his lip—and he shook himself out of it quickly.

"Dane. Nice to see you, man," Reid said in fake admiration. Why did I think he was faking it? It wasn't like I knew Reid that well…it just felt off, like I could feel the vibes Reid was giving off and was absorbing them in my chest.

"What do we have here?" the Dane guy asked, shifting to the side to see me better. He was tall with dusty blond hair that was buzzed like he was in the military. Big muscles, wide mouth, stinky breath.

Reid put his arm around me and pulled me until I was tucked under his arm, against his body. "This is Layla Carter," he said, giving us no title of friendship or more, just leaving it out there for Dane to assume what he would.

"Layla, huh? I haven't seen or heard of you…must be new." Dane narrowed his greedy gaze on my chest and then lower. I felt slimy and gross under his perusal. I wrapped my arm around Reid's waist to hopefully show this idiot I wasn't on the market. Dane's eyes tracked my movement, and he took a step back.

"I'm newish, have four kids. Nice to meet you," I said with a small smile, still tied to Reid. Dane winced at my comment, as most people did when they heard 'four kids.' He looked over to someone who had called his name and gave us a half-hearted smile and wave then took off. I dropped my arm but allowed Reid to keep me tucked into his side.

"Hate that guy," he whispered into my hair, and I nodded, having known it the whole time.

"Why did he call you Reid the Speed? Is that a nickname or something?" We shuffled forward until we were climbing onto the back of the wagon. Since it was colder now and a bit later, most people had gone inside or stuck by the outdoor fire pit. The driver had a spare blanket and offered it to the two of us. Greedy and thankful, I huddled closer to Reid as he put part of the blanket around his shoulders then tucked me under his long arm as the wagon started moving.

"It's a nickname. I went by Reid the Speed while I did the rodeo circuit." He laughed into my neck with his face angled. "In fact, Reid is a nickname too. My real name is far more serious and ridiculous."

I tried to look up at him, and it brought our mouths dangerously close. "What's your real name?" I laughed and watched the white puff of air leave my lips.

He smiled wide and shook his head. "That's not first-date-conversation material. I don't want to scare you away."

I cleared my throat and dared to look up. The moon was white and bright, centered in the sky. I could see my breath and feel my heart lurching violently in my chest, screaming at me to be careful. I was too distracted to care about his real name or why he thought it was so horrible; instead, I focused on the bomb he'd just dropped.

"Is this a first date?" My voice came out strained.

Reid looked down, covering me and watching me with those calculating eyes. "It is to me," he whispered back. His hot breath fanned my face and made everything tingle with reluctant desperation. I watched him, refusing to break his stare, and tracked him as he lowered his face to mine. The closer he came, the more turbulent my thoughts got, but I didn't stop him.

His lips carefully touched mine, like when the sea dusts the land with the slightest splash, warning it of what's to come. He was cautious and curious like he knew we were seconds from all my thoughts catching up with me.

I felt something inside me shift, break open, and crash. I felt liberating freedom only to be reminded that it was still attached to a guilt-laced prison. I pulled back with a gentle hand on his chest. His heart was beating erratically, matching the rhythm of my own. His frantic green eyes searched mine and begged me to stay. They asked a silent question of me that I couldn't answer. I was frozen, torn between the lust filling my veins and the pain slicing through my soul.

I used the hand that was on his chest to fist his shirt and leaned forward. I rested my head against his chin and relished the warmth of his hand coming up to rub my back. A stray tear slipped free, falling into the small space between our bodies that was closing fast. Reid pulled me closer until his arms were fully around me, holding me. A sob I had been battling since those lips landed on mine worked itself free and sounded like a siren to the quiet, cold air. More tears flowed as I nestled my face into the crook of Reid's shoulder.

"Shhhh, it's okay, baby. I know it's hard," he softly cooed in my ear as he brushed the hair from my face, disentangling the sopping wet locks from my lips. Him understanding why this was so difficult only made it worse. My heart beat for Travis so hard that sometimes I thought it had turned to stone and I'd died with him. Sometimes I didn't want to be alive without him, but that was so much better than feeling my heart beat for two men, than being split in half for a man I could never have and a man I should never want.

My throat burned. I was sure it was my wedding vows coming back up in tiny flames to remind me that I'd sworn an oath to only one man in this lifetime. I had no words to give Reid. They were all for the man I had buried. So, I let him hold me, let him kiss my forehead, and let him into a very dark and lonely place, somewhere no one had been yet, and that alone made the moment more intimate than any kiss ever could.

24

Reid

"YOU THINK HE'LL BE OKAY ALONE ON THE DAYS I WORK?" I ASKED KIP while the small ball of fur tried to scale my chest to lick my face. Kip crouched down next to me with his Carhartt jacket zipped up tight. The temperatures had dipped again and we were all feeling it, especially on the concrete floor of the kennel.

"I think so, but maybe Landon will let you take him with you for a bit?" Kip suggested, reaching out to pet the tiny little fluffball. "You sure you want to do this? Getting a dog is a big responsibility," he asked, scrunching up his eyebrows in concern.

I didn't know if I wanted to do this or not; I just knew I was trying to avoid my feelings and the woman next door, so getting a pet to fill the emptiness of my life felt appropriate.

"Yeah, I need some company."

I picked up the small dog and headed toward the front desk, where I started filling out papers. Rhett was a mixed breed who'd been abandoned on the front steps of the shelter a few days earlier. He was about ten weeks old and perfect for me.

I paid the fees and we headed to a ranch and supply store, where I picked up a leash, collar, and food.

"You'll need a bed for him too," Kip noted, snagging a stuffed dog bed off the shelf.

"Shouldn't it be a bit bigger?" I eyed it skeptically. It looked like it might be for a cat.

Kip turned it around in his hands. "How am I supposed to know?"

We moved down the aisle, me still carrying my little pup and Kip walking next to me. He hadn't asked about what'd inspired me to suddenly hang out with him every free chance I had. I drove to his house, went to the bar with him, and even the gym. He was thankful for the company since things between him and Star were a bit icy at the moment. From what he said, it was a "massive misunderstanding."

We'd been going on about a week of this and, as desperate as I was to have my mind stay off of Layla, it drifted back to her often...back to that wagon and the tears that had sprung to her eyes when I kissed her.

"Here we go." Kip gestured toward a bigger bed.

"What do you think, Rhett?" I asked my new buddy, and he licked my face. "I think he likes it."

I RUBBED my lips while watching my reflection in the mirror. My eyes were red and irritated, my beard had overwhelmed my jaw, and my hair was a disheveled mess. I looked worse in that moment than I had that night I'd left Jen's apartment. That night I had looked nice—black tie, slate suit. I had come home early to put together the baby's crib because Jen had absently mentioned it that morning while she was applying her makeup, trying to get as close to the mirror as her swollen belly would allow.

I looked down and turned on the water, splashing my face and trying to get those memories to stay at bay. It had been ten days since my kiss with Layla and seven days since I'd taken a break from going inside the house to see the kids or spend any time around where Layla might be.

The kids had caught on quicker than I'd thought they would. Jovi was the first to show up on my porch with her homework and her coloring book. I sat out there with her, drinking a root beer while she nursed her own and cradled little Rhett in her lap. She slid her coloring book toward me, a full page of color reflecting back, two horses running in a field together. Her note at the bottom said: *Do you think Samson will ever talk back?*

I swallowed and tucked the piece of paper into my flannel pocket because I wanted to keep these little silent conversations going for as long as I could. Jovi was precious to me, and her hurt weighed heavy on my shoulders.

Steven came next, a soccer ball under his arm. He asked if we could do drills in my backyard. Henley finally made his way over with Michael, and they'd join in whatever it was we were doing. The kids would play in my backyard with Rhett, laughing and playing, filling my soul up with more happiness than I deserved.

Sometimes, I would go into the barn with them to help care for the horses and teach them about keeping them safe in the winter, a lesson I assumed Layla's sister would teach her, but the kids needed to know too.

I grabbed a long-sleeved shirt and pulled it on then made my way downstairs to let Rhett out. My phone rang from the counter, and I absently answered while I ducked down to grab my dog so he didn't pee on the floor.

"Hello?"

"Reid?" My mother's worried voice sneaked through the three tiny holes of my phone and struck right at my heart.

"Mom, hey." I grabbed at my hair and pulled, wishing I had checked the ID like I normally did.

"Honey, how have you been? I haven't heard from you since you got back," she asked, sounding hurt.

"I'm okay," I stated firmly. I had been avoiding my mother. As much as I hated it, I was…I just couldn't face her. Not her optimism, not her excuses for my shit decisions, not her endless love for a son who didn't deserve it, any of it.

"Well, how's the house?" She stayed off hot topics, and I let out a tight breath of relief.

"It's good. Thank you for sending everything here. I wanted to call you sooner, I just…"

"Honey, it's okay. I understand," she said softly then paused.

I waited, trying to ready my answer for whatever thing she wanted to dredge up that I didn't. I opened the back door and gently put Rhett down, watching him make his way toward the yard.

"So…have you sent it yet?" my mother asked, speaking carefully, cautiously.

"No." I thinned my lips as anger began bubbling up inside me.

She let out a heavy exhalation. "Son…I think you should send it," she encouraged gently, and I hated her for it.

"Mom, let her move on. I know I need to," I bit out, irritated and ready to hang up.

"Reid, honey, try to hear me out." I could picture her with her hands up, trying to calm me, just like she had the last horrible time I had seen her. Memories were like a trap I couldn't ever see coming. "Mom, I need to go…I need to go check on my neighbor." I headed toward my front door, not lying at all. I just left out the fact that my neighbor was fourteen years old. "Sorry, I'll call soon," I lied, cutting her off.

I hit the red end button and ignored the twitch of guilt that swarmed through me at the action. I brought Rhett back in, set him up in the laundry room with food and water, and then headed toward the door. I pulled on my work boots and grabbed for a hat. Shoving my hands in my pockets to ward off the chill in the air, I headed toward Layla's house. I wanted to shake the funk those memories had put me in. I looked out toward the fields to my right and saw a low-hanging fog clinging to the trees and outlying structures. *Shit.* That meant snow was headed our way.

I turned my head toward Layla's place and saw a red truck pulling up just as my feet made it to the driveway. Her sister Michelle jumped out of the truck wearing brown Carhartt work overalls and a soft blue fleece zip-up. She eyed me warily and shoved her black-rimmed glasses farther up on her nose.

"Hey…" I muttered, nervous she might have heard what I had done to her sister.

She gave me a weak smile. "Hey…" She glanced up at the house then her brown eyes drifted back to me. "You should really talk to her…" She trailed off, pursing her lips.

I nodded, unwilling to give any words to the situation because I'd fucked up. I shouldn't have kissed Layla. I shouldn't have broken the boundaries of our friendship, but I wasn't ready to talk to her and hear that she needed space.

Michelle gave me a small nod and headed up the steps. I tried not to think back to that night in the wagon, to the moment I knew I'd screwed everything up between us, but there in front her house, it made me want to do things…things like tell her I would wait for her to heal. I'd wait as long as it took.

I eyed her door, considering the words I might use if she ever let me. I watched the quiet house and my heart…the damn thing beat frantically at the idea of Layla being in there. Was she dressed in sleep shorts and that flimsy robe she liked to walk around in? Was she bare-foot or wearing those tall Harry Potter socks that went past her knees? I loved it when she wore those socks with her short sleep shorts; she'd done it a few times while making dinner, thinking I wasn't paying any attention to her. She was wrong—I always paid attention to her, even when she was ignoring me.

I must have been standing outside too long because the front door opening caught me off guard, making me jump. My gaze snapped up, expecting Michael, but it was Layla. She was wearing black leggings with tiny slippers on her feet and a long, off-the-shoulder shirt. Her hair was thrown up into some kind of array of chaos, and it was the most stifling thing I'd ever seen. No air was in my lungs, no blood in my veins. Everything just stopped at the sight of her.

She stepped forward, getting to the porch steps, and stopped. She held on to the railing like it was a rope tossed to save her in the ocean.

I swallowed and watched her as she slowly descended the stairs, step by step, until she was standing in front of me.

My eyes immediately went to her pink lips, because that kiss had been everything to me. It had changed something inside of me. It was like feeling the sun again, but she'd pulled back, and I understood. I really did, but it still hurt. It still ripped me open and burned me alive, scarring me for everything and everyone after.

"Hey," she whispered. A loose honey strand fell to her shoulder at the tip of her head in my direction.

"Hey," I whispered back, hating how shaky my voice sounded.

"Where have you been?" Her tender tone was as shaky as mine. It made me want to reach for her and pull her toward my house until we were alone and away from everyone, until we could whisper to each other in the dark and she could break as long as she let me put her back together.

"Around." My eyes drifted from her lips to her brown eyes, which also looked red and irritated, like mine. *Interesting.*

"Heard you got a puppy." She crossed her arms like she was trying to ward off the chilly air.

I nodded. "Yeah, he's a tiny thing. Named him Rhett." I watched her, hoping she didn't ask to meet him, because I'd have to explain that I couldn't do that without trying to kiss her again.

She looked back toward the house and suddenly grabbed my hand and pulled me until we were walking toward the side where the tool shed was. She tugged me until we were both standing nose to nose inside the cramped space, concealed from the world. It was cold, and our breaths were coming out in harsh puffs of white air.

"What are you doing, Layla?" My voice was raspy with need and frustration. I knew she didn't mean to toy with me, but I had my limits, and pulling someone into a tool shed implied things to a man. She looked up, panicked, tortured…whatever it was, it was something I was achingly familiar with.

"How come you've been avoiding me?" She sounded like she was on the brink of tears.

I looked around, holding back the urge to laugh maniacally. "You know why."

She looked down and tried to cross her arms, but there wasn't enough room for such luxuries. "I didn't mean to—"

"Don't. I'm not mad at you. I'm mad at myself for pushing when you weren't interested. I'm trying to show you that I get it. I'm backing off," I said, raising my hands slightly.

She grabbed my hand and brought it to her heart then covered it with her other hand.

"Reid..." She swallowed, sounding like she was barely holding it together.

I swallowed too, waiting...not hating that we were touching.

"I can't explain what I feel. It's like I'm torn in half, like a sheet of stiff paper, but with you gone...it's like..." She stopped and gulped air in, like she was running a marathon.

I stepped an inch closer, my hand still pressed to her chest.

"I don't want you to stay away from me," she finally got out.

"I can't keep being around you, not when I have feelings like this for you, not when I've tasted you and know what I'm living without." I leaned closer to her, invading the space...pushing her. Her brown eyes were so dark, and they roved between mine, testing and weighing the moment. I was about to step back when she rose up on her toes and pressed her lips to mine.

I didn't allow her to pull back or give her any time to second-guess it. I grabbed her face and pulled her closer, molding my lips to hers. I moved my head to the side and deepened the kiss, and she met me move for move. When I felt her tongue dart out and lick my bottom lip, I nearly fell apart. I opened for her and let our tongues dance, let our teeth clash. I saw lights dancing behind my closed eyelids—from what, I had no idea, but it had never happened before, and it made me crave more of her. I moved one hand to her waist and then slid it further south until I was cupping her perfect ass.

I expected her to pull back, but she shocked me and nearly killed us both when she jumped up, threw her arms around my neck, and gave me a split second to catch her. I grabbed a handful of her, steadying us, but the jump made me step back, which led to me stepping on a rake, which made the hoe fall over onto us, hitting Layla in the face.

"Ouch!" Layla put her hand to her head while she was still in my arms and began laughing. I needed to set her down, but I couldn't find a clear space to set her. I turned, tripped on a white bucket, and nearly fell over. She laughed harder and put her feet on the ground, trying to help me stabilize. Finally, I found my balance and put one hand on Layla's hip, because after all that, she wasn't getting away with me not touching her.

She straightened her shirt, fixed her hair, and turned around, heading for the house. Before she got too far, she threw over her shoulder, "Don't be a stranger."

25

Layla

I had never done drugs, had always been more of a straight-and-narrow kind of girl. I went to college, got married, and got pregnant all within my first year, but I had a few friends who did recreational drugs and one who did the hard stuff, the ugly stuff that couldn't be quit just by self-control and determination. That one drug led to several others, and before I knew it, she was dropping out of school and moving into some apartment that had no furniture and a bunch of ratty mattresses on the floor.

She had been a close friend of mine, and I remembered trying to chase her down, trying to reason with the addiction. She gave it a try once, but the withdrawals were too much for her, and by the end of the week, she'd gone back to that disgusting apartment. I remembered Travis telling me we couldn't force what worked for us on anyone else, saying we'd never know their battle until we walked in their shoes.

I thought of Shannon and her withdrawals during the week Reid was away, avoiding me. I'd see him drop Michael off, but instead of coming inside like he used to, he'd just go home. The first day he did it, I nearly threw up. It was the most insane thing. My stomach twisted so painfully I had no appetite for dinner that night. I couldn't stop thinking about how he'd held me in that wagon, how he'd left room for my brokenness. I wanted him closer to me, not farther away, and yet day by day, he was pulling back more and more.

Finally, I broke. He was standing out there, in front of my house, looking all kinds of terrible, exhausted, and alone. He looked like he was waiting for something, and whatever it was whispered that it was the same thing I had been waiting for all week. I hated myself for wanting him so badly, for suddenly needing him, for feeling the frayed edges around my heart so intensely that I couldn't take it anymore. I didn't understand how I could be in love with one man so deeply but desire the presence of another with just as much passion.

I needed him, like a drug, a fix. My withdrawals from Reid were like wilting when I had the chance to flourish. I refused to wither away when he was my own personal sunshine, ready to help me bloom. It had me telling Shellie I'd be back in a second and walking out to meet him. It had me grabbing his hand, dragging him to the tool shed and kissing him.

And holy shit, did he kiss me back. I wasn't ready to dissect that kiss yet. I was still torn in half, and that kiss didn't deserve to be compared to anything in pieces; it needed one hundred percent of everything. Now he and Michael were supposed to be driving up the road any second and I had an angry swarm of bees attacking my insides. Everyone got butterflies, and that was what I'd say I had felt with Travis, but that was too tame for what I felt for Reid. It was an angry, desperate feeling.

I set the warm casserole dish on the table and smiled at Jovi as she readied the salad and bread. I planned on asking Reid to stay for dinner, and there was something so perfect about not having to worry about the kids' reaction. They loved Reid. He was more therapeutic for them than the horses were. He was in no way a replacement for their dad, but he was an amazing friend and mentor, someone they could rely on and look up to.

"Mama?" Henley called, walking into the kitchen with his cowboy hat on.

I smiled and hid a laugh. "Yes, bubba?" I grabbed a few plates and handed them to Jovi.

"Do you think Reid will teach me how to ride those sheep at the rodeo?" He tilted his little head and my heart nearly burst. He was getting bigger, taller, his baby voice wearing off, and he'd lost two teeth already.

I drew in a steady breath and smiled. "We could ask him tonight if you want."

Casper had a big rodeo happening in December, something about a tribute to someone who'd passed. I hadn't paid too much attention to the kids going on and on about it. They wanted to take a weekend at my sister's and go to the rodeo all three nights. Henley and Steven had found out there was such a thing as riding sheep like they were crazy horses, and they hadn't stopped talking about it since.

"They're here!" Jovi yelled from the living room; she had sauntered over to look out the window. While I wanted to kiss Reid again, there was that tiny part of me that had cried in the wagon and still existed inside of me. A subdued sob, a painful agony, it was grief that would live in my soul as a forever thing, but I'd have to learn to live alongside it.

"There's no way!" Michael's booming voice met us first when he had barely opened the door.

Reid smiled down at him and said, "Just watch, bud." They laughed at their inside joke and private conversation, took off jackets and boots, and then made their way toward us. My heart beat erratically as I watched Reid's white-sock-covered feet walk toward my kitchen sink, where he gave me a sly grin while he scrubbed his hands. Where would he put those hands once they were clean?

He stood, and I wanted to sit. I needed a second to acclimate to him being so near. He'd been in my home for weeks, kicking back on my couch, laughing with my kids, comfortable and relaxed—and yet now, I was nervous.

The kids milled around us as Reid slowly walked toward me, green eyes blazing with need. I wanted to wrap my arms around him and kiss him, taste those lips I had devoured earlier, but I looked down and straightened my shirt instead. He chuckled, which made me look up. He pulled a chair out and sat down just as everyone else filled in around the table. We'd all had meals together before, but now that Reid was touching my toes under the table and making me feel like a hive of bees lived in my stomach, things were different.

I nervously laughed as the kids joked. Michael talked about his job at the ranch, a place that had changed my son for the better. He talked about how several of the owners who boarded their horses were coming to check on and ride their horses before winter set in, how one of the rich kids snubbed him but he only laughed at how spoiled they were to have expensive horses but never the time to actually ride them. "The jerk didn't like it when I reminded him that I get to ride his horse more often than he does," Michael joked while stuffing a big bite of casserole into his mouth.

Reid gave him a warning with a smile. "Just remember that those expensive boarding brats are what help get your paycheck printed."

Michael canted his head in a *yeah, yeah* kind of gesture. Once dinner was through, I told the kids to each take a job while I took Reid out to the barn to have him check on a few things for me before the first snow fell. Of course, Henley begged to come with us, but I told him he had to help first.

It wasn't going to be easy to find time alone with Reid, but when I was determined, I was also creative. We slipped out through the back door as the last of the sunlight clung to the horizon. The cold air was turning colder as November approached. I knew that meant snow and, from what I understood, a harsh Wyoming winter, but it also meant newness and a fresh slate for me to create memories and monuments, places I could look back on and measure how far I'd come, how much progress I'd made.

Reid followed without touching me as we headed toward the barn, the place where our lives had connected and clashed together like the lightning over our heads that night. Once we were inside and out of eyesight of the house, Reid crowded me against a wall.

"Missed you today," he whispered in my ear as his lips touched the sensitive flesh there. A shiver ran down my spine at his nearness, and my back answered his whisper by arching into him on its own. He wrapped his hand around me and, with one arm above my head, leaned in to kiss me. It was dark in the barn as the sunlight fled the world and dusk replaced it. All I could see were shadows. I brought my arms up to wrap around his neck, intertwining my fingers, gripping, holding, retreating.

He broke the kiss for a second, but only to smile against my lips and pull me closer. "Give me some words, Layla. I need to hear you, or else I'm going to think you don't want me to do this."

I brought my finger down to trace his lips. "I want this. I want you...I want a fresh start," I whispered then pushed forward to kiss him. I poured my hope into the kiss, hoping he'd catch all the fervor I had for this, for us.

We moved our mouths to the beat of our hearts, frantic, crazy, and desperate. We only broke apart when we heard Henley's little feet running toward the barn. Reid took several steps back, crossing to the far wall to flip on the lights, and I adjusted my shirt and my hair. Henley rushed in, looking worried that he'd missed something fun.

"Did you guys go riding yet?" Henley's little voice had Reid and me staring at each other in a hilarious stare-down.

Reid never once looked away from me as he lifted a brow and said, "Not yet, bud, but I'm hoping your mom will agree to it soon."

My face heated and my stomach churned, but somewhere lower, everything burned. Reid wanted to sleep with me at some point, and I had no idea if I was prepared for it. Kissing and grasping at each other like high schoolers was one thing, but sex? My breathing turned shallow. I looked back over at him and relished his shy smile. I didn't want him to think he'd pushed me too far, so I smiled and tucked some hair behind my ear to reassure him. If Reid and I kept going, sex was going to be a discussion at some point, but tonight all I wanted to do was be in sweet and innocent denial.

A THIN BLANKET of snow covered the ground as the kids and I piled into the SUV. Their school day started at seven in the morning, which meant we had to leave our house at six forty-five. It was horrible and cold and dark. I wanted a blanket and sleep.

"Michael, didn't I ask you to start the car fifteen minutes ago?" I asked through chattering teeth. Our SUV wasn't brand new by any means. It didn't have seat warmers or a fancy steering wheel warmer, and I was learning that I'd need gloves to drive if the car didn't get started in time.

"You never asked me to do it," Michael deflected, blowing hot air into his cupped hands.

"She did too," Henley called from the back where he sat in his booster, wearing a hat, gloves, and winter jacket. He was always more prepared than I was. He also always knew exactly where all his winter-related clothing items were. Don't ask me why or how, but that kid loved the prospect of playing in the snow and treasured his protective wear.

"Shut up," Michael spat from the front.

"You shut up!" Henley said with a twist of his mouth, mimicking his older brother.

"Boys!" I warned as I reversed away from the house, but just as I turned the car, I felt a slap on my window.

Startled, I turned toward the sound and found Reid there, smiling. He was holding two traveling mugs of what I prayed was coffee. I rolled my window down as my stomach sloshed with anticipation of caffeine and of seeing Reid.

"Hey guys," he said, looking over my shoulder and into the back.

"Hey Reid," everyone yelled in greeting.

His gaze turned back to me, his solid green eyes searching mine for something, but I wasn't sure what. "I was wondering if you guys had room in this beast for one more?"

Michael was already unbuckling, likely all too eager to make room for his new BFF. I smiled and nodded my head, encouraging him to get in. *Should I have offered last night?* I'd thought he had driven his truck to the ranch.

Reid climbed in and shut the door, and Jovi popped into the third row, where Steven was already reading by himself. Michael took her spot and buckled. The middle console separated Reid and me, but I could feel the heat from his body and from his gaze.

I put the car in drive and maneuvered to the road.

"Sorry to shove in uninvited," Reid softly said from his seat as he bumped my knee with his fist. My stomach wanted out of my body from the movement. I looked over at him and smiled. Stupid—he made me stupid and unable to form words.

"You're always invited. If you want a ride, just come over and get in the car." I smiled as we continued down the snow-covered road. The world was dark but awake. Headlights shone from farms that were already moving and starting their day, and if I'd rolled my window down, I'd have heard the low hum of tractors started, keeping their diesel warm. It wasn't winter yet, and from what Reid had told me, no one was closing up shop until at least December. Even then, it would still be busy, just a different kind of busy.

"I'd like to ride with you guys, if for no other reason than to see you every morning." Reid gave me a side smile then quickly amended his statement. "I mean all of you, the whole family."

I swallowed and focused on the road. He was so present, so there, and I both hated and loved it. While in the past Travis was the only one to drive us around, it felt strange to have a man in the front seat. His scent tickled my nose and triggered memories of his lips on mine. It made me squirm in my seat and sneak glances at his mouth to remind me that it was still there. He was still there. I could pull the car over and pull on the front of his shirt, drag him toward me, and kiss him senseless, the only problem being that the kids were all in the car, and—*oh*...

Not used to seeing Reid so early, I had completely forgotten I was in my robe...and slippers...and *oh God!* My hair was in a sloppy mess on top of my head, and my glasses were perched on my nose because I wore them every night after I removed my contacts. I had no makeup on, and dark eyeliner was still smudged below my eyes. I also had not brushed my teeth yet, and suddenly I wanted to die.

How could I be so comfortable with Reid that I had totally forgotten I wasn't even wearing a bra? I had just jumped in the car to take the kids to school like I did every day. I normally didn't shower until after I got home and had worked out for a while in the form of stretching and doing yoga, and sometimes I just vegged out and watched the workout videos while I drank water. Sometimes putting on workout gear was a feat in itself.

I slightly turned my body away from Reid, trying to shield him from my crazy, but the instant I did, he noticed.

He cleared his throat. "Everything okay?" He said it quietly so the kids didn't hear.

I quickly glanced at him and then straightened my spine. "Yep, fine. I just, uh...I kind of forgot I'm in my robe, and it's slightly horrifying." I kept my eyes forward as we neared the ranch Reid worked at. I put on my blinker to turn, but he reached over and put his hand on my knee.

"Let's drop the kids first," he said softly while watching me with that hungry stare I had seen the night before.

I continued forward and tried to relax as Reid engaged Henley and Michael in conversation, taking the focus off of me. Once we pulled up to the old, red brick building, the kids all began piling out of the car. I normally stayed put because it was a carpool lane, and while it was a small school, I still didn't want to see or be seen by the population of Douglas. Reid, however, got out and individually hugged each child, giving them a small pep talk on how to be amazing. There were six cars behind me and the crossing guard was furiously waving us forward, but Reid didn't act like he saw or cared.

My eyes watered at the sight of my little Jovi tucked under his chin and a wobbly smile plastered on her face. Hot, stinging tears fell, fat and unapologetic when Michael smiled at him and gave him a high-five. Reid would never try to replace Travis and never could, but he could be the sun that would drive the rain out of my children's grief-stricken world. He could be a helper, a friend, someone who would...

I placed my hands on my cheeks to wipe away the remnants of my reaction to witnessing what I'd seen. I tried to clear my mind of long-term ideas and images of Reid being a part of our lives down the road. It wasn't fair to him or us to put that kind of baggage on him. I had no clue what his plans were or what he saw happening with me.

He climbed back into the car and smiled as he buckled. I pulled forward and out of the school parking lot. It was silent between us, no words, no sound...just breathing lungs and beating hearts.

"Pull off up here?" he asked, glancing over briefly. I would have preferred he not get a close look at me in this condition, but I would have also preferred not to have to go the entire day without his arms around me.

Putting my blinker on and turning, I safely put the car in park off the main road and away from any local farms. We were in the middle of nowhere. Reid turned toward me, and I turned too...reluctantly, unsure of how horrible I smelled but too scared to lift my armpits to find out.

"Hey," he said quietly as he exhaled, pulling my attention to him. I shoved my glasses up my nose and crossed my arms, tightening my robe.

His dark hair was tousled on top like he'd run his hands through it with water but just a small amount. He'd shaved since the previous day, which revealed his firm jawline and full lips. His dark long-sleeved shirt tucked under a dark green puffy vest made him look like some camping model. He'd have convinced me to buy all the sleeping bags and tents in the entire store, especially if they had him smolder like he was right then.

"So, you're nervous about being around me like this?" He lightly waved his hand, gesturing to my appearance, and I felt my face heat. Before I could respond, he half climbed over the console until he was crowding me and close enough to whisper in my ear. "Because seeing you like this does the worst things to me." His hot breath caressed my skin and sent a delightful shudder to my core. He adjusted his body until his hand molded to my waist. "Seeing you like this makes me think about things I shouldn't be thinking about." He leaned closer and landed a gentle kiss to the shell of my ear. I waited, and he pulled back, just a few inches or less from my lips. He searched my eyes and said, "Ask me what I shouldn't be thinking about, Layla."

I drowned in his gaze but came up for air long enough to ask, "What does it make you think about?" I shouldn't have asked, shouldn't have allowed my mind or his to go there, but my body was already begging me to drop my guard and let him in.

In every possible way.

Reid's hand on my waist flexed and tightened, his other hand came to my hairline and tugged on one of the loose strands, and his nose skimmed the space right next to my mouth.

"It makes me think about what it would feel like to wake up with you..." He closed his eyes briefly, as if he was savoring something sweet. "Opening my eyes to see you like this, unguarded, unprepared...no walls up. Just your thin pajama pants and these barely-there straps of your tank top." He slipped his hand into my robe, near my collarbone, and pulled the thin strap of my tank tight until it snapped. "It makes me think of what it would be like to..."

He lowered his lips to the side of my neck. Pressing kisses against my skin, gentle and possessive, he made his way from my neck to my jaw. When I thought he was going to come for my lips, he went back down, and this time he pressed the tip of his tongue to my skin, tasting me. I heaved in a sharp breath and brought my hands up to grip the sides of his face, holding him in place lest he try to stop the perfection his mouth was creating.

I arched my back, pushing my neck and chest toward him, desperate and hungry for more of his kisses and whatever else he wanted to do. He sat up, drawing his face away. His eyes were focused on my lips, his brows drawn in tight.

"Are you going to let me kiss you, or are you going to tell me you have to go home and shower first? Because I really want to kiss you." He searched my eyes with his own and breathed in and out heavily.

I sat up just a fraction of an inch, let my robe go, and slammed my lips to his. It was wild, uninhibited, bypassing all the places we'd gone in the barn and in the tool shed. This was something so different, something on the edge of dangerous.

Two strong hands gripped my waist and pulled me over the console. I gripped his neck and willingly went into his lap, straddling him in my thin sleep pants and robe. Our kiss deepened as our mouths slid to the side and back, his tongue invading my mouth, his teeth biting and demanding. Heat radiated through my entire body as I worked relentlessly not to be affected by the hardness underneath me. My body was completely amped up and ready, but my heart was beating frantically for me to stop.

With all my strength, I pushed on his chest and pulled away. I relished the image of the way he looked: lips red and glossy, green eyes dilated and hungry, hair messy from my fingers tugging on the ends. He was beautiful, and some tiny place in my heart whispered, *He's mine.* That same place whispered that I wasn't his...I was lost to a ghost, a man who could never hold me again, never kiss me or touch me.

"I can't do this." I panted, gripping his forearms. My robe was open, my small tank revealing exactly how ready my body was for him. I carefully pulled on the split fabric and covered my chest with it.

Reid let me go, and almost immediately, I could feel him retreat. He was already building a wall, someplace safe where I couldn't get to him. Panicked, I reached out to cup his jaw.

"I like this...what we're doing. I'm just worried about it escalating...I'm not ready for..." I trailed off and looked up, trying to hold off the awkward emotions that had started clogging my throat.

A warm hand gripped my chin and drew my gaze down. "Then let's just stick to this." He smiled, and my heart pounded with a painful thud in my chest.

I nodded, not able to respond, and leaned forward to hug him. He wrapped his strong arms around me and held me tight. I let a few tears out and let Reid hold me, like he had that night in the wagon. Worried he'd stay away again, I sat back. "Will you come over for dinner tonight?"

He cracked a big smile. "I'll be there." He leaned up to kiss me one more time before helping me back over the console. We both swallowed the words we owed each other regarding this situation, what was expected, and the kids...I didn't bring any of it up because I was terrified of Reid, scared of what it meant that I was feeling things for another man and scared of what could happen if I ruined it all.

26

"Okay, I'll only be an hour..." Layla stammered, messing with her hair. It was one of her nervous ticks I'd come to recognize. Since we still hadn't told the kids about us, I pushed back the urge to reach out and grasp the rogue strand that had fallen to tuck it behind her ear.

"We'll be fine. In fact, I think I might take them out to a friend's ranch and let them see some bulls and farm animals." I gripped my belt buckle, a normal-sized one that just had my name on it.

Layla watched my movements and smiled at me. "You really are a rodeo cowboy, aren't you?" she joked, pushing at my shoulder.

"Luckily for you, all the bad habits of the rodeo life have been purged from my system, except for this pesky tick of grabbing my belt buckle." I smiled and leaned in closer to her, causing her to take a step back and blush.

She looked around, making sure the kids hadn't seen, and cleared her throat. "Okay, well if you're gone a bit longer, I'll just head over to the local coffee shop and get some work done. Actually, that sounds amazing, so please stay as long as you want." She brought her hands together in a prayer-like fashion.

I smiled and laughed. "Go to your appointment, woman."

She turned and walked through the glass door of a smaller brick building.

I turned toward the four kids who were climbing all over the boulders that lined the parking lot and clapped my hands. "Who's ready for some fun?"

"ARE you sure we're allowed in here?" Jovi whispered while gripping the black bar on the side of the large train engine. It was a big tourist spot for anyone who was passing through Douglas, a few stray train engines parked on the grass in front of some federal buildings. People could look around and take pictures in front of them, but for the people who grew up in the area, we knew you could also climb inside them.

"Yes, it's fine. Just keep going," I assured her. She had three large steps to climb up and a big door to push open, but that was it. When she faltered again and I saw the look of panic on her face, I gently grabbed her by the waist and set her back down on the grass. "Here, why don't I go first so you know it's all safe," I offered then set Rhett in Jovi's arms and moved around her to start climbing the steps. I grabbed the lever on the outer door and heaved it open, creating a rusty squeak and loud echo. I smiled down at the kids. "See?"

"Whoa, that's awesome," Henley said excitedly then started scrambling up the steps. Steven followed, Jovi carefully stepped up, and Michael brought up the end. Henley was hopping from one place to another. The space was large, all painted a cream white with a tall ceiling and windows, and it had a very distinct, empty feeling like a tank. There were a few black seats stationed around that resembled bus seats, but otherwise just a few knobs and levers. It was fun, but not too much that the kids could get in trouble with.

"This is awesome!" Henley yelled from his seat before running toward the back.

"It's pretty cool, isn't it?" I asked, smiling at how the kids were reacting to the thing I used to love as a child. Rhett sniffed the ground and ran after the kids. I technically wasn't supposed to bring the dog in there, and technically we were supposed to wait until the tourist hours started and a guide was there with us.

"When I was a kid, this thing looked a lot bigger," I muttered, pulling myself up into a pull-up on one of the low-hanging bars.

"Can we try the other one?" Michael asked from the open door, halfway hanging out of it.

I smiled and nodded. "Go for it."

WE SPENT NEARLY an hour checking out the trains and seeing who could successfully climb to the top of one. I made sure each kid was spotted and not doing anything dangerous, but also, they were kids and needed to smile. Hearing their continuous laughter all day had me eager to figure out what else would excite them.

I was traveling up a bit of a grade on the outskirts of town where the vegetation thinned a bit and it was mostly just dirt and yellow fields. I saw the old white house first, the paint chipped, a few discolored boards in place from different seasons of weathered storms. The roof looked newish, but there was an addition to the side that looked much newer, like it'd been added in the last few years.

I put my blinker on and turned down the dirt road that led to the ranch that had defined my childhood. Dirt kicked up as the tires pressed into the path. To the left was a small set of bleachers set up right outside of the horse arena, enclosed by aluminum fencing. There was a large reader board that showed an empty place for stats and numbers; I doubted it was connected with video like some of the newer rodeo grounds were. I'd be put off if it was. The Wildes' ranch was where I'd learned how to ride broncos, and where I'd learned what fear felt like and how to control it.

I put the car in park near the house and smiled at the kids as they looked around in confusion.

"Where are we?" Jovi asked while Rhett slept soundly in her lap. I liked that the kids had taken so well to my dog and vice versa, especially because I'd been thinking forever kind of thoughts about their mama lately.

"I grew up learning how to ride here. This was where I did my first rodeo," I explained, opening the door. The front of the house opened, revealing the man who had been like a second father to me growing up.

He wore a tall, cream-colored cowboy hat on top of his withered gray hair. He had a thick mustache still in place and wore a button-down shirt that was tucked into a pair of faded Wranglers, along with a pair of dusty old pointed-toe cowboy boots that crunched the gravel near his front steps.

"I'll be..." he mused, nearly in awe. I ducked my head as I took a few steps closer.

"Gary..." My throat constricted as I greeted my old mentor. His family had been a safe harbor for me more times than I could count. When Dad died, Gary was the one who stepped in to help my mom figure out property stuff and life insurance hell, and more than anything, he and his wife were pillars for us.

"Reid Harrison?" he whispered, stalking closer, and shit if it didn't actually feel like my own father was wrapping his arms around me. I hated myself for not coming to see him sooner, but when I'd left, it had been him who was the most hurt by my need for the city life.

Country air was the only air he'd ever wanted to breathe, rodeo the only thing he ever knew.

"Yeah...sorry it took me so long to come see you." I clapped his back as he wrapped me in a tight hug.

"That's all right. We all gotta wait until it's right to get out and see who needs seein'."

He leaned back, releasing me, and allowed his gaze to drift over the car and the kids who were now slowly exiting it.

"What on earth have you got here?" He laughed as all four of them stood in front of the truck with Rhett running around it.

I leaned back and brought a few of them forward by their shoulders. "These are my students and neighbors." I introduced each child and smiled as Gary laughed at each one. "I was hoping I could show them some of the bigger bulls and a bit of the farm." I looked up, catching the question in Gary's eyes as he looked over the kids again. He knew there was more to this story, but I wasn't sure what else to tell him. I wasn't ready to talk about anything else that had brought me here.

"Well of course. The baby sheep need bottle-fed here pretty soon, same with the goats." He lifted his hand and gestured toward the bigger barn off to the side.

I walked with the kids down to the sheep pens and smiled as Henley and Jovi fawned over the babies, wrestling with each one to feed them the bottle. Once they were finished, we walked over to the largest barn and I stopped short with the kids on my heels.

"Before we go in here, you need to be prepared. These bulls are big. Up close, they're pretty scary, and they aren't exactly nice. Out in the pasture, they're much more relaxed, but here in this pen, they're amped up. They will charge you. Do not crawl inside the pen under any circumstances. Do not put your hand in to pet the bull. Do not try to touch its horns. Am I clear?" I quirked a brow and checked that each one of them had heard my warning.

Once they all nodded furiously, I slid the door open. The first pen held a huge Plummer bull, long white horns on his head, snot dripping from his nose. As we entered, he kept his head straight forward but canted to the side and let out a loud exhalation through his nose. It made Jovi jump. She backed up once he started stamping his hoof and giving us the side-eye. All the kids backed up a bit.

"You've ridden one of those before?" Steven asked absently while staring the beast down.

"Actually no, not one of those. I've ridden several that are like it, but I'd love to get on one of these bad boys. Should we ask Gary if I can give it a shot?" I smiled wide at the kids and they all snapped their head in my direction.

"No way." Henley was in awe.

"Come on, let's do it." I threw my thumb over my shoulder.

"What about one of the smaller ones? That one seems like it's pretty big. You could get hurt," Jovi squeaked out.

I laughed and headed toward the gate where some rope was resting. "Nonsense. I grew up on the backs of these guys—rode my first one when I was just six." I scoffed then realized my error too late. Henley's eyes got really big and his gaze bounced back forth between me and the bull. "I was with another adult, though, and had on a helmet and pads. It was all very official and safe," I explained, hoping to rid Henley of the thoughts. "Gary, we wanna ride your Plummer bull," I called over to him as he talked to a few other guys who worked there.

He gave me a knowing look that said I was full of shit. "That one is for people who've been on a bull in the last five years."

I winced at his tone and looked around the barn. "And for people who haven't been on one in ten?" He pointed a finger toward the back, so I walked around a few more pens and let out a loud groan. "Lyle? You want me to ride Lyle?"

The bull was ancient and barely moved at a snail's pace. He didn't buck, kick, or do anything but move his head from side to side.

"You know better than anyone that you can't walk into the world and expect to be handed all the keys you once held. You have to earn those back, son." He said it jokingly, but there was a bit of bite to his tone.

I waved him off. "I think I'll stick with the Plummer," I joked, but Jovi tugged hard on my hand, stopping me in place. I looked down and saw her little eyes were brimming with tears. I crouched to her level and gently calmed her down. "Hey, what's wrong?"

"Please don't ride it. You could get hurt, and I don't want you to die." She sobbed and flung herself around my neck. I hugged her back, all while catching Gary's knowing gaze. I rubbed her back softly, trying to soothe her.

"How about we go find Vonny and see if she's baked some cookies?" Gary offered, leading all the kids back toward his house.

My heart felt all fluttery and jittery. I hated that I had just made Jovi even consider that she might have to deal with death again. I hated that I loved the warmth in my chest that sparked at how much the idea of something happening to me bothered her. I was falling for these kids, and I wasn't sure I'd survive it if I ever lost them.

27

Layla

I PRESSED THE BACKSPACE BUTTON ON MY LAPTOP WITH FORCE AND planted both hands on my face. The cup of coffee I'd ordered was cold, had been for a while as I sat there trying to come up with ideas for this list. My therapy appointment with Dr. Vox had been different than any of the other ones we'd had, leaving me feeling unsettled.

Usually, every single appointment was dedicated to my grief and how I was coping as a single mother in a new town, or how I hadn't come to terms with the hate simmering in my soul for the man I had avoided talking about for the past year. Vox would usually ask how I was taking time for myself and not just the children, how I was letting go and trying to move on. Today had revolved solely around the fact that Reid was on my mind and slowly inching his way into my heart.

I had been panicked, outright crazed with confusion as I laid it bare for my therapist. He had smiled, nodding his head, and eventually came up with this hairbrained idea to make a list of five things I could say yes to with Reid.

I had already confessed that sex was a big no for me, and it seemed to consume my thoughts because I wasn't sure how else I could be intimate with a man. I didn't even know if I wanted to be intimate with a man. So, there I was an hour after the appointment and no closer to coming up with a list of things I could say yes to.

I knew I liked kissing Reid, so I slowly typed out the word after number one. I tilted my head and contemplated what else I was comfortable with.

"You gonna be in here all afternoon?" the barista boomed from her counter across the room. I startled and looked up, thankful I hadn't been drinking coffee at that moment.

"What?" I asked, a little confused.

"You're Reid Harrison's new girl, right?" she asked with unveiled vehemence.

I was too stunned to answer. I had seen her eyeing me distrustfully at the town dance, but how did she know Reid and I were together? We hadn't told anyone, not even Michelle.

I grasped for something to say so I didn't have to say yes. "Um… have we met?" I didn't want any rumors getting back to my kids before we had a chance to tell them. But also, why the hell was she being such a bitch to me?

A snarky scoff met me while the girl examined her nails. "You know he and I were together before he moved away, right?" She had sleek brown hair and large side bangs, glaring while popping her gum. How old was she? She looked about my age, but her maturity and professionalism (or lack thereof) suggested a much younger age.

"Okay?" I said, confused why she'd bring that up. I started gathering my things because, at this rate, I wouldn't be staying there.

"Okay, so are you staying here all day?" she asked again, more urgently and with a wave of her hand.

What the hell is happening?

"I'm a customer, so…is it a problem?" I argued, getting a little frustrated that she was being so rude. No one else was in the coffee shop, but several patrons had come and gone throughout my time there.

"It's just that I usually close up early if no one comes in." She popped her gum again. She was wearing skintight jeans, a low-cut tank, and a large flannel over her slender shoulders. Her bright pink lipstick stood out as she chewed and popped her gum like a cow. I resisted the urge to roll my eyes because she'd just had a customer not even ten minutes earlier.

"If you want to close early, just say that," I curtly replied then stood to gather the rest of my things. A second later, the glass door opened, causing the bell to jingle loudly in the empty space. Barista girl's eyes jumped to the tall, handsome specimen of humanity entering with a grin the size of Texas pointed directly at me.

"Hey, baby, you ready?" Reid stepped close, kissing me on the lips. I smiled at him and decided maybe kissing could go down on my list twice.

"Yeah, just packing up." I piled my laptop into my large purse and snagged my headphones. "Where are the kids?" I asked, scooting my chair in and peeking at the gaping barista, who was turning a few different shades of red.

"All in the car, ready to go." He grabbed my hand and threaded our fingers. "Hey, Meina." Reid half-smiled and nodded his head toward her.

She closed her mouth, turned an angry glare on me, and spun on her heel to walk away. I smiled to myself as I followed him out, and just as we exited the door, he spun me around and crowded me against the wall. There was still a corner we'd have to turn in order to be seen by anyone in the parking lot, so there was no way anyone but maybe Meina could see what we were doing.

"Did you have a good appointment?" he asked while trailing kisses down my neck.

I grabbed his hair and smiled as his lips branded me. "I did. I actually wanted to talk to you tonight, so would you mind staying after dinner is over?"

He pulled back and smiled down at me, his green eyes dancing with excitement. "Of course, I will." He moved in with a slow and steady kiss, one that made my toes curl in my shoes. His lips sang of desperation; it echoed through me and demanded to latch on to what was rioting in my chest. It was screaming that we matched, that what we felt was the same, that we were in sync.

THE SCREEN DOOR snapped shut as I cradled my mug of tea and softly walked toward Reid, who was slouched on the porch swing. I handed him the mug as I wrapped myself in a large blanket and snuggled into his side. It was freezing, the kind of cold that required a fire and thick layers to be outside, but I needed some time alone with him. Reid had cleaned everything up, washing dishes and sweeping up crumbs from around the table while we all did our bedtime routine.

They'd all said goodnight as I headed upstairs to tuck them in. Jovi waited a second before walking up, watching Reid's back as he cleaned. Before I could ask what she was doing, she jogged over to him and wrapped her little arms around his back.

He stopped moving and twisted his frame until he was in front of her. He bent and picked her up, and she burrowed her face into his neck as he rubbed her back and whispered something into her ear. My breathing got really pained and shallow as I watched my little girl embrace him, as I watched her open her heart up to another man. It unleashed the flutters of winged creatures that were sure to be in my stomach somewhere and tugged on all my heartstrings.

He'd set her down a moment later and smiled at me before turning back toward the sink. It was in that moment that I realized Reid had already taken a huge chunk of my heart. Regardless of what I allowed to happen between us, he'd already hooked my kids. They were too far gone, and there was nothing I could do to stop it.

"So, what did you want to talk to me about?" Reid asked, bringing me out of my thoughts and back to the chilled but perfect moment with him. I shifted closer to his side and retrieved my hot mug from his grasp.

"I know this whole thing is a little complicated. We haven't told the kids about us…" I trailed off and could feel him shift next to me.

"Layla, it's only been two weeks. We can take it as slow as you want."

I smiled as we swayed in the dark. The crisp night still held so much beauty. The white stars peeked out of the dark sky, casting a glorious view for us to drink in from our swinging perch. "I know, but I want more than stolen kisses, hushed whispers, and frantic hands. I want something deeper, but I'm not sure how much more I can give you."

He made a humming sound as his hands found my hair and started playing with the ends.

"Do you want to define what this is first?" he rumbled softly as his leg kicked out in front of him.

I inhaled a steadying breath. "No, I'm not ready for that yet."

He laughed, tilting his head until he was kissing my hairline.

"Then what exactly did you have in mind?"

I shuddered a careful breath before gathering enough confidence to tell him. "Something I hope doesn't confuse you, or me, or make this worse."

"Hit me with your worst, baby." He kissed my forehead again, and I relaxed into his side as I revealed what I had in mind.

28

Reid

THE SOUND OF SOFT CHIMES AND BUZZING WOKE ME AS MY CELL PHONE alarm went off next to my bed. I haphazardly reached for it and ended up knocking it off the stand. I had been setting this alarm for the last week, and every day started with a strange fluttery feeling in my stomach. I'd get up early, shower, dress, take care of Rhett, and jog over to Layla's house. She'd laid out her idea on that porch swing, and I had eaten it up.

Finishing my shower and dressing in simple jeans and a flannel, I shoved my feet into some slippers and started across the gravel driveway. A white sheet of snow covered the ground again, but the dirt was still peeking through, so it wasn't deep, just a friendly reminder that winter was coming. I tilted my wrist just a fraction of an inch as my legs carried me closer to Layla's sleepy house. My watch showed that it was just after four thirty in the morning; I was right on time.

I carefully and very lightly stepped onto the front porch, taking each step quietly. I took the key from my pocket, the one Layla had given me last Sunday night while she awkwardly stumbled through her suggestion. She had offered me something in place of sexual intimacy. I'd smiled, taken the key, and greedily accepted this new arrangement.

I unlocked the door and silently shut it behind me, flipping the deadbolt and removing my slippers. I looked around to be sure none of the kids were awake. The lights were off as usual, and the place was tranquil. I rounded the stairs, creeping up one at a time until I stepped into the hall and found Layla's door. Dim lighting met me as I nudged it open. She was sitting cross-legged, smiling at me, waiting for me. That smile drove me to my knees most days, the one where her nose wrinkled and her eyes widened in anticipation like she was a little kid about to get an ice cream cone or a pony ride. It did something to my chest, made it lighter somehow.

I padded to her bed and crawled toward her on my knees. Her blonde hair was tossed on top of her head with little strands hanging down. She wore those thick-rimmed glasses and...

Holy shit.

Is that my t-shirt?

I crawled until I was in front of her, the warmth from her full coffee mug spreading between us as my face lowered toward hers. I drew my eyebrows together in concentration as I stared down at her.

"What?" she whispered, suddenly acting self-conscious. She patted her hair and wiped at her mouth. It made me smile but my gaze stayed locked on hers. "What, Reid? Tell me... You're freaking me out." She used her free hand to shove at me.

I caught her wrist and held her hand. "Is that my shirt?"

She blushed and looked down, withdrawing her hand. "You left it last time...it smells like you, so I sleep in it."

Before I could say how much it affected me to see her in my shirt, especially this early in the morning, her head turned toward her closet and a somber silence filled the room. When she got that look in her eye, I knew it had to do with her husband.

"Did that trigger something?" I asked, carefully taking the coffee mug and setting it next to her bed.

She tucked a few stray pieces of hair behind her ear. "It's just that I used to sleep in his shirts...nearly every night. I'd wear them during the day too...and I hadn't even thought about the fact that I had started doing the same thing with your shirt. I just missed you and wanted to feel close to you." She lifted her slender shoulder in a shrug.

I pulled her into a hug and lay down with her, cradling her in my arms. Most mornings she'd have coffee waiting for me and we'd whisper to each other about our plans for the day then we'd kiss and cuddle. I'd play with her hair and she'd touch my stomach, which most often required me to abandon my shirt...at her request. The last time I had just pulled my sweatshirt back over my head, forgetting about my shirt because Henley had woken up and I needed to make a quick exit. Some days Layla would talk about her husband, but sometimes she'd say it hurt too much. I wanted to be sensitive and careful, so I waited and just tried to support her.

"Should I steal one of your shirts so I can sleep in it?" I joked while taking the elastic tie out of her hair.

She laughed and let out a heavy sigh. "No, but I do think we need to tell the kids about us."

My hand froze in place. She was the one who had wanted to be careful with them and not do anything to mess with their emotions, not until we figured out what it was we were doing.

I turned toward her. "Does that mean...?"

She was already watching me, those brown eyes dancing with answers. "Yes, Reid. Let's define this thing." She cupped my face with her hands and kissed my lips quickly before pulling back.

I sat up enough to support my body with my elbow and rested my face in my hand. "I want to date you, exclusively. I don't want to share you with anyone but your kids," I said in a rush, unsure of how much time we had before the kids woke up.

She looked relieved, the line between her eyebrows disappeared, and a small smile cracked her lips open. "I would like that," she responded on a breathy sigh.

"So, we tell the kids they might see me kissing you occasionally?" I clarified while pulling her closer to my chest.

"Yes, let's tell them that, and I want to be sure they understand you aren't replacing their dad...you're just coming alongside us in your place, separate from anything their father ever did. I'll still love him.

I'll always love him." Her words came out tangled, rushed, nearly panicked...as though she was trying to reassure herself of all these things, not just her kids. I hesitated about moving forward when this was still such a struggle for her, but I also knew how important these little steps were to her.

Looking at her nightstand clock, I realized I only had thirty minutes of kissing time left before Michael was supposed to wake up. The clock was the only thing there aside from her lamp. She told me she'd had a picture of her husband there but had moved it. I hadn't been sure what to say when she told me that. I still hadn't seen what he looked like, and I wasn't sure if I ever wanted to. All the pictures were gone from downstairs, which she'd mentioned at one point was due to the kids needing the closure. I had no idea what that must have been like to have to tuck away a piece of her life like that. When my dad passed, we'd actually increased the number of photos around because we always wanted to be reminded of him, but I knew everyone grieved differently, not to mention I was much older when I lost my father.

I leaned over her and brushed her hair back until her face was bared to me, those lips on display, ready to be kissed. Her eyes searched mine as her breathing hitched. I loved this, loved how her back arched on its own like she couldn't help it. I loved how her cheeks went rosy from what I liked to imagine was her thinking dirty thoughts about us. Ultimately, I just loved how eager she was for my touch.

I ran my hand down her arm and relished the goosebumps that arose. I used my nose to trace the column of her throat and then pressed a kiss there, strong and firm. My tongue skimmed the creamy skin she had on display, which wasn't enough.

"Would you be willing to take this off?" I whispered into her neck while tugging on the hem of the shirt. She sat up and tugged it free, revealing a pink spaghetti-strapped tank underneath. It was much like the one she'd had on the first time we'd pulled over and made out. The thin fabric revealed too much and not enough; it was maddening. She had no idea what she did to me on a regular basis. This waiting, this restlessness—I loved it and craved every second of it with her, but I always wanted more.

I slid my tongue farther down her throat until it was flat against her collarbone. She let out a low hiss and arched into me, begging for more. I knew if I surprised her by letting my hand travel south, I'd feel exactly how much she wanted this, how much she wanted me. She said she wasn't ready for sex, but there was a lot of gray area between here and there. She ran her fingers through my hair and tugged on the ends, and this time it was me who hissed. All my fucking strength was being dedicated to not tugging her shorts down.

"Reid," she whispered, voice raspy.

I nodded, knowing she wanted more and hated herself for it. It was something I was well versed in now. She missed her husband and wished she could pine for him forever, but she had feelings for me that were raw and terrifying. As much as she hated to admit it, she was attracted to me and wanted my hands on her every time we were alone.

"Just tell me to stop if I'm going too far," I whispered into her skin as my nose traveled down her throat again, tracing a line and making a memory. I brought my finger up to her shoulder, gently lowered the strap of her tank top, and waited. I noticed her breathing was chaotic with the way her chest was rising and falling so quickly, which meant she was nervous, and I knew if I looked up to her eyes, there'd be a shine to them from the tears she was likely shedding.

She didn't have to say anything; I already knew this was still too much for her. I carefully pulled her strap back up and placed a gentle kiss on her shoulder, then on her nose, and then I kissed away the tears that lingered on her cheeks.

She grabbed my face with both her hands and held me still, whispering ever so gently, "Your willingness to go slow and be careful with me…you're going deeper inside of me than you ever could physically. This means everything to me, Reid." She kissed me hard and, in that kiss, I could feel her turmoil, the pain of letting go of her past and the fear of imagining a new future. I held her for fifteen more minutes before I let her go and went back home.

WRITING THIS WAS LONG OVERDUE. My mother knew it, and I knew it; I just hadn't had the words until now. I didn't want to face this part of myself again, and I certainly didn't want to face the wreckage I'd left behind me. I just wanted to pretend none of it had happened, but the longer I was with the kids and with Layla, the more I realized how badly I wanted to move on. I wanted a clean slate. While Layla had been drawing lines in the sand and building walls for us to stay within, my own heart abandoned all of them for her.

It was an odd realization—that no boundary existed where she was concerned. No fears, no trauma from the past leaked into my future. So, really, I had no reason not to send this letter. I was moving on with my life, I was happy, and I needed to stop pulling my past into the present.

I finished writing the last line, folded the white paper into thirds, and then slid it into an envelope. For whatever reason, I felt the need to put a tiny sticker I'd gotten from Henley on the back, as though to seal it with some sign of my life as it now was, some flag to wave saying I'm at peace and I hope they can be too.

I kept the front blank for my mother to fill in the address and then slid that envelope into a larger one and addressed it to my mother. She would see that it was mailed, and she'd be proud of me for finally closing out this chapter. I was almost tempted to call her, just to tell her about the letter and my life now, how tonight I was headed to Layla's house so together we could tell her children we were a couple, tell them we were in a relationship. My heart had grown wings; I was sure of it because I had never felt like this, not over anyone. I had never felt so free and wild and in...

Shit.

I cleared my throat and ignored where that train of thought was headed, walking outside to my mailbox. All I could focus on for now was this damned letter and an end to a very ugly chapter of my life.

29

layla

"GUESS WHAT I HEARD DOWN AT THE SALON YESTERDAY?" STAR whispered from behind me, resting her chin on my shoulder.

I nearly dropped the bag of carrots I'd grabbed. "Geez, Star!" I held my chest to calm my heart rate.

She walked around me in the grocery aisle, laughing and pushing her red hair behind her ear. "Sorry, didn't mean to scare you." She laughed, swinging the black grocery basket in front of her.

"It's okay. What's this about hearing something?" I looked around, trying to ignore how Star seemed to always gather attention.

"Well, it's all about how you and your sexy neighbor are a thing now—an official thing." She shoved me in the shoulder playfully. "When were you going to tell me?" Star's voice rose three octaves or so, causing a few more heads to turn in our direction.

Today I had decided to visit the larger grocer in town instead of the smaller one across from the coffee shop. They occasionally had better produce, but also, I figured I'd have less chance of having to talk to anyone. No such luck.

"Shhhh, I haven't told anyone yet. Who told you?" I asked, trying to corral her closer to the natural food section while eyeing people around us.

Star thankfully went without a fight and hushed her tone. "Wilma from the cake shop said Beverley heard it from Mrs. Traylen," she explained, searching my face as though all those names would make perfect sense. My blank expression must have brought her up to speed. "Mrs. Traylen is Meina Traylen's mother. I'm guessing she heard the story from Meina, seeing how the story revolved around Reid Harrison coming to pick you up at the coffee shop then ravishing you against the wall once you two were outside." Star fanned herself, giving me big eyes and a flirty hit on the arm.

Shit. This wasn't supposed to get out before we told the kids.

"Star, we're telling the kids tonight—you've got to help keep a lid on things until then so nothing leaks back to them," I pleaded, gripping her shoulders like I was about to drown.

"Honestly, I'm tempted not to help you at all. Serves you right— how could you not tell me? I'm your best friend."

I stood back and let out a sigh. "I don't have a best friend."

"Perfect, then it's an easy decision. I'm your best friend, and you can't keep stuff like you hooking up with Reid a secret from me." She swatted my arm again.

"Ow! Stop hitting me," I scolded, rubbing my arm.

"Stop omitting delicious details then." Her blue eyes dared me not to spill every last one, so I gave in.

"Let's go to the bakery section and get some coffee cake or something. I'll fill you in." I moved away from the aisle and pulled my phone free. I wanted to be sure I had enough time to grab Henley from his shuttle since they still only had half-days for kindergartners.

"Sure, let's have coffee cake because calories don't matter when you get to burn 'em all off with that stallion, Reid the Speed." She waggled her eyebrows suggestively and forgot to use her inside voice. I felt like I was trying to wrangle a child.

"We aren't... Oh for shit's sake, just come sit down and stop speaking so loudly," I said, trying to push her toward the baked goods. Hopefully after this, I could keep it somewhat contained before my children found out.

I BRAIDED my hair for the thirteenth time and strangled the ends with my black hair tie. My flyaways wouldn't stay put, my makeup wouldn't stop smudging, and for the life of me, I couldn't stop stress-tidying the house. Each of the kids had commented on it, knowing it was what I did when I had to tell them something.

"Uh-oh, get ready, everyone—Mom is going to lecture us about something," Steven joked as he tossed a chip into his mouth. I rolled my eyes and moved the centerpiece on the table to the left about three centimeters. *There, much better.*

Jovi joined in next. "She's stress-tidying—everyone hide!"

I stood and walked to the stove, checking on dinner for the millionth time. The timer said it still had ten minutes to go but I was an overachieving freak who just needed to be really sure.

"Mom, stop. What's going on? Just tell us," Michael finally said, gripping my shoulders and shaking me. I knew it wasn't possible, but I wondered if he could shake hard enough to make all my secrets fall out... I moved past him and was about to calmly explain that nothing was wrong when there was a knock on the front door and my heart kicked my lungs in the face and demanded to be set free.

Holy shit, I'm doing this.

I was going to tell my kids I was seeing someone—not just someone, but Reid, *their* Reid.

I tried to regulate my breathing, just like the yoga video on YouTube said to, but what she did didn't look like what I was doing. My breathing was more labored, more intense, like an entire house made of straw and wood would tumble any second if I was close enough.

"Reid is here!" Henley came in shouting like it was the return of Jesus. I laid a hand to my stomach and tried to relax, but the sight of Reid walking in wearing his dark green shirt with his puffy cowboy vest (one of the terms I used to describe his clothes; I was sure the vest had an official name, but I had no idea what it was) made my heart kick in my chest in a different kind of way. It didn't want out so much as it wanted to settle in, real nice and slow with this guy. I stared into Reid's mossy eyes while I scrambled to find something to say. My tongue was glued to the roof of my mouth, totally unprepared for him.

Ninety-five percent of me wanted to just shout to the room that Reid and I were together and that was that, but the tiny five percent wanted to do things right. "Hey, everyone go ahead and take a seat," I yelled then gave Reid a knowing smile, which he returned. I liked when he smiled at me like that, when he saw things down deep that no one had ever bothered to look for before. I turned my back and began scrubbing at a dish for no other reason than pure stress. I needed something to do.

I thought over the last week when I'd started this crazy idea with Reid about how we could squeeze in some time together away from the kids. For whatever reason, I wanted him to come over to the house and spend the mornings with me, and while they'd mostly been just a bunch of whispered secrets and cuddling, there was no denying that things were escalating. I knew it when I started waking up half an hour before my alarm clock and getting those excited flutters in my stomach. I was secretly showering and then getting dressed back in pajama shorts and making my hair look cutely loose and flowy, my teeth were brushed, and I even applied a tiny bit of concealer under my eyes.

I knew it was stupid and I should just be real with him, but I liked Reid. I liked him so much. He had me doing these crazy things, and the more I wanted a boundary in place, the more I'd find some back door or secret passage for him to get through because I didn't really want any boundaries with him. I wanted him to have all the access he wanted, but every time I thought of giving him the keys to my heart, I'd feel a tug on the other end that belonged to the guilt I still carried for Travis.

"This smells delicious," Reid said while pulling out a chair. It brought me back to the moment, and I hurried over to the table with the steaks. I had contemplated talking to the kids alone, but honestly, I felt like the more I thought about it, the more I would chicken out and just say never mind to this entire thing. I needed Reid's strength.

"So, what's going on?" Michael asked accusingly, eyeing Reid and me.

"So observant, Mikey. Always so observant," Reid joked, breaking out in a huge smile.

I cleared my throat as the silence at the table grew and everyone shifted awkwardly in their seats. "Reid and I have something we want to tell you guys…or ask. Um…" I looked up at Reid, suddenly unsure of whether we were telling them we were together or asking them if it was okay.

"We have something to tell you guys." Reid covered for me with a patient smile. He was making a point to remind me that there was no backing out of this.

"Are you guys finally going to tell us you're boyfriend and girl-friend?" Jovi pointed her fork at us and raised an eyebrow. My heart stopped. I looked up and noticed Reid had stopped chewing as well.

I cleared my throat for the hundredth time and asked, "Why would you say that?"

"We aren't blind, Mom," Steven joked while snagging a roll and stuffing it in his mouth without adding any jelly or honey. He never ate them without something on it, which meant he was nervous or sick…or both.

"Yeah…ugh, you guys do know there's a window on the side of the house where the tool shed is, right?" Michael said with a small laugh and a blushing face.

Oh my God.

I was going to die from embarrassment. Heat slammed into my face as I imagined how many times Reid and I had snuck away to make out in that shed.

"Plus, Aunt Shellie told us your heart was a tangled mess over Mr. Reid and that we needed to be nice to you about it," Jovi added while taking a sip of her milk and sounding way older than her nine years. I hadn't told my sister about Reid yet, not more than the vague details of him being over and hanging with the kids. I hadn't told her I had started kissing him or that I had started grieving my husband in an entirely different way because of him.

"What else do you guys know, you little detectives?" Reid asked jokingly, moving that strong jaw around as he chewed his food. Why did that look sexy? Why was I looking at his jaw?

Henley piped up, scooting his little leg under his bum. "Well, we know Mom looks out the window an awful lot and she thinks we don't see that she's trying to look for you."

"We know you bring her flowers and coffee and the smiles you give each other aren't friendship ones. We know Mama was hiding from you because she liked you, all those times you'd come over and she'd go upstairs." Jovi pointed her fork around the room like a little lawyer.

Shit, these kids knew everything.

"I know Mama cries while looking at Daddy's picture and says she didn't mean to move on and she still loves him. She says she's sorry to him a lot," Henley said somberly, and that tone settled around the room like a heavy blanket, suffocating us.

My eyes slowly met Reid's, and he had the same look on his face he did every time I needed us to go slower like he didn't want to lose me and he'd wait for me. It made my heart beat faster.

My eyes locked on his, I finally spoke up. "I have feelings for Reid, deep ones I don't fully understand yet. I love your father. I will always love your father, but Reid makes me very happy and I would like to be his girlfriend if that is okay with you kids?" I finished, breaking eye contact and scanning the room.

Before anyone could say anything, Reid spoke up. "You kids matter to me. I wasn't hanging out here because I thought your mom might like me one day. I hang out here because I like hanging around you guys. Jovi, your presence is like a warm breeze on a cold afternoon, soothing and comfortable. Henley, your stickers and smiles make my day better by a thousand percent. I put those stickers everywhere." His eyes moved to Steven. "You've got a gift for compassion, kid, and it makes me want to be a better man." He looked over to Michael, who was already sporting a small smile. "Mikey, you know I love ya, kid.

You're my favorite coworker and you tell the best jokes. With that said, you should know that I respect your mother *and* your father. I'd never want to take his place. I will never be him, but I would like to be your friend, and I would like to be more than that with your mom."

His eyes landed back on me and I could see he was hoping with me, waiting with me. Silence filled the room while the kids chewed, and it felt like none of them wanted to go first, as though whoever did might be betraying their dad somehow. It made my gut twist.

"Reid is the silver lining of our sad days. I miss Daddy, but that hole in my belly feels smaller when Reid's around. I like that he wants to make you happy, Mama, but please don't make us see you kiss because that's gross," Henley said while twisting his lips to the side and scrunching up his face.

Everyone laughed and the silence broke.

"I like that you're moving on, Mom. I want to see you happy," Jovi said, simple and sweet.

"I agree, just as long as you're happy, Mom," Steven added, and then Michael let out a heavy sigh.

"We never assumed you'd be single forever. You're not a troll, so we knew there'd be some guy, someday. If it has to be anyone, I'm glad it's him." He nodded toward Reid and then lowered his head to focus on his nearly empty plate. The knot in my stomach began to unravel and an excited energy took its place.

"You know that might mean I spend more time over here, and I might hold your mama's hand and maybe even kiss her a time or two," Reid joked. Henley smiled but acted like he was putting his finger down his throat in disgust.

"We know, just don't pull a tool shed moment in front of us any time soon," Michael said, getting up from the table. Steven followed him, and they both began clearing the table, which was odd. They never cleared the table without being told at least fifteen times. I was going to need to talk to them privately because they were off, and I had a feeling if I watched Jovi, she might be too. I knew this was going to be hard on them, and I slightly hated myself for doing it at all. Why couldn't I just be a lonely spinster, fine with spending my life alone?

Reid slowly got up from the table, walked his plate to the sink, and started washing the dishes. Michael and Steven stood there watching him, frozen in place. My heart thundered in my chest as I watched the lost look on their faces. I was about to get up and move, about to do something when Reid turned the water off, turned toward the boys, and wrapped them in a hug. He whispered something to them as he patted their backs.

I couldn't see Michael's face, but Steven was crying and gripping Reid's vest with force. I turned back toward my other two and saw that Jovi was crying too and Henley was picking his nose. I got up and walked over to Jovi's side, pulling her in for a hug.

"You okay?" I whispered into her hair.

She nodded against my chest. "I just miss Dad, that's all."

"Me too, baby girl. Me too," I murmured, wishing so badly I wasn't in this moment, wishing I wasn't telling my kids I was falling for a new man.

"WELL, WE DID IT." Reid let out a heavy sigh as he settled in next to me on the couch. His puppy was asleep on the floor, near the couch. It was nine at night, and he'd stayed to clean up dinner, play a video game with the kids, and then help check the horses with us. It was nice because the horses weren't tied to Travis. They were ours, and we'd invited Reid into it. He had made us each laugh as we brushed them, and he'd wrapped his arm around my waist a time or two. It was a perfect start for us.

I leaned into his shoulder and closed my eyes. "Thank you for being willing to do this."

His heavy arm cradled me in and held me close, and it made me feel completely perfect and safe. The room was quiet as we just sat there and processed the evening.

"Hey, what happened with the sink hug tonight?" I carefully turned my head toward him as he looked at the blank television. He let out a sigh I felt but couldn't hear.

"I don't know...I just saw it on their faces. Being lost, afraid, a little confused...I just felt like they needed a hug. I told them it was okay to miss their dad and I would only ever try to help them remember him..." His soft voice trailed off and the silence settled back in. My throat was tight with how many words I wanted to say to him, how much I loved that he was so sensitive toward my broken boys. Instead of focusing on how much I might be falling for him, I redirected.

"Have you ever felt like that before? Lost and afraid?" I gently whispered while tugging on his hand, intertwining our fingers.

He did another one of those big silent breaths before responding. "Yes, once." He paused for a second and I waited, hoping he'd open up. There were way too many details I didn't know about him.

"I was engaged once, a while back... We had been together for two years when she found out she was pregnant. I was excited—beyond excited. From what I knew, we were happy. Our wedding was planned for that following summer. She'd have a baby bump, but she'd still be a beautiful bride, and I didn't care either way as long as she was having my kid and marrying me." He paused, taking in a big breath of air, but it was the slight tremble in his hand that made me wonder if he was ready to talk about this. Whatever it was, it had obviously affected him very much.

I waited, not wanting to push him.

"The first sign that things were slightly off between us was her postponing the wedding. She said she didn't want to be fat on her wedding day but refused to set a new date, saying she wanted to wait to have the baby and feel it out." Reid shook his head as though he was still back in that argument...in that brokenness.

I snuggled deeper into his chest to try to comfort him.

"I went to every doctor's appointment with her. I fell in love the second I saw our daughter on the sonogram...I helped pick her name and went and bought Jen all the things she craved. I read books on being a birthing coach and partner. I read books on how to be a dad... I was invested." Reid's deep stare sent goosebumps down my arms, and there was this sharp pain in my stomach that made me want to tell him that was enough, I didn't need to hear the rest...but he kept going. "Seven months was all I had with her, seven months to believe I was going to be a father." He stopped again and rubbed his hand down my shoulder.

My heart was beating painfully slowly.

He waited a second before continuing. "One day I came home early from the office so I could put the crib together like Jen had asked me to. I knew she wanted it up and the nursery complete in case the baby came early. When I got there, she was with people...a man my age and an elderly couple. The man stood when I walked in, and he looked enraged by the sight of me...like I had just walked into the wrong home or looked at the wrong woman. I felt like the wrong man. I knew I was when Jen put her hand on *his* arm to calm him down. It was like my world tipped over and everything came crashing down. Jason, that was his name...the actual father of my little girl," Reid croaked, seemingly trying to keep the emotion out of his voice. "He was an ex, and she had gotten together with him while I was away on a business trip. They were always meant to be...according to her, but when he wasn't sure, she told me the baby was mine instead." He let out a harsh scoff and brought his free hand up to run through his hair.

I wanted to reach into his heart and put him back together. To lose a child like that, one you loved and wanted to hold and be with only to be told it wasn't yours and you'd never be in its life...I couldn't imagine. Tears streamed down my face at the betrayal he'd lived through. I wanted to tell him I felt his hurt and I would be careful with him, tell him I would never hurt him, but the grief in my soul warned me not to.

Grief is an unpredictable bitch.

"That was the worst night of my life, for more reasons than one..." He trailed off again like he was seeing a ghost.

I turned toward him, disconnecting our bodies. I took his face in my hands and kissed him. I molded my lips to his and poured emotion, adoration, and devotion into my kiss. It quickly built up speed, and Reid wasted no time in pulling me flat against his chest where we'd be hidden by the couch.

He ran his fingers up the back of my shirt and then lowered them until they were dipping into my jeans. He carefully skimmed the skin there, causing a fire to ignite in my core. This thing with Reid felt like remembering a language I used to speak. Obviously, I'd had sex before. I knew how to go from touching to actually getting all the parts moving, and as I was sprawled across his chest in the dark with just a few glowing lights lit around the living room, there was a primal need down deep telling me to do what I used to do, to do what came naturally. I resisted the urge to grind down on the hardness under me that was getting firmer by the second. Reid's low hiss surrounded us as his touch skimmed higher and moved away from my jeans.

I knew we were dancing closer and closer to this line I'd drawn in the sand. I knew I couldn't hold this man off forever, but tonight wasn't the night, and I had no idea when that night would be. I leaned back just a bit to look at Reid's expression and asked, "Is this hard for you...to wait like this? I don't want to hurt you or make you feel like..."

He shook his head back and forth and grabbed my wrist, pulling it to his lips and giving it a long kiss. There, in the low lighting, he was beautiful. His green eyes seemed to catch what little light was the room offered, and they were like a beacon. It was like staring at a tiny glimpse of the future I wanted, one full of peace and perfection.

"Just breathing the same air as you is enough for me, Layla." His voice was raspy, low, and desperate, and it shifted something in my chest. He was still holding my wrist when he continued. "I know that sounds intense, but I'm serious...it's enough for me. Whatever you can give me, will give me...for as long as it takes...it's enough."

I rested my head on his chest and fell asleep listening to his heartbeat, knowing each thud inside was for me. I was humbled and honored that he was essentially declaring something to me, something he maybe hadn't felt since his heartbreak with his ex.

30

"How about we get our gear on and go sledding? We can take the horses up to the ridgeline. It's pretty steep and an awesome spot to go down," I suggested, smiling at the excited faces greeting me. Even Michael seemed intrigued by the prospect of sledding.

We made a plan to hit the local grocery store to get ingredients for Thanksgiving then head out to Regret Ridge, aptly named by me as a child, and go sledding. Layla's sister wanted us to go into Casper for bulk shopping, but we'd finally gotten our first dose of snow, causing the roads to close.

As we moved through the store, I tried to focus on avoiding things the kids didn't like. Jovi hated anything that had celery in it, which ruled out a specific kind of stuffing. Henley hated cranberries, and Steven couldn't stand marshmallows. Michael thankfully just asked that we not make him eat anything that wiggled, so Jell-O was a big no for him. I found Layla laughing at me a time or two as I concentrated on coming up with substitutions for side dish options and alternate things we could put on top of the yams.

"You can never try to get them all right because before you know it, they'll turn on you and all like different things just to drive you crazy." Layla laughed and reached for the cheaper version of boxed stuffing, putting two boxes in the cart.

I looked at her and smiled. "Just watch." She gave me a smile that made me feel warm and took me back to the night I'd told her about Jen and the loss of my baby girl. I thought about how she'd fallen asleep on my chest that night, how we'd woken up at three in the morning and made out again for thirty minutes before I snuck back home.

I was falling in love with Layla Carter, and I had no idea what to do about it. She wasn't ready for love, and I wasn't ready to lose her.

TURNED out the kids had never gone sledding on a hill like Regret Ridge. It was a sharp incline with a nice flat platform at the top, perfect for getting on the sled and zinging down the hill. There were little to no trees or rocks, which also added to its appeal, but more than that, the ridge was on our ten acres of land, so no one else was there. After a long day of sledding, the kids were exhausted.

I told them I'd put the horses away and care for them while they headed in and showered. I was alone in the barn when my phone rang.

"Hello?" I held the phone to my shoulder as I pulled a warm blanket over Thor.

"Reid?" My sister's tone caught me off guard and had me stopping where I stood.

"Sarah?"

"Yeah…sorry it's been so long. I should have called a lot sooner." She sounded sad, broken…how I had felt before I met Layla.

"It's okay. How's Europe?" I milled about the room, trying to get things tied up. I tried not to focus on how it felt so good and hurt so much to finally hear from her. We had always been so close growing up, but after the night with Jen, we'd fallen apart, and nothing had been the same.

It wasn't the same for me, for her, for my mother or my soul. I was shattered, and I didn't know how to come back.

"It's…getting a bit old, if I'm honest." She slightly laughed. "Mom told me you sent your letter…"

I slowly sat down on a bale of hay as I registered her words. Sarah hadn't talked to me since our big blow-up after that night, not after what I'd done. She was a supportive sister, but I was being a self-destructive ass. I could understand it, but it still hurt. It hurt to be drawn back to that night.

"Yeah, I did," I somberly replied.

She let out a small sigh. "That's good…sounds like you're finding healing then."

I smiled. "I am. I'm moving on. I'm…happy."

She was quiet for a second before sniffing. "That's good. Really good. That's all I want for you… What will you do if she writes back?"

I hadn't thought of that. I froze, unsure what I would do in that scenario. Part of me assumed I'd send my letter and that would be that.

"Not sure. Guess I'll cross that bridge when I get to it."

"Maybe it's best if you don't read it. Maybe you should just let it be and move on. Mom says you're the happiest you've ever been. Just let the past go, Reid." Her tone was soft but urgent like she knew something I didn't. It made me oddly uncomfortable.

I nodded to no one.

"I better get going. Have a happy Thanksgiving, brother. Love you." She ended the call without waiting for me to respond. It was strained and confusing, this new existence she and I lived in. I could have and probably should have tried to fix it, but I didn't know how. I just wanted to forget and leave it in the past.

"You aren't so bad at all this holiday stuff." Michelle gently nudged my shoulder with her beer bottle and laughed.

"Yeah, not so bad. If only your pie-baking skills were as good as your teepee-making skills," Star joked from the foyer where she was pulling on her boots. It was about an hour after Thanksgiving dinner had ended, and we were just relaxing and getting ready to play board games. Star had joined us for a large portion of the day, which was entertaining as always, but she was leaving now to head to her family's house. I had spent the day playing football with the kids and building a kickass tepee we could actually use in the winter with a fire pit and everything. The ladies had cooked and I'd offered to help, but they had shooed me away, saying me keeping the kids entertained was helping.

It was a good day, but I didn't miss the few times Layla excused herself to the bathroom and came back with red, watery eyes. I didn't miss the way her somber attitude stretched and covered the tone of the room. I wasn't an idiot; I knew it was about her husband, but I felt helpless. I felt like I was in the way, like she resented me for the fact that he wasn't here and I was. It made me unsure of where we were, and I hated those moments because it was the closest I ever felt to losing her, like she was slipping through my fingers and there was no way to close my fist.

I turned toward Michelle and smiled, trying to be encouraged by the comment, and then turned toward Star. "I happen to prefer my pies crispy," I joked, knowing full well I'd overdone them over at my house. No one had really seemed to care as long as enough ice cream was piled on top.

Michelle adjusted her glasses on her nose and quickly glanced over toward her sister, who was still scrubbing dishes, unwilling to let anyone take over. Star looked too, gave Michelle a knowing look, and then turned toward the door.

"I'm off, beautiful people! Happy Thanksgiving," Star called out. The kids all sang goodbye in unison, Layla waved from the sink, and Michelle shut the door behind her.

Michelle and I both slowly turned to watch Layla return to the dishes. I knew the real reason Layla was scrubbing dishes, and so did Michelle. She was crying, missing the husband who wasn't here tonight, regretting the boyfriend who was. I knew I needed to love

Layla through this like I did every time she missed him, but there was a selfish part of me that was getting tired of being the regret in her life.

"I'm going to head home. I'm pretty tired," I said to the room with a sigh. I wasn't trying to run away, but I also didn't want to make this night any harder on Layla, and having to hide her tears would be hard on her.

"Goodnight, Reid." Jovi jumped up and ran to hug me.

"Night," Henley started, but Michelle cut him off.

"Actually, I was hoping to have a movie night with the kids. There's a Christmas movie showing at the Princess Theatre."

I eyed Michelle curiously. She wasn't from here, and I had no idea how she even knew about the Princess Theatre or the showtimes. All the kids yelled excitedly and got up to grab their shoes and coats. Layla made her way over, wiping her hands on a dishtowel.

"Shell, you don't have to do that. I'm fine..." Layla's eyes flicked to me and then went down to her feet.

"No, you aren't, and you need a little time to yourself to figure that out," Michelle responded while grabbing her phone and coat. "I'll be in the car, warming it up. Send the kids out please." She gave me a small smile and a wave then headed outside.

I liked Michelle. She was cool, and I especially liked that she wasn't a jerk to me when I knew, in situations like these, she could have been. The kids all left one by one after Layla placed kisses on their heads. Each one stopped to hug me too and then dashed outside into the cold, which just left me alone with Layla.

31

Layla

I FELT TATTERED, EMOTIONALLY TORN AND RIPPED APART FROM THE TOP of my head to the soles of my feet. All I wanted to do was cry, and I hated myself for it. I hated that I couldn't just enjoy a fun holiday and be with my family and be happy, be with my new boyfriend and create new memories with him. He was so patient, and although I wanted him there, I had been pushing him away all day.

Thanksgiving had always been a big deal to Travis—huge, in fact. It was more than football, food, and family. Travis had a tradition each year where each family member had to pick a person, kind of like secret Santa, except instead of gifts, we each had to write something we appreciated and loved about him or her. Each one was required to be at least a full sentence long, so it was more than just someone being nice or fun, which two of the kids had always tried before the rules were in place. Travis and I took turns helping Henley, and every year it would bring our little family closer together. The previous Thanksgiving was the first year we tried doing the tradition without him, and it was so empty and difficult to get through that we promised not to do it again—just one more thing from my life with him that I was forced to bury and leave behind.

"Hey," Reid cautiously said from behind me.

I was furiously wiping at surfaces and purposely facing away from him because I couldn't risk falling apart in front of him. I was sure he was exhausted by my emotions, by my constant back and forth and me *always* putting a dead man first. I knew if the tables were turned, I'd walk away. I wouldn't be able to handle being second choice, second best in someone's heart.

"Layla," he murmured in a raspy voice, this time closer. I continued to ignore him; eventually, he'd get it. Eventually, he'd see I wasn't good for him. I was broken, and he was already living in his own upturned version of heartache, so there was no way he deserved to stay trapped in mine. The idea of losing him, though, the idea of doing the right thing and letting him go...it made me physically ill.

Strong hands came around me from behind and gently clasped mine, stilling them mid-wipe on the counter. I froze as his warm body moved closer, pinning mine in place. His lips met my neck, gentle, firm, and reassuring. This wasn't fair to him. He couldn't have my heart because I didn't yet have it back from the last man who owned it. I had nothing to offer him. Tears dropped without any warning, fat salty drops of exhaustion, and grief spilled down my face onto the counter.

As one left, another took its place until I was sobbing. I bent over the counter and hit it with my hand, a loud slap echoing through the quiet house. Reid's arms came around me and held me tight. I was making sounds I had only made after I lost Travis. Agony mixed with terror of spending the rest of my life without my husband ripped me open and revealed how raw, how vulnerable and alone I felt.

Reid turned me as more sobs cascaded loudly through me. My eyes were closed tight as more and more tears came. My throat was too tight to let any words free, and I wouldn't have wanted them to be spoken even if I could manage it. I wanted to lock every part of this grief up tight and keep it so I would never have to move on, never have to forget my husband.

Reid picked me up and began carrying me, letting out comforting sounds. We walked upstairs, and then I heard water running. He set me down and placed a Kleenex in my hand. I wiped and wiped and wiped but didn't open my eyes and didn't stop crying. I wanted to scream, to shout, to hit and maim something…to somehow give physical definition to how unfair this was, how unfair it was that I had to live here and be without him. We'd promised each other we'd have one another forever, and I was so angry at him, at God…at the other fucking driver. I was just mad at everything and everyone, and I couldn't figure out how to fix any of it.

Reid squatted down in front of me, took off my slippers, and gently ran his hands up my thighs until they were at my waist.

"Baby, let me put you in the bath. I don't want anything from you, but let me take care of you." His soft words washed over me, and some of the pain receded. I nodded and opened my eyes but was blinded by tears and mascara. His warm fingers tugged on my leggings until they were being pulled ever so gently down my legs. Once those were free, he stood and carefully pulled my top over my head, and I assumed he discarded it. My eyes were downcast on the white tile at my feet. Reid waited a second, for what I didn't know, but if I had been thinking and in my right mind, I'd have known he must have been hesitant to see me naked. He probably imagined the first time being romantic and sweet. Instead, he got this, a hot mess of emotions and an ugly tear-stained face marked with regret.

He squatted in front of me again, and I could feel his hot breath on my exposed skin.

He didn't wait or hesitate, just grabbed my hands and helped me stand.

I assumed he was going to help me get into the tub alone, but a second later, while I was looking at the floor, I saw his bare feet. His socks were kicked off behind him. Reid crawled into the tub first, fully clothed minus his socks. He stood then reached for my hand and helped me in. He sat me in between his legs and let me cry. I brought my legs up to my chest, wrapped my arms around my knees, and cried until I couldn't anymore. Reid just stayed put behind me, rubbing my back and whispering soft encouragement.

Having Reid there with me like that…it was different than anything I'd ever felt before. Having his strong arms around me, not vying for a sexual connection, just a supportive one...it helped me calm down. He helped me breathe again. He was showing me he was there for me and wasn't intimidated by my scars. As helplessly in love as I was with my husband, the feeling I had now felt similar...felt like a fresh dose of the good kind of hope. He was like my very own burst of sunlight in a darkened room.

Once I finally stopped enough to talk and think clearly, I used the water to wash my face and finally addressed Reid.

"Thank you," I said with a raw tone, my voice scratchy from the crying.

Reid played with the ends of my hair that had gotten wet then trailed a finger down my spine. "Not hating this at all, Layla."

Something in his tone caught me, and it felt like nose-diving on a rollercoaster—terrifying but exhilarating at the same time. He leaned forward and kissed the shell of my ear, and the touch melted me and made my core heat with need.

"Do you want to tell me what's going on? I have a pretty good idea, but if you want to talk about it..." He trailed off while dragging his finger up and down my arm. I shut my eyes and pushed the emotions of the day away, instead allowing myself to feel something else.

"Reid..." I turned my head slightly. He waited, and so did I...for nerves, for bravery, for something. "Can you make me feel something else? I hurt...and I don't want to hurt. Can you distract me, get my mind off this day, these emotions? Make me feel *something*." I leaned my head back against his chest, exposing my breasts and everything else to him, hoping he'd catch my hint. Tonight, I needed his touch, his heart, his soul...I needed him to give me something because I was about to push everything away if he didn't find a way to save me.

Nothing happened. Reid didn't move, just stayed behind me and breathed in and out. I wanted to turn my head to see his face, but I also didn't want to shatter this moment. I'd asked him for something, and I was hesitating to see if he'd answer.

"Layla, I'm not..." Reid trailed off. His tone sounded...hurt. Before I could say something to fix it, he was moving from behind me and getting out. "Layla, I'm not just some guy you can mess with. I thought we were serious with each other. I thought…" His eyes were boring into the tile on the floor, and a red flush of anger was tickling his jawline.

My stomach dropped, and a horrible feeling crept over me.

"I'm in love with you, Layla…and while I'm content in waiting for you to be ready for me physically, I'm not the kind of guy who will endure being ignored all day, tossed around emotionally like a secondhand ragdoll. I know I'm your second choice." His hand was pointing forcefully at his chest, and I hated how his green eyes were accusing me. Tears pricked my eyes again, but this time they were only for him. "I'm always second choice, nothing fucking new there, but you're my first choice—my only choice. I'm willing to wait for you, but don't ever reject me, cry over your husband, and then ask me to fuck away your bad thoughts, because I know by tomorrow you'll have sobered up and you'll put it on me that I didn't push back."

His voice was carrying through my bathroom and I wanted to scream back and tell him I loved him too, but I didn't. I just sat there and waited.

"I'll do anything for you Layla, but not that." He shook his head, disappointment leaking out of every harsh sound that came out of his mouth.

He was about to leave, so I quickly stood up, carefully stepped out of the tub, and wrapped a white towel around me. "Reid, stop. I'm so sorry. Please just let me explain."

Tugging on his hand did nothing to stop him as he stormed down my stairs and out of my house. He'd done it, had managed to make me feel something different. I was beyond the grief that had strangled me all day; now I was just heartbroken and sick with how I'd treated him.

I was terrified he wouldn't let me say I was sorry. I knew I should be even more terrified by the fact that I loved him too, but I couldn't bring myself to care. Right then, all I could do was get dressed and pray I wasn't too late.

32

Reid

I'D DONE MY BEST TO AVOID LAYLA, BUT MY LOVE FOR HER WAS LIKE A self-detonating bomb. She showed up on my doorstep that night, begging to talk to me, crying again, telling me she was sorry. I let her in, hugged her, and asked her to go back home. We obviously needed space, and she needed time to work through her emotions and feelings for her husband. I refused to be someone's second choice again. I didn't want to be that guy where someone pretended to be happy with me just to fulfill something they needed until they didn't anymore, and then I was like the trash—clutter, disposable, a frustrating reminder of what had been but was no longer. The week dragged on, and I hated how much I missed her. Every time she saw me, she'd try to catch my gaze and smile. She was trying, but I didn't smile back. I just turned the other way.

All the emotions from that day would come back, the rejection, the hurt...the fact that I had been there for her in a way I had never been for anyone and at the end of it, she tried to use me to get past her own hurt.

But with each passing day, I began to forget why that mattered.

One week turned into two, and I hadn't found the words to tell her I missed her, but I also wanted to protect what was left of my heart, what was left of my life. I didn't have the right to be angry with her; I realized that, but I knew I deserved someone who actually wanted to be with me.

It was Tuesday and I was packing for the Casper December Dust N Bash, a charity rodeo event honoring a legend who'd recently lost his battle to cancer. Everyone had loved Big Bill, and all the people who'd been connected to the rodeo over the years had been asked to pay tribute in some way. I'd even been asked to ride a bronc, regardless of the fact that I hadn't been on one in ten years. They had laughed, said it'd add to the appeal. I'd spent a few days up at Gary's place practicing, just to be on the safe side.

Now I was leaving, and it was hard to get the looks on the kids' faces out of my head, their little furrowed brows and turned-down mouths. It was like a punch to my fucking gut.

Our connection had been strained as I worked through things with Layla. I never wanted them to feel like things were bad between us, so I made sure to spend as much time as I could with them, but I knew they still felt it. Regardless of how many pictures I colored with Jovi, how many model airplanes I built with Steven, how many video games I played with Henley, it was strained.

I had found a tiny coloring page stuffed in the pocket of my coat. It was of a black horse running in a field with a little note from Jovi at the bottom.

Please don't forget us.

Another fucking punch to the gut.

Once I was in Casper, I settled into my hotel room and tried to relax...except my mind kept going back to Layla.

Her laugh, her smile, how she felt in my arms...how we all make mistakes and maybe I was being too hard on her. She'd tried so many times to apologize to me, but I kept pushing her away. I snagged my cell phone, about ready to text her, but I got a call from Bill's wife instead.

She kept me on the phone for nearly an hour, going over details for the big day, and by the time she was off, it was time for dinner. My thoughts kept circling back to the same conclusion, that I needed to forgive Layla. I needed to move past this, but I wasn't sure how.

THE LIGHTS WERE bright and obnoxious as I made my way to the starting gate. The stands were full to the brim with people, and so far, we'd had one hell of a show. Since this was an indoor arena, it was humid and hot, and I felt sweat stick to my skin as my leather vest and chaps moved against my clothes.

"Harrison, you're up next!" a burly older man yelled toward me. This wasn't exactly a competition, more like an exhibition, so it was more relaxed, more fun. I gripped the railing and pulled myself up to the starting chute, maneuvering around the guys up there already dealing with Hellraiser, the bronc I was going to be riding.

"This one is a son of a bitch, so be careful!" one of the guys shouted around his wad of chew. I nodded my understanding and mounted the horse while pinned in by the enclosure. Hellraiser shuffled to the back as much as he could, which wasn't much. I tried to steel my nerves as I recalled how I used to get into the zone.

I wrapped my gloved hand with rope six times then fastened it to the horn and tugged to ensure I had a firm grip. I leaned back and prepared for one hell of an adrenaline rush. There were hundreds of people in the stands, and a huge video monitor showed everyone a big close-up of me on the horse. The announcer had already gone through the stats and accounts of my glory days, all of which I'd mostly ignored because it'd just mess with my head.

Then I saw the same burly man wave his hand and the chute flew open. Hellraiser pranced to the side with a huge lunge, kicking his back legs out too close to the guys up on the bars. A collective sound of astonishment was made as they dove to safety. I strangled the rope and kept my body weight in the back as I was tugged and pulled by the force of the horse thrashing. I was thrown back into memories of how it felt to have my heart in my throat, my stomach flipped and entirely thrown off-kilter by the fear that clawed its way through me.

I didn't see the board, didn't hear the announcer; it was just this beast and me in that dirty arena. I could feel my bones shift and my stomach twist as the turmoil intensified and the horse increased his tempo. Finally, a loud beep sounded in the air, signaling the time, and another rider came alongside me. I let go and jumped onto the back of his horse.

We cleared the arena as people stood to their feet, shouting, screaming, and losing their minds. "Holy smokes, eight amazing seconds, ladies and gentlemen. What a treat to get to see Reid the Speed pop out of retirement for this event."

I was trying to get my gloves off; my hand was throbbing, and I needed to get some ice on it, stat. I wasn't paying attention when the crowd started to make a different kind of buzz.

"Would you look at that? Looks like our retired bachelor has a bit of a fan club." I snapped my head up to the large jumbo screen where the camera was zooming in on little Jovi with a huge poster that said, *Reid the Speed is our Hero!* Then it panned over to Henley, who was wearing a cowboy hat and holding a sign that said, *Reid is our favorite! We Love You!*

My heart thudded painfully fast in my chest as the cameraman moved up to the blonde decked out in western gear. Her hair was curled under that brown cowboy hat, her lips a glossy shade of red, and her sign said, *I Love You, Reid—Come Back to Me.*

Layla.

I was running up the aluminum steps of the bleacher stands, past raving fans and girls screaming at me. I jogged over through one section and then the other as the entire crowd was up out of their seats, making oohing and aahing sounds. The announcer was commenting on my quick approach. Layla kept looking around, and three steps up, I was there, wrapping her in my arms, holding her face in my hands, and kissing her with all the passion, anger, and forgiveness I had in me.

I wanted her. I needed her.

"I'm sorry," she whispered as we broke apart.

I shook my head, my face still inches from hers. "It doesn't matter.

I love you so much, so fucking much," I whispered against her lips before I was claiming them again.

We all went to dinner afterward, not wanting to stick around for the huge crowds or traffic. Henley didn't stop asking me questions about how I stayed on the horse and how I didn't die, and Jovi was a bit emotional as she talked about how scary it was to see me ride the bronc. Layla held my hand under the table, threading her fingers with mine as Steven and Michael asked questions too.

We were like a family, eating pizza, laughing, and joking with each other. My heart was full as I traced the inside of Layla's fingers under the table.

IT WAS a Saturday night in December, a week since the rodeo, and things were slowly settling back into place for us. We'd all just finished a superhero movie at nearly midnight. Henley, Jovi, and Steven were all passed out on the floor, and Michael stretched then went up to bed. Layla was curled under a blanket, lying on the couch with her toes in my lap, and Rhett was snuggled under her arm, sleeping as usual.

I turned off the TV, carried Henley and Jovi up to their rooms, and tucked them in. Steven had woken by then and trudged up on his own. I gave him a simple, "Night, buddy," and mussed his hair. Once I returned downstairs, I picked up Layla, letting Rhett follow after us as we walked upstairs.

Her room was dark, but with the light of her charging port, I could see the bed well enough. I laid her down and tucked her under the covers, and just as I was about to leave, she tugged on my hand.

"Stay with me."

I looked down at her and waited, not sure if she was actually awake.

"Baby? You awake?" I crouched down to her face, which was planted in her pillow.

She turned her head fully toward me and tugged on my shirt.

"Please, this is on my list. Maybe I'm not ready for sex, but I want to sleep in the same bed as you. Will you stay? Please?"

I buckled...not that I really had anything against staying anyway, except that our last intimacy conversation had ended so badly. Since returning from Casper, we'd been cozy and politely kissed, but nothing had escalated past that. We were lukewarm, floating, waiting, not sure who should make the first move.

I took off my shirt and slipped out of my jeans, staying in my boxers, and crawled in next to her. She snuggled into my arms and tucked her head under my chin.

"Right here...this is what I want," she whispered groggily into my skin. My heart was hammering as I processed this huge step we were taking. I was sleeping over. I would wake up here, with her, the kids, the family.

I wanted this so badly it ached, but instead of freaking out, I just closed my eyes and tried for sleep.

33

Layla

WAKING UP WITH REID EVERY MORNING WAS SOMETHING NEW AND perfect. Each night before we went to sleep, he'd read to me. It was always a classic, and he'd rub my toes or my thighs while his eyes focused on the pages. Rhett, who was getting bigger by the day, was usually in my lap or scampered off to sleep with Jovi. The sleeping over part—from Reid to the reading and touching, the playing house —it was sexy as hell, and for the past five nights, things had slowly been escalating between us.

The first night, we just slept. The second night, we kissed heavily and groped a ton but drew the line there. By the third night, I crawled into bed in just my panties and night tank. He groaned and laid his hand over his face for a solid twenty minutes while he digested the information before pulling me close and touching all the available skin.

The night after that, I'd grinded against him in my sleep pants. We were like frantic teenagers, slowly getting closer and closer to things imploding and getting lost to our lust.

Lust was an odd thing, one I was learning to process.

My therapy sessions were helping. I had told Dr. Vox about my attraction to Reid and how things were progressing. I'd decided I was finally ready, but I didn't want to make the big leap with the kids home. So, I called my sister and asked her to come stay the weekend while Reid and I went on a getaway. We were going to stay in a small resort just outside of Casper, and I couldn't have been more excited.

The kids were still at school while I packed my things, and Reid was at work but was planning to get off early. Since it was Friday, I wanted to snag the mail once it came and see if I'd gotten anything from my mother; she was supposed to forward me the letter I'd received from *her*. The letters she used to send me so frequently had become nearly nonexistent, and I wondered if it was because of my mother or if it was just because a year had passed and she felt like she didn't need to write anymore. Maybe she felt I'd grieved enough.

The snow kept barely kissing the ground each morning, but by afternoon it would melt. That didn't mean it wasn't freezing, though. Just the jog from the mailbox to my door had my teeth chattering. I sorted through the bills and manila envelope that had arrived then headed upstairs with the personalized letter in my hand.

She'd written. I was so relieved that I tore open the letter with my finger, which made it rip awkwardly. I pulled the blue-lined paper free and tried to take comfort in the fact that I was getting this sign, this omen of sorts on this monumental weekend when I was choosing to move forward with my heart in a big way.

I settled into the oversized chair near my window and began skimming.

Dear Mrs. Jacobson,

I stopped there and quirked an eyebrow. I had never gone by my husband's last name. It was a joke between us because of Travis' past. Travis legally went by Jacobson, but to everyone we knew, he was Travis Carter. He'd taken my last name as a symbolic gesture when we married. My daddy was a man with no sons and had a desperate desire to carry on his legacy. Travis' dad was an asshole who'd left his mother. So, Travis had said we'd use my name. As such, looking at the letter, it made me even more intrigued. More importantly, the person who usually wrote had never once addressed me by anything other than Layla.

I hope this letter finds you well, although I have no delusions that you are well at all...not after what I took from you.

My stomach dropped.

This letter was from *him*. I didn't think I was ready to face anything from the man who'd taken my husband from me...but oddly enough, instead of fearful, I felt...brave. I continued to read, ready for whatever this man had to say.

I have wanted to reach out to you so many times but have always felt the lack of words to be terrifying. I wrote you several letters over the year but each of them felt too insignificant. I would never dare to water down what happened or give you excuses, but you should know that I am not an alcoholic. I rarely drink, but that night...that night I made the worst decision of my life. I found out I had lost my baby girl. Her name was Emma, and I loved her with every breath in my chest and every single part of my soul. Her mother broke the news to me that I was not the father, that I had been lied to for seven months, and had been falling in love with another man's child.

My head started to spin, and my stomach churned as I wondered what the actual fuck was happening.

I got in the car that night and just started driving south. I stopped in Vancouver at a bar. I drank too much, but I stupidly thought I was sober enough to keep going. In my head, I was almost to my mother's house in the central part of Oregon, but as we both know, that wasn't the case. You should know I went to him. I did everything in my power to ensure he could make it. I wanted to trade places with him. I wanted to die. When I heard he had a wife and kids, I think a part of me did die. I'm so sorry for what I've taken from you. I'm so sorry for what I've done to you, to your children. I hope you can find solace in this lifetime, and I'll never ask you to forgive me because I know that's not fair or possible, but I do ask that you at least know that I care, that I'm sorry. I thought I wanted to die for a long time, but then I found hope in the form of a broken woman who also lost her husband. I love her with all of my heart, and as I try my hardest to walk with her through this grief, I can't help but wonder if it's somehow connected to the penance I owe for what I took from you, to love someone who is in love with someone they can't have. I hope you find peace and the strength to move on from this. I'm so sorry.

Sincerely,

Jameson Reid Harrison

I read the letter over and over again, pausing at the name Jameson. Somehow in my mind, I was trying to give Reid an out, but that night in the wagon came rushing back. He'd told me Reid was what he went by but he had a different first name…

Agony ripped through me, hot and angry. I felt like I'd just been injected with something lethal, and it was working its way through my veins, breaking and shattering everything along the way. My legs wanted to give out, my body slowly giving up.

How the hell did this happen?

How is this…

I heard someone running up the stairs, and my breathing was so shallow and erratic I started seeing spots. I prayed it was Michelle because I couldn't face anyone else.

"Baby, you up here?" Reid called from the hall.

He was here.

My husband's killer.

The man I'd fallen in love with.

My heart beat irrationally hard in my chest, confused and angry. I tightened my grip on the letter as he stalked into my room. He looked so happy, so excited. His face was bright with a small hint of red from the cold outside. He'd gotten off work early like he said he would just to help me pack.

I was going to be sick.

His eyes danced along my body, taking in my posture, the letter, and then his gaze slowly dropped to the floor, where he paused. He crouched down and picked up the discarded envelope, the one that had a racecar sticker on the back. I saw the moment it registered in his eyes. Those iridescent orbs narrowed and then widened.

He knew.

And I was destroyed.

He didn't say anything; his face was losing color by the second as he took one step back and focused on the floor. He was standing there in tight jeans, snow boots, and a soft, black sweater. His hair was disheveled, and he had a few days' worth of beard growing on his jaw. I wanted to hug him, wanted to have him hold me and tell me we could get past this—but another part of me wanted to slap him, wanted to hurt him the way he'd hurt me.

"It was you..." I whispered, not asking, just sadly declaring.

His eyes watered as he stammered a pathetic response. "I...how... your last name isn't the same," was his big response, his big moment to reclaim me from the darkness that was swallowing us both up.

I narrowed my eyes as that rage I'd carried around with me began to surface. I stepped forward, and he took a half-shuffled step backward.

"Layla..." He spoke as though he already knew he'd lost me. It cleaved the repaired pieces back into two. Two men, one heart...it wasn't enough.

"You should leave," I whispered, the rage calling the shots as my heart sang to the tune of something else, something closer to forgiveness.

But in that moment, right there, I couldn't find it.

His eyes went wild, searching the room. "Don't..." He choked out. I watched him, unsure of what he was going to say. I was desperate for something... for him to fight, but my pride wanted him to leave. I waited, silently begging him for something, but he blinked away a few tears and stepped backward. "I can't ever forgive myself for this. I can't ever move on from this...but you have to know I'm so fucking sorry." Those green eyes finally met mine, and the sorrow I found there nearly broke me. He swallowed, dipped his head, and backed out of my room.

I stepped forward, frenzied and insane for something more in that moment. I wanted to fight with him. I wanted to hear him tell me why he did it, why he took my husband's life, but no words would ever satisfy the anger lacing that savage part of my soul.

"Reid..." I called, but he'd already made it halfway down the hall.

He stopped mid-step and looked up at me, eyes red and watering. My heart lurched.

"Just know...as you wish for the asshole who did this to you to get what he deserves, know he did. He fell in love, so hard, so entirely that he didn't want to breathe without her. Know he pictured marriage and Christmases, graduations and soccer practice. I wanted the entire thing with you, and it's so fitting to have it all ripped away. I deserve this. I'll never forget you, Layla. I'll never stop loving you."

He dipped his head again, ran down my stairs, and slammed the door behind him, slamming something shut in my soul as well. He didn't let me say what I needed to say, didn't let me fight with him... didn't let me tell him...

I thought back through the facts: Reid drove his car into my husband's lane, causing him to run into a telephone pole. He killed my husband, and I had already given him my heart. They say love can conquer anything...how would it conquer this? I thought back to a little letter of my own that I had sent just weeks ago...how I was now being called out on what I'd confessed there. God, or fate...maybe Travis himself was calling my bluff, asking if I meant it, if it was the honest truth. Right then, I wasn't sure, but seeing Reid leave me again felt like maybe I was wrong, like maybe I hadn't forgiven the man who'd killed my husband.

34

Layla

WITH SHAKY HANDS, I LAID OUT THE SIX LETTERS IN FRONT OF ME ON the table. They were a little wrinkled because I'd gripped them so hard over the past twenty-four hours. My tear-stained face was dry at the moment because I'd needed to collect myself. Michelle had come like she was supposed to, and with one look at me, she'd known something was wrong. So, she'd helped distract the kids and care for them, just like she had when I'd lost the first man I loved.

I traced my finger over the first letter, dated August of the previous year, roughly a month after the accident.

I unfolded the edges until I could see her black handwriting and read.

Layla,

You don't know me. I'm the sister of the man who took your husband's life, and I'm sure you're wondering why on earth I'm writing you or where I get off feeling entitled to even reach out. Truth is, I don't really know. I know I'm devastated on your behalf. I'm beyond torn up by the choice my brother made that altered your lives.

I guess I just wanted you to know you have a friend. His family doesn't somehow secretly harbor resentment or ill will or blame anyone but my brother for this. It was his choice, and I wish I could turn back time to give you your husband back. I wish I could do so much more, but for now, I'm offering an olive branch. Please reach out to us if there's anything you need.

Sincerely,

S

It was her.

His sister.

The one who'd lived here before me. I closed my eyes tightly at how unbelievable this entire thing was. I suddenly remembered a very specific letter from her that came after I'd responded about being broken and needing an outlet for my children.

I shuffled a few pieces of paper until I found the third one from her.

Layla,

I'm glad you reached out. I'm glad you're seeking help and getting the support you need. I think getting a new perspective on things would be beneficial for you. When I lost my dad, I turned to horses for therapy. I had emotions I wasn't sure how to process. I had feelings that were too big and I didn't know how to handle them, but the horses never judged me for it.

Here's a link to a house for sale in a small town near where I grew up. It's beautiful, peaceful, and I think it could help you and your family. This place is for sale and at a great price. Please feel free to call me if you have any questions about it.

Sincerely,

S

She'd led us right to him. She had to have known.

Anger surged through my veins as I processed all the information. I took a deep breath and tried to calm down as I slouched in the chair.

I'd never followed up on whether or not we moved, so she didn't technically know it was us. She'd already put it up for sale before we came into the picture, so there was a tiny chance she didn't know.

I brought my hand to my face and rubbed the exhaustion out of my skin. I hated this. I hated how much hate was vying for a position in my heart. Tears stabbed the corners of my eyes again, but I pushed them closed, tight and unyielding. I was done crying over this. I didn't want this pain or this ache in my soul.

I thought back over details about Reid I'd learned since knowing him, how he walked everywhere, never drank, didn't want to talk about his past. Suddenly curious and angry that I'd avoided this particular detail for so long, I pulled out a blue folder that had the trial information inside, details I'd ignored because I didn't want to hate the man who'd killed my husband.

I drew out one paper that explained the verdict.

Six months in prison for reckless driving, three months of probation, a few fines, and that was it. His name was printed there at the bottom: *Jameson Reid Harrison*. I had held the truth the entire time and I'd ignored it. I'd fucking ignored it because I was a coward.

A discussion with my mother finally made sense now as I recalled her arguing with me about how the state had screwed us on this. Out of curiosity, I looked up the consequences for reckless driving in Oregon: minimum one-year sentence.

One year and Reid got six months.

No wonder Mom was so angry that I didn't show up to the hearing. She wanted the judge and the jurors to see the kids, to know Reid deserved more time.

I felt sick.

So sick and exhausted.

The deal I'd made with the devil had finally come back to finish my soul. Simmering there under the surface was a deep love for a man who'd stolen my life from me. It didn't make any sense, but I missed him as much as I currently hated him.

It was entirely different than what Travis had left behind. It was nearly worse.

"Mom, did you hear me?" Michael asked, waving his hand in front of my face.

I blinked, trying to focus. "No, sorry. What?"

He let out a heavy sigh. "You've been so out of it for the past few weeks—what is going on?"

"It's the breakup, jerkface," Jovi scolded, narrowing her eyes at her brother as she put a dish away.

The breakup…right.

Reid was gone. I hadn't seen him again after that day on my stairs. His house had gone up for sale, and the sign just hanging there made me feel like it had slapped me in the face. I'd snuck over to see if it was actually empty, to see if this was actually real, if he was really gone without a word, without a trace. I had a feeling he'd send the kids letters later because that was the kind of man he was—a good one who considered my children's food preferences at Thanksgiving and who had thought of graduations and Christmases.

Tears pricked my eyes, but that wasn't new. I hadn't worn makeup since he left because all I'd done was cry. Somehow Reid's letter offered some kind of closure on my husband's death. The grief hadn't exactly eluded me; it had just lessened. It was a dull butter knife scraping at my nerves now, a reprieve from the steak knife it had been for so long.

"I said I need a ride home from work tomorrow. Now that Reid isn't there, I don't have a way home. I can't walk in this deep snow shit," Michael barked out and stalked away. I didn't even have enough steam to correct him about the language. It was his tone that struck me. He was back to being stormy, angry Michael. His friend was gone, and it was my fault.

I didn't respond to him, and he didn't let me anyway. I walked toward the living room and started cleaning up.

"Mama, wanna play video games with us?" Henley asked, and I was getting sick of turning him down, so I didn't. I grabbed a controller and sat down. He beamed at me and started explaining what I had to do next. "Okay, so Reid always says to make your thumb go this way and it will help control your car." I moved my thumb the way he'd described and ignored the tightness in my chest. Henley stopped suddenly and asked, "Mom, how come Reid left us?" His tone was dripping with sadness, and I crumbled at his expression.

"Honey, he didn't leave us." But that was all I could say because I couldn't bring myself to tell my children that the man we'd all fallen in love with was the reason their father was dead.

"He did. He left." Henley cried into my shoulder, and I broke. I shattered all over again, and I was so tired of this, so tired of hurting.

THE WINTER in Wyoming wasn't a joke. Thank God for my sister, who had been staying with me for the last week helping ensure the horses were okay from the blizzard that had hit. My car had gotten stuck in the snow and I hadn't been able to dig it out, so I'd called Shellie and she had come to my rescue. Her old truck was apparently a machine, impervious to drifts and packed snow. It had been two months since Reid left, and his house still hadn't sold. It was something that put me at ease each day, deluding myself with ideas that it meant he might be coming back. I wished I knew where he was. I wished I could talk to him...wished he'd left some form of communication open between us.

Michelle didn't comment on my heartbreak or the fact that Reid had left. She seemed to be in the same silent boat that I was, where she wasn't sure what to say. No one did, not even my mother. I'd left her speechless at Christmas when I explained everything that had happened.

She had replied with, "Well fuck a duck."

My feelings exactly.

"Are you okay?" Michelle stopped brushing Thor and furrowed her eyebrows at me.

I stopped and looked up at her. "What? Why?" I didn't even bother lying, because I knew I wasn't okay. I just wanted to know why she was suddenly curious.

"Look, I think you need to track him down," my sister argued while lifting the horse's leg to inspect its hoof.

I scoffed and put the brushes away. "How? And *why?*" I spread my arms open and shook my head. It was insane. I was torn between both questions. I hated that Reid had left me with no way to contact him, and I hated that I was even thinking about contacting him.

"Because you miss him and you're a miserable mess. This kind of miserable is entirely different from Travis. I'm worried about you," she muttered quietly, her face softened with concern.

I shrugged my shoulders in frustration. "He didn't leave me a way to contact him."

She stared for a second then lowered her head, accepting defeat. Yeah, exactly. There wasn't any finding him, and this was how our story would end. My heart ached for there to be more, but I couldn't reconcile how it would happen. Once I missed him more than I was angry with him, I knew I'd forgiven him. I just wanted him to return, and in my mind, we would work through all the details as long as he just came back.

But he hadn't. He was gone, and the sooner I could accept that, the sooner I could heal.

35

IT WAS DARK WHEN I STUMBLED HOME FROM WORK. I HAD BEEN working long hours, as long as they'd let me. I had a remote job for Microsoft I worked during the day, but it wasn't enough to distract me from the thoughts that threatened to tear my mind apart at night. So, I got a night job doing millwork near Crescent, Oregon, where my mother lived. I needed to be near family, and that was where I should have headed after the accident, not Wyoming.

I should have never met Layla Carter or her amazing kids. Jealously sliced through me at the idea that they all belonged to a man I'd killed. I hated the familiar feeling because I had been working so hard to get past it, but the current jealousy I was feeling was proof that I wasn't over it. The weeks had helped to reveal how much I loved Layla and how much she preferred Travis to me, how much I was a second choice and now, more than ever, she'd never pick me. She'd never forgive me, and I didn't blame her.

I turned the silver knob on the shower with force and washed the night off of me. It was nearing three in the morning, and all I wanted to do was sleep. I stumbled into my small bedroom and ensured that my alarm was set on my cell phone. I stopped cold when I saw I had an unread text message.

(307) 333-6789: I got this number from your mother...don't ask.
We need to talk. Call me tomorrow, please. – Michelle

I sat there and stared, reading it over and over again, and eventually, I fell asleep watching the screen, as though Layla's sister could somehow offer me some solution to this new fucked-up existence I was living.

THE NEXT MORNING, I made coffee and breakfast then sat and stared at my phone just as it started to ring.

"Hey, Kip," I answered, feeling relieved to put off the Michelle thing a bit longer.

"Hey, man, how you holding up?" He sounded somber like he felt bad for me, but he didn't need to. I deserved this, and when I'd asked him to take my dog for me and look after a few other things as I got the hell out of Wyoming, he'd listened in a confused daze. I still wasn't sure he'd caught all the details of what exactly had happened, but I didn't need him to.

"How's Rhett?"

"You just going to keep ignoring my questions every time I call?" Kip asked, irritation scratching at the surface.

I leaned forward on my knees and put my hand over my eyes. "There's just not much to answer them with..."

"You just assume no one wants anything to do with you then? You're just done with existing and mattering to anyone else in the world?" He sounded hurt, and I felt it deeper when I heard a small bark in the background. I'd abandoned my dog because I was too chickenshit to allow my heart to be worthy of even the love of a pet.

"Kip, did you need something in particular? Is Rhett okay?" I stood, stalking toward the fridge, trying to find something to replace the emptiness in my stomach.

He waited a second before letting out a heavy sigh. "No, man, I don't need anything, and he's good...but I know for a fact your girl isn't."

"No shit, Kip. She just found out I killed her husband," I scoffed, sounding entirely like the asshole I'd become.

"No, you shit. I think you need to talk to her."

"She told me to leave." I drilled it home, wondering why afterward, wondering what the hell the point was. It didn't matter. Even if she hadn't told me to go, I would have anyway.

"Look, just be good to yourself, man. I'll talk to you later." He hung up without a goodbye. I gripped the device, desperate to fling it across the room, but the damn text from Michelle was still burning a hole through my pocket. I let out a heavy sigh, pressing in the number listed in the text.

I held my breath as I listened to it ring. Was she near the kids? Would I hear them laugh in the background? Would I hear *her*? I wouldn't be able to bear it. Having someone else's kids ripped from me again was the final nail in this coffin that I called life.

Michelle answered on the fifth ring or so.

I let out a heavy sigh. "It's me, Reid."

She exhaled what sounded like a relieved breath. "Reid...finally. I had to sweet-talk that barista girl for your mama's number, and truth be told, she thinks I want to try to talk her into talking *you* into coming back now that you and Layla are over. Seems like she's a fan of yours."

I brought my hand to my eyes and groaned. "Michelle, I appreciate you explaining, but how can I help you?"

I felt bad about being so brusque, but even hearing Michelle speak had my gut twisting due to the knowledge that she likely knew what I'd done and who I was.

"Look, I get it—you're pissed at yourself...hiding and running. It took me some time to get past it myself, but now all I care about is my sister." Her tone was slow and tired.

I shook my head to an empty room. "How the hell am I supposed to respond to that? You got past the fact that I killed your brother-in-law? Good for you, Michelle. That was Layla's husband, the kids' dad. There isn't a fucking chance in hell we're ever getting past this." I stood, getting frustrated.

"I'm not past it, like it was easy or anything, but I can get past the fact that something horrible happened. You were brought into my sister's life and my niece's and nephews' lives… They adore you, Reid. They love you. They miss you like crazy, and the kids are blaming themselves for you leaving," Michelle argued back with just as much steam as I'd put out.

"Did she tell them?" I asked, breathless, pained to the point of fucking exasperation by how their faces must have looked when they learned what happened.

"She did. She told them two nights ago…which is why I called." She stopped and waited, and damn my curiosity because I needed more details.

I slowly sat back down and ran my hand through my hair when she continued.

"Henley said you were the silver lining in their life…said their daddy chose you to protect them and love them since he wasn't able to." Her voice was shallow and sharp, like she was holding back emotion. My throat clogged up as I imagined little Henley's face twisting as he explained his theory. "Jovi said even God had to let his own son die to save the whole wide world…and if they can get past that kind of thing, she thinks you and Layla can get past this." Michelle let out a little laugh, followed by a sniff.

Tears welled in my eyes, ready to fall if she listed one more reason why I should let my heart hope this might not be over.

"Reid, they miss you, all of them. Michael said you were a good man and he didn't care what happened…he's just hurt that you left. Steven said much of the same. I stood by Layla through her grief for Travis, but this is different…she's broken. She can't function, can't remember things. She gets this far-off look in her eye all the time, and whenever we're outside, she just stares at your house."

I let out a shuddering breath as emotions overwhelmed me. "What do you want from me, Michelle?"

"I want you to call her. I want you to let those kids know you haven't disappeared. I want you to give her a chance to talk to you about this instead of just running. Reach out to her. Personally, I think you should move back, move slow…do whatever you have to do, but just come back to them. You took their hearts with you when you left."

THE CRACK of wood filled the empty air as I lifted my arms and swung the ax down hard on the log. I'd been at this for an hour now, cutting wood in the back of my mother's yard behind her cabin. The physical movement was good for my busy mind, and the extra wood would help keep her stocked up through the rest of winter. I leaned down to snag another log and lined it up, took a step back, and raised my arms again.

A soft voice broke the silence. "You're gonna throw your back out if you don't take a break." I let my arms come down in a heavy swing and cracked the wood in half then lifted my eyes toward the porch. My sister was standing there, her small shoulders wrapped in a thick sweater. Her dark hair was tied back behind her head, leaving her pale face blank and open. I hadn't seen her in so many months. Back before the accident, we had been friends, siblings who loved each other, who called and texted and laughed together.

That day in court, she showed up, and once she saw that my sentencing was being reduced to reckless driving, she was quiet…too quiet. That night, she lashed out. She didn't understand how I could be so stupid, so thoughtless. She reminded me that he had a wife, kids, a life. I couldn't argue with her, because she was right. I had been thoughtless. I had been selfish. She didn't know what had happened with Jen, but it didn't matter. I had no right to drink and get behind the wheel.

"It's good for me to move," I quipped before lining up another log. I didn't understand why she was here. I didn't need my nose rubbed in the mess I'd made or to be told I didn't deserve the woman I'd fallen in love with, and I feared that was all my sister had come to do.

"Do you think you could stop long enough to talk to me?" she asked, leaning her elbows on the railing of the porch. I turned, eyed the strong beams she stood next to and tried to push the image of my father out of my head. He'd built the cabin when he was fifty, knowing he and my mother would be retiring soon and needed somewhere to settle. He died of lung cancer a year later. He only finished half the house, but these beams were ones he'd cut and prepped before he passed. Instead of selling the place, my mother had hired a team to come finish the house, and she'd been living in it ever since.

"Depends on what you want to talk to me about." I turned back toward the log and swung the ax. "If you're here to tell me I deserved to lose Layla and the kids, you can fuck off."

I lined up another log while she clicked her tongue and moved off the porch. She walked toward me with her arms crossed and her eyes downcast. I ignored her until she was just a foot or so away, watching me line up another log.

"I was wrong that day, after the hearing. I shouldn't have said those things to you, and I'm sorry, Reid. I'm sorry I haven't been around and haven't been there for you. I was selfish...confused, still hurt over losing Dad, and..."

I turned to look at her, curious about what else seemed to be haunting her these days.

"And?" I asked, encouraging her to continue.

She kicked at the frozen mud near her boot. "And I guess I was hung up because...Charlie cheated on me right around the same time everything happened with you. Blamed it on being drunk."

"Shit, I'm sorry, sis." I winced, lowering the ax.

She slowly nodded, keeping her gaze on the ground. "He ruined everything between us, for a drink...guess I was just a raging bitch at the time and your incident made it all flare up again. I'm so sorry, Reid."

I leaned toward her, pulling her into a tight hug. We stood there, in the cold of winter, with the silence of the forest at our backs, and held one another. It felt good to have one part of my life back in place, stitched together after so much had been ripped apart.

"I came here to give you something," Sara murmured, pulling back and wiping at her eyes. She dug into her sweater pocket, retrieved a thin letter, and gently held it out to me.

"What is this?"

She let out a lungful of air. "This is a letter from Layla. I received it about four months ago...before Thanksgiving.

I gripped the white paper with my freezing fingers and drew my eyebrows together in confusion. "What in the hell are you talking about?"

"After the accident, I started writing to her. I never told her my name, just that I was the sister of the man who'd..." She trailed off, likely sparing me from having to hear the harsh title I'd earned: the man who'd killed Layla's husband. "Anyway, she wrote back about a month after I first wrote to her, and we just kind of fell into a routine of writing letters to one another. I think you need to see this one. Mom told me what happened."

I pinned her with a glare as cold as the air that hung between us. "You mean you knew this entire fucking time? You knew I was living next to her? You knew I was making a fool of myself, falling in love with her kids, with her?" My voice caught on the betrayal that was cutting through me.

"No!" She held her hands out in panic. "God, no. I had no idea she'd taken me up on the suggestion to buy the ranch. I had someone else deal with all the paperwork, so I didn't know the name of the person who'd bought it. I did give her the listing of the house because I was trying to sell it at the time, but she never told me if she actually moved there. She told me she moved close to her sister, that's all. I swear I had no idea she was your neighbor. I suppose I would have if I'd called you or asked." She lowered her eyes, face blanching, hopefully at the realization that she'd abandoned me.

Her soft blue eyes lifted to mine a moment later. "Reid, I was trying to help. I know it's all a mess. It's my fault she found the house. I didn't think you were headed back. You hadn't been back in ten years—how was I supposed to know you'd go back? I figured you would sell it...I thought you were here with Mom."

"So, I guess you cut Mom out of your life too then?" I stomped toward the porch steps, more than fucking ready to leave.

She raced after me. "I'm sorry, Reid. I screwed up. I moved to London, ignored my family for an entire year, ignored everyone. I'm sorry...I'm trying to make up for it."

The urgency in her tone stopped me short. I turned to look at her and realized I had no room to pass judgment or be angry. She hadn't actually known or done anything wrong, and I'd never regret meeting Layla.

"I'm sorry too," I whispered then pulled her back into a hug.

"Just read it...and forgive yourself, brother. You deserve to move past this."

She kissed me on the cheek and headed inside, leaving me alone with the letter in my hands.

36

layla

RIDING THOR IN THE SUMMER WAS NOTHING COMPARED TO HIS arrogant ways in the cold of winter. The asshole was even more frustrating than normal. It was nearing sunset. The kids had fed and watered the horses and put them away for the evening, but I was antsy. I needed to get out of the house, to feel the cold wind in my hair and the crisp bite of winter on my face.

The snow had lessened over the last week, leaving us with just an inch or two left on the ground. I rode Thor around the fence line, purposely getting close to the shared one with Reid's property...or whoever had purchased his house. The big fat 'Sold' sticker had been plopped on the white sign the previous morning, and I'd lost my breakfast after seeing it.

He was really never coming back. He was really, truly leaving me alone with this heartbreak. I was so exhausted from the war being waged in my heart by my feelings, from trying to figure out whether I wanted him to come back and fight for forgiveness or stay away so I could honor Travis' memory. After this time away from Reid, after seeing that sold sign, I knew who'd won the war.

I wanted Reid back.

I wanted him to come back to me, to us. I'd wanted him to be there when I had to explain to the children why he'd left. A deep anger surfaced at the memory, at how he'd left me to explain to my children that he was the man whose car had drifted into their daddy's lane, causing his car to swerve. Reid had left me there alone to shoulder the burden of this honesty I didn't want. He hadn't helped me through it, hadn't helped me understand it or helped me heal. He had just left.

Tears fell, and the cold wind dried them up. The sun began to set, and I steered Thor toward the barn. I'd had enough of my own company for one night and was ready to talk to my sister or head into town and punish myself with copious amounts of alcohol at the local bar. Star had been trying to get me to go out with her for weeks, maybe it was time I take her up on the offer.

After I took care of Thor and put him away for the night, I headed into the house. The kids were supposed to be reading or getting ready for bed, but when I walked in, they were laughing, all huddled around something in the living room. I peeled off my gloves and jacket, stashing them in the laundry room, and moved toward their little giggle fest.

I stopped cold when I heard Henley gush, "Reid, guess what? I rode a sheep!" I closed my eyes, not ready to hear his voice, not ready to feel the tattered pieces of hope I'd managed to gather crumble.

"That's so awesome, buddy. I can't wait to see it." Reid's voice echoed through the living room. The kids were all watching a screen, which meant he was video-chatting with them. I tucked my body behind the door frame and stayed out of sight, not ready to interrupt their conversation or admit I was secretly dying to hear his voice again.

He hadn't called me. He had called them. I wasn't sure what to feel about that yet. It put a smile on my face that the kids were so happy. It made me think about the night I had told them about what had happened with Reid.

I remembered tentative faces pulled tight, clouded with confusion. They'd all stared at me, silent for minutes, until Henley spoke up and said he missed his daddy, but he thought maybe his dad had given him Reid as a present, a way to feel better since he couldn't be there anymore. Michael was the one I worried about the most. His face had twisted in impatience as the kids all talked, but once they were through, he'd approached me.

"Is that why he left? Did you tell him he couldn't be here anymore because of it? How dare you, Mom...after all Reid has done for us... wasn't it you who said hate is an addiction and we never have room in our lives to feel it for anyone?" He'd spewed all his anger at me, pointing a finger, and I had just stood there taking it.

I *had* asked Reid to leave, but I hadn't meant it. I'd just needed a second to adjust to the news, but it didn't matter because he'd left anyway, and I hadn't stopped him. I did wonder if I felt hate for Reid after he left, but the more I tried to hate him, the more I realized I didn't at all. I loved him. I loved him so much it terrified me, and it ached in an entirely different way than losing Travis had.

"Mom has been getting way better with the horses. You'd be really proud," Steven softly said to the screen, and Reid went quiet. I wanted to see his face, see what the last two months apart had done to him, if they had been as hard on him as they had been on me. There was a part of me that worried this was the only call he'd make, worried it would be the only way to connect with him, and it made me want to run out there, screaming at him to hold on and talk to me.

But I stayed put, holding up the wall, biting my lip to hold off pent-up tears.

"When are you coming back? Mama told us about how your car was the one that went into daddy's lane. Is that why you're gone?" Henley asked, curiosity coloring his tone. My heart shuddered as silence followed his question.

Finally, after a long pause, Reid gave his response. "I can't tell you kids, how sorry I am." His voice caught, sounding strained. "There're reasons why I got into the car that night, although none of them matter. I left because I figured your mom and you kids wouldn't want me around. I was trying to do the right thing." His voice cracked, and I nearly crumbled to the floor.

The tears couldn't be held back, so I let them free.

"How was I supposed to see you guys every day when you can't ever see your dad again, because of me?" Reid asked, still sounding strained, like he was breaking apart.

"But we love you too, Reid. We miss you too…I have no one to color with, or to leave notes for," Jovi said, starting to cry. I peeked around the corner and saw she had her hand on her chest, her blonde hair looking wild along with her wild eyes. She was so passionate.

"Yeah, shouldn't we have gotten some say in how you two ended things?" Michael asked, folding his arms across his chest.

"Mommy misses you. She's sad in a different way now," Henley added, sniffling and wiping his nose with his arm.

Silence stretched on, and I could imagine Reid running his hand through his hair.

He let out a sigh. "Trust me, you guys…I miss you too, but this is for the best. There's no way your mom could ever look at me the same after this. I'll call again in a few days, but I have to go for now. Love you…talk to you soon." Then he was gone, and all the kids were letting out disappointed sounds mixed with, "Don't go," and "Love you too."

I sucked in a deep breath and closed my eyes. He was gone again, and I had no way of finding him or telling him to come back.

37

"See you tomorrow, Reid?" Jeff, my supervisor, called over his shoulder. I nodded and gave him a small salute before heading out of the office. Jeff wasn't sure when I was going to leave, and I wasn't either, so at the end of every workday, he asked if he'd see me tomorrow.

The last three months had been lonely and horrible but efficient. Sarah had stayed for two weeks, visiting, awkwardly asking each day if I'd read the letter yet. Each day I'd smile and say, "Nope."

Because I wasn't ready. I couldn't face whatever was in that letter, and as much as it would gut my sister to know it, I didn't trust her entirely. I didn't know if Layla's letter talked about loving me or missing Travis. Honestly, neither would really help, because I couldn't have her.

The snow had stopped falling but still stuck to the ground in patches. The air was frigid, and the city was quiet. Crescent only had about three hundred or so people in it, making it peaceful and private. It was the perfect rehab for me to try to heal my broken pride and wounded heart. My soul was beyond repair, so it was also a good place to let my demons settle.

I drove two miles south and flipped my turn signal on, drove a few more miles down a dirt road, and turned onto the private drive. I was renting a small one-bedroom house on the edge of town. I had two neighbors a few miles away, but that was it. The woods butted up against my backyard, but otherwise, it was all open land.

I parked my new truck under the carport and trudged inside. I'd gotten a new one because my old one held memories of long talks with Michael, Jovi picking the radio station, Henley bouncing in the back seat...me kissing Layla. I'd needed a new one with zero traces of the life I left behind.

The day had waned, and the sun had almost set, creating a nearly purple sky, but it wasn't enough to let any light into my house. I'd opted for overtime, so I was working day shifts every weekend. It was too much work, but not nearly enough at the same time.

A gloomy house greeted me, as usual, and I ignored how lonely it made me feel. I swallowed the thick emotion down and pulled my phone out. All I wanted to do was call the kids and hear their voices and, if I was lucky, maybe see a wisp of Layla passing by the screen or hear her call one of the kids in the background. I just wanted to hear her voice, but I couldn't bring myself to call her. I'd typed out text messages a million times, had let my thumb hover over the send button only to drift to the backspace instead. I couldn't do it. I refused to insert myself back into her life when I'd taken so much away from her.

Just as I settled into my recliner, someone clicked on the lamp across the room. I froze as a familiar figure materialized in the lonely gloom that was now my home. Brown eyes frantically searched my face, and those pink lips quivered as she inhaled a sharp breath. My eyes moved down, from her long, curled hair draped over her shoulder to the neckline of her black sweater that dipped into a V.

I inhaled, making my breathing match hers, and brought my hand to my jaw. She was here...in my home...looking more gorgeous than ever... My brain was jumping to all kinds of places with what that meant.

"What are you doing here?" I asked, leveling her with a hard stare.

I didn't want her here, not when I knew what the outcome of this conversation would be, not when I'd have to watch her leave.

She dipped her head, causing her hair to fall forward. "You look good, Reid." Lifting her face, she gave me a sad smile. My stomach flipped and churned at the uncertainty of what was happening. I waited her out because she didn't need to be told she looked good. She always looked good.

"You should go," I whispered, closing my eyes, shutting out the sight of her.

"You don't mean that," she whispered back, and the pain in her tone pierced me.

"Of course I don't fucking mean it, Layla." I stood, throwing a couch pillow across the room. "But you're sitting here in my living room after all these months...and I..." I turned and stomped toward the front door. "Please just go. I know I don't deserve even that kindness, but whatever you have to say, just assume I've already heard it." I pointed at my head. "I hear it in my head every fucking night when I try to sleep, every day when I go to work. Every time I breathe...it's in there, taunting me..." I trailed off and snapped my jaw shut as emotion clawed its way through my voice.

Layla stood and walked toward me, slowly and cautiously. She had on the same brown boots she'd worn the night of our first kiss, and tucked into them was a pair of sinfully tight blue jeans. My gaze traveled up and saw tears wetting her face and smudging her makeup. I stood still, frozen and terrified of being this close to her again, breathing in the same air as her.

She walked forward until she was just a few feet away from me, and even in the dim lighting of the room, she glowed. I dropped my eyes to the floor so I didn't have anything else about this moment to commit to memory.

"Reid," she whispered, speaking my name like it was a prayer. "I didn't come here to hurt you or to do any of the things you think I'm going to do. Will you come sit with me?" She held out her hand, and damn it all, I nearly took it.

I clenched my jaw tight and kept my hands at my sides. "I don't think that's a good idea."

More tears fell from her dark lashes and it made me want to wrap her in my arms, but I wouldn't...because I couldn't.

"Fine, I guess we'll have this conversation standing here, where the draft from the cold air is hitting us the worst." She crossed her arms and stood rigid, unrelenting, her lips turned into a frown and her eyes narrowed on me.

With a resigned sigh, I nodded my agreement to head back toward the couch. I grabbed a bottled water for her and a box of crackers in case she was hungry, slipped my boots off, and clicked on an additional lamp to illuminate the room a bit more.

When I returned to the living room, she was on my couch, had removed her boots, and had her legs tucked underneath her with a blue throw blanket covering her. I wondered what she must think of my mismatched furniture, empty walls, small television, and miniscule floor space. The house was bleak, to say the least, but I spent most of my time at work, in the woods, or at my mom's.

I set the water and crackers next to her on the small table then stood there awkwardly. I eyed the spot beside her but couldn't make the move to sit there on my own, not when she smelled like watermelon and sunshine just like she always had, but when I was about to turn toward the chair, she stopped me by pulling on my hand and tugging me down next to her. The touch was like an electric shock to my system, sending chills down my arms.

Fuck, I missed her.

I settled in next to her as best as I could and waited for her to begin.

She cleared her throat and turned her body halfway toward me. "How come you haven't called me?"

I kept my eyes off her face and stared straight ahead. "What would I say? Sorry about ruining your life, but I miss you and want the future with you that I stole from your husband?" I laid my head back against the couch and turned it toward her. Her brown eyes were still brimming with tears, and she had her hands in her lap, tugging on the threadbare blanket.

"You would ask how I was and tell me you were coming back. You would tell me you were sorry but we could work through it." She lowered her voice and stared down at her lap.

I scoffed and lifted my head, only to shake it. "Layla, we can't work through this. You'll hate me. If you don't now, eventually you will. You'll resent me for it, and I wouldn't blame you. I resent me for it." I pointed at my chest and nervously bounced my leg in place. I wanted to get up and leave. I wanted to run.

"I'm not saying it would be perfect. I'm not even saying it would be easy, but it *would* be worth it," she snapped, and it was like she reached into my body, gripped my lungs, and squeezed.

I held her gaze and waited for what she might say next. She fiddled with her blanket some more before she continued.

"We're both guilty here, Reid, both of us carrying around our own baggage of shame. It's uncomfortable and difficult at times, but I'm carrying it whether you're with me or not because whether you accept me or deny me, I fell for you. I fell for someone other than my husband, and that alone makes me feel like dying a thousand deaths." She took a steadying breath in and closed her eyes. "But I love you, Reid. I love you so much I hate myself for it. I love you so much I can't stop thinking about you, and I can't stop wishing you'd just come back to me. When I realized you were the one who...the one who was in the car, I hated myself even more, because instead of feeling disgust or hate toward you, all I felt was loss. I didn't want you to go. Sure, I needed time, needed to process the news, but I wanted you there with me while I did it." Her breathing shuddered, and I could see her chest rising and falling harder than before. "It's illogical and may be unreasonable, but the hate I want to feel for you isn't there. I feel it for myself, but I can't summon that kind of emotion for you. All I have is the pain from losing you."

She stopped and narrowed her gaze until she was just focusing on my hands. I wanted her to touch me so badly it ached.

Fucking ached and ached.

A second later, she pulled my hand into her lap, quick as lightning.

"Reid, please," she whispered as she gently shut her eyes.

I looked down at our joined hands and noticed how soft and pale hers looked. I examined her nails and thought of the last time I'd touched her like this. Closing my eyes, I let her go and stood up.

"This can't work...this won't work," I started, shaking my head and pacing the small room. How could she honestly think it could?

She quickly stood and let out a heavy sigh. "You are seriously pissing me off. Do you know that?" She raised her voice, bringing her hands to her hips.

"Look, it's just that there's no way—"

"There is, if you'd just give it a chance." She glared with those daring brown eyes.

I narrowed my gaze and stepped closer. "Layla...aren't you angry? Aren't you mad about the fact that I took him from you? I wasn't innocent...I took him from you because I got into a car drunk. I was selfish, and your entire family is paying the price. I know you're angry, so don't stand there and pretend you aren't," I snapped.

Her eyes teemed with tears as she worked her jaw back and forth, and a wheezing sound came out of her as she demanded, "Stop it."

"It's true," I yelled, opening my arms, daring her to stare at my ugly truth and still say she loved me. "Just admit it. Tell me you're angry with me. Stop pretending," I yelled again, and I hated myself for raising my voice at her.

Tears slipped free and ran down her face, adding to her streaked makeup. "Yes, I'm angry, okay?" she yelled back, lifting her hand and gesturing toward me.

"Finally, we're getting somewhere," I snapped back, stepping closer. This thing between us was charged and dangerous. It was full of pain and laced with agony, and it was ready to explode.

"I'm angry with myself, Reid—for not being angry with you, for not hating you. I'm angry that you left me to sort this out alone. I'm angry that the man I fell in love with turned out to be such a coward." Her face twisted in disgust and her eyes flitted toward the door. She wanted to leave, and none of what she'd just said had anything to do with the fact that I had killed Travis.

My heart skipped, slowed, and nearly burst. I needed to slow this thing down and try to fix it before she left, because I didn't actually want her to.

"I'm angry that you won't hear me. I'm angry that you left my kids without saying goodbye or telling them yourself that you were the one that night. I'm angry that you won't let me love you," she cried, pointing both her hands at her chest, desperate and panicked.

Her words were knives cutting and slicing me open, and I was bleeding out, ready to die if I didn't get this fixed.

"I'm angry that you're being so selfish. I'm angry that you won't let me have you..." She stopped, wiped her face, and then quietly added, "There isn't much left of me...but whatever there is, I want you to have it. I want you to have the rest of me, Reid, the rest of my mornings and my nights, my good days and bad. I have them to offer, and I want you to swallow your pride and take them. Because without you..." She trailed off and dropped her hands as though she was giving up, losing steam...ready to leave.

I stood there, not even realizing tears were streaming down my face until a cold drop hit my arm. *Shit.*

Fuck my pride and my protective notions. I lifted my hand and pulled her to me. She came willingly, frantically pushing her hands into my hair and molding her lips to mine. She tasted like salt and desperation. I moved my face to the side, deepening our kiss, and she did the same. She was pouring her reasons why this would work into the kiss, and I was pouring out all the reasons why it likely wouldn't.

We waged a war with our mouths and drew battle lines with the way our arms wrapped around one another. We fought over the hate that should have been between us. Her frenzied kisses were telling me it wasn't there, but I pushed into her and insisted that it was. I wrapped my hands around her ass and lifted without breaking our kiss. Her legs went around me as her hands clung to my hair, all while her mouth continued its assault against mine.

I walked us back to my room and carefully lowered her to my bed, a place I had wanted her since the first time my lips tasted hers. Shadows danced across her soft features while light from the outside porch poured into the room. She was lying with her hands above her head, and her sweater had inched up enough to expose her flat stomach. My greedy eyes took in the way her hair fanned out behind her and how it looked like the moon had wound itself into each and every strand.

Her pink lips were slightly parted, and her brown eyes were daring me to take the next step.

"You're perfect," I whispered on a heavy breath, standing in between her legs. She looked up at me and smiled. It was brilliant and bright, and I wanted to marry her, so fucking bad that it was going to ruin me. At the end of all this, I wouldn't regret her.

"Where'd you go?" she asked, sitting up and bringing her hands to my stomach.

I cleared my throat and looked down. "I don't deserve this...I don't deserve you."

She stared up at me and gave me a soft smile. "You can't earn me, Reid. You can't rationalize love. It doesn't make any sense, and we can't..."

I bent down and slammed my lips to hers, violent and panicked. Whatever part of me that wanted to be careful or go slow had just gone out the window with the way she looked up at me and said we couldn't rationalize love. Because we couldn't. Love wasn't ours to fix or force, to make any sense of or use to erase things that shouldn't even exist.

I broke the kiss in order to tug her sweater over her head then reengaged her and slowly pushed her back. Her hands roamed under my shirt, pressing firmly into my abs and chest. In turn, I pushed my fingers into the soft flesh of her sides, sliding one hand down to her ass. I pulled on the back of her thigh until her leg was wrapped around me.

"Reid," she whispered, looking up at me with that desperate gaze. Without a word, I pulled my shirt over my head and carefully brushed my fingers over her lips.

"I missed you so much." I pressed my lips to her neck and continued making a path down to the swell of her breasts. She pushed her fingers into my hair and let out a moan. I reached behind her and unclasped her bra. Her little gasps and moans were making me impossibly hard, and the second her hips began to buck against me, I let out a low groan. "Are you sure you want to do this?" I growled against her skin because I couldn't deal with her regretting this come morning.

She cradled my face in her hands and made sure I was making eye contact with her.

"Reid, you get all the rest." She smiled sensually and added, "Make love to me."

I lowered my lips to hers and kissed her, creating a new memory, one I'd never be able to purge from my mind. I flicked the copper button on her jeans, slid her zipper down, and moved my fingers to the tune of her moans.

She came apart and it was the most beautiful sound, the most perfect thing I'd ever heard. Her soft hands moved across my waist as they rid me of my jeans, mine did the same with hers, and once we were bare, open and exposed to one another, I slid inside her. That first gasp was like a siren in my head. It was the sound of surrender, of breaking. I slid out and pushed in again, desperate to hear it again. She let it pass through those perfect lips again and it shattered something open inside of me.

I looked down at her, those dark eyes begging me to jump into the deep end and drown with her. I smiled and gave in. Bending low, I kissed her long and deep as she pulled at my hair. As I pushed, she pushed back, and what had started like someone testing out a cold lake turned into diving in with frantic and heated movements. She watched me as we moved with hungry eyes, watched with awe where our bodies joined and moved desperately to a different kind of rhythm.

One that was just ours.

Hope and hunger ignited between us as we clung to one another.

"You make me insane," I whispered against her shoulder. "I've wanted to be inside you like this for so long."

She let out a moan, one that only amplified the gasp I'd heard.

"Do you like this?" I asked, pushing harder into her.

"Yes," she gasped, and I was shattering open again.

I whispered all my desperation into her skin, like my words were ink, branding her forever. I thrust all my pain, my hurt, my anger into her, and she met me with each arch, every moon-shaped nail print into my back, each gasp and muffled scream. It was ours, and it was perfect.

I leaned in to kiss her again, because it was like I couldn't get enough of her lips, of her taste, or the sounds she made when I owned her like this.

She was so beautiful; she was so perfect and so mine.

If only I could keep her.

LAYLA WAS CRADLED in my arms, the light from outside lighting up her soft features as she slept. She looked peaceful and perfect. The heat in my room was nearly nonexistent, so she was bundled under my comforter and clinging to me as tightly as possible. It was beyond anything I'd imagined.

I stared up at the ceiling as the hours gave way, and I refused to let this moment with her go. I knew as soon as the sun hit her face and she realized what she'd done, she'd clam up and go home. She likely just needed to see if she could do this, and now that she'd slept with the enemy, her curiosity would be satisfied.

Near dawn, I slowly slid from the warm bed and tugged on my boxers and sweats. I walked to my dresser and carefully opened the drawer that held the letter my sister had given me. I walked toward the living room as I gently unfolded it then began reading as I leaned into the recliner.

Dear S,

The last letter I received from you, you were hoping I'd found my solace in the anniversary of my husband's death, hoping maybe a year into grief I'd be finished with the worst of it. I have to be honest; I didn't read your letter until well after that day had passed. Truth is, I was quite lost after my husband's anniversary. I was lost the entire year before, too...that is, until I met someone.

An innocent friendship...my kids' horse instructor and our neighbor...he rescued my horse one night, and then my son. He rescued me in the process, too, and I don't think he was even trying to.

You mentioned in a past letter that you'd lost your fiancé to infidelity and how that pain had become a part of you, how it was something you lived with now. I know it's different than losing someone to death, but I still feel like maybe you can understand where I'm coming from. You likely understand the pain of living in a world without the one person who made the most sense of it.

But what do you do if you've accidentally fallen in love with someone after your person is gone? Is that something you can relate to?

Because I have, and I'm not sure how to fix it, how to work through it. I have no idea what I'm going to do, but I know it feels different...this thing growing in my heart, new and scary...but right.

It feels like a future I was too scared to want, and I'm clinging to that feeling and pulling it close. I'm not letting him go, and I wanted to tell you that and thank you for writing me and trying to connect the broken pieces of my shattered past. I wanted to tell you that somehow, through the love of this man, I've found a way to forgive your brother. I know it seems strange, know it seems highly unlikely, but this love I've found...it's enough, enough to swallow darkness and hurt, to make room for new things. I want fresh starts and happy memories. So, I guess I just needed to let you know...so that maybe in some way, you'd forgive him too.

All my love,

Layla

I gripped the edges and reread the entire thing twice, homing in on the words that stood out to me.

I wanted to tell you that somehow, through the love of this man, I've found a way to forgive your brother.

The same question ran through my mind over and over again.

How? How could she find a way to forgive me through my love? It wasn't perfect, wasn't good enough or constant enough. There was no way I was enough for her or the kids, but it didn't change the fact that she'd written it. It was her truth, and I couldn't argue with it.

Instead, I decided to take it for what it was: a second chance.

It was a new beginning, the love of a woman I didn't deserve.

38

Layla

SUNLIGHT BROKE THROUGH MY HALF-PARTED EYELIDS, AND THE SMELL of coffee forced the heavy things all the way open. I blinked and looked around. My first question was why Reid had no curtains in his bedroom. A single-pane window revealed tall trees and a small patch of frozen dirt behind his house, still slightly covered in bits of snow. I reached behind me, trying to feel for the man I'd come here to retrieve, but the bed was cold and empty.

I slumped back into the softness of the mattress and pulled the blankets up, desperate to avoid the cold a bit longer.

I thought back to the night before, to how it had felt to have Reid inside me in a way he hadn't been before. He'd already owned my heart; regardless of whether he knew it or not, he'd been inside me for a long time. I thought of his expression, of how Reid had stared down at me with that stunned, hungry look in his eyes.

I thought of how I'd held his face to my chest and kissed the top of his head after he roared his release to the room and after I'd cried out my own. We were sweaty, broken, a mess of limbs and skin. It was perfection in chaos, heaven in hell, my future tangled in the barbed wire of my past—and I wanted more of it.

I wrapped the sheet around me and padded across the cold floor toward the kitchen. Reid was standing with his back to me, a pair of gray sweats hanging low on his waist and a dark green t-shirt clinging to his firm back, those two defined lines visible and drool-worthy. The old, worn coffee maker was bubbling and dripping liquid goodness into the glass pot.

"Morning," I said, running my hands down his back.

He turned halfway, wrapped me under his arm, and murmured, "Morning." He kissed my forehead, and it made my stomach buzz with those damn bees he'd left me with. I'd missed him so much.

"What are you up to today?" I asked hesitantly. For some reason, it felt like he'd pull away again. After we had finished the previous night, Reid had drawn circles into my back, quiet and reflective but withdrawn just the same.

"I was thinking…" Reid pulled away from me, pouring me a cup of coffee and handing it to me. "I want you to come meet my mom…" He trailed off and brought his hand up to his hair, running it through those messy strands I had tousled hours before. "I want to see her before we head back." He paused and gave me a small smile. I set my cup down and launched toward him. The sheet dropped, but I didn't care. He was coming home, to me, to the kids, to us.

He kissed me frantically then pulled me up into his arms and walked us back to his room.

REID'S MOTHER'S house smelled of roast and was warm from the large fire he'd started. The cabin had a myriad of couches, plush pillows, and throw blankets, and at the moment, I was relaxed next to him on a small two-seater sofa. I was nervous. I had no idea what she would think of me or what she might have heard. I had already pieced together that Sarah might have spilled the beans about our conversations, but I didn't know how that might have made his mother feel. Reid put his hand on my knee to try to calm me down. His mother had yet to come home, which was partly what was making me so nervous. When Reid had called and asked if he could swing by, she had said she'd be back in about an hour.

We'd waited and come after the hour had passed, but she still wasn't there. She'd apparently put a roast in the crockpot before she left, and it smelled all kinds of ready to eat. If his mother didn't show up soon, I was going to help myself.

"Should we head back to your place and wait for her to call? I don't want to make it seem like we're imposing." I strained my neck to check the front door.

Reid laughed and moved his hand up my thigh. "We aren't imposing. In fact..." He leaned in to kiss me. "I could carry you to the guest room right now..."

"I'm here! So sorry for the delay." His mother's singsong voice filtered in from the doorway, heading straight for the kitchen. I shoved him away and quickly stood, eyeing the space where she had entered. I pulled my fingers into my palms and cleared my throat. Reid stood too, taking my hand in his, leading the way to the kitchen. His mom was unpacking what looked like a large brown box of groceries, likely from Costco. She looked up briefly and smiled, quickly doing a double-take when she realized Reid wasn't alone. She dropped the bouquet of flowers she was trying to trim and stared at me.

"Are you...? Is this...?" Her eyes jumped from Reid to me.

I cleared my throat. "I'm Layla."

Her soft green eyes that matched her son's began to water as she took the few steps that separated us and drew me into a hug. "I'm so sorry, my sweet girl, so sorry for what you've been through," she whispered into my ear as she rocked me in her arms. I didn't want to cry, but the force of her hug shifted something in me. She was so maternal and loving, something I'd never felt from my own mother.

She leaned back, and I wanted to tell her I loved her hair, the graying pieces that framed her face, her soft skin that had a few crow's feet and wrinkles. She was gorgeous, and her kindness only amplified it.

"Thank you," I squeaked as I took a step back.

She turned her gaze to her son and pulled him into a tight hug, whispering something to him that had him nodding into her shoulder. After the introductions, Reid gathered me in his arms and kissed me lightly on the lips before running outside to get the rest of his mother's groceries.

We ate dinner together. We laughed and didn't bring up the accident, which I preferred. Reid talked about the kids, and from the way they talked, I knew he'd brought them up before.

"Jovi is the one who colors pictures with you, right?" she asked Reid, and it made my heart flutter. "And Henley is the youngest?" she asked around her bite of stew.

The fact that he had already talked about them, not knowing if we would ever work out, just made me love him even more. There in that moment, I wanted to whisper to my husband that I was going to be okay, that in an odd way, this whole thing had worked out and he could rest in peace. I would always love him, but I was going to be happy with the time I had left. I was going to forgive, let go, and embrace the gift God had given us: a man who cared for us, loved us, and would make us whole again.

I WAS SITTING on the counter digging into a tub of ice cream, something with mint and cookies. Reid was standing in between my legs, stealing bites and kisses.

"Stop it." I swatted at him.

"We're supposed to be sharing," he muttered, diving for my spoon.

I laughed and tossed my head back. "No, we're supposed to be packing, but you keep getting distracted."

"I was doing a really good job of packing until you came out of the shower with that tiny towel wrapped around you. What was I supposed to do?" he said against my neck as he mauled me with his lips for the millionth time that day.

We decided to head back together once I'd told him I hadn't driven but had taken a taxi and really didn't want to have to pay for one back to the nearest airport, which was about an hour and a half from where his mom lived.

"Maybe I want to stay in this little paradise with you," he whispered. His kisses were moving south as intense pleasure wound its way through me, tugging and pushing all the way into my heart and down to my core. I needed to stop him because my poor body couldn't handle another round. I was so sore and out of practice that I was going to break if he did anything more to me.

"I would love that, but we have four kids waiting for us at home." I cradled his jaw, lifting his eyes until they met mine. His soft expression nearly did me in.

"They know I'm coming back?" he asked, a little breathless.

I nodded. "I called them while you showered this morning."

He grabbed me by the ass and helped me to stand up. "You take the kitchen, I'll pack up the living room. I'm not taking any of this furniture," he yelled over his shoulder.

I laughed and grabbed ones of the boxes he'd loaded up earlier in the morning. "Thank God! Maybe we should do this place a favor and leave a burner on?"

"Hey, don't be mean. It was all I could find. Hopefully, I can find something at least a little nicer when I'm back in Douglas," he joked from the other room, but it had me stopping short.

"You're moving in with us," I said with the kind of finality that left little room for argument.

He stopped loading his DVDs into a box and looked up at me. "I figured you'd want to take things a bit slower," he said quietly.

"Slower than spending the last three months apart?" I scoffed. "No thanks. I love you, Reid Harrison, and I want you in my bed, making love to me or just snuggling with me for as long as you'll have me."

He dropped the box and took measured steps toward me. "And what if I want forever with you, Layla? What if even that wouldn't be long enough for me?" He was right in front of me, and I was having a hard time controlling the lust filling my veins.

"That would make me happy." I looked up at him as his face drew closer.

"How happy?" His voice was all dark and delicious.

I leaned up on my tiptoes and pressed my lips to his, winding my fingers through his hair. His hands landed on my hips and lifted me, just like he had the night before.

He walked us back to his bedroom and I giggled into his mouth, saying, "See! Distracted!"

39

Layla and I had been gone for five days. That was how long it took for us to stop being "distracted" enough to pack the house and make the drive to Wyoming. I'll never forget the way the kids emptied onto the porch as the truck pulled up, or how they threw themselves at me when I exited the vehicle.

Each one had something to tell me about the few months I'd missed. There was a new neighbor they didn't particularly care for; she was a girl and only seemed to show any kindness to Jovi. As I passed Michelle, she gave me a sly smile and punched my arm playfully.

We walked inside and ordered pizza, which gave everyone enough time to share their stories and for me to build up the nerve to say what I needed to say to them. We were all crowded around the couch, Layla tucked into my side as I leaned forward and began.

"I need to say a few things."

The kids all moved to where they could see me. Layla grabbed my hand and squeezed it.

"You all know what I did. I won't try to hide it. In fact, I will never try to hide it. I won't ever ask you to brush it under the rug or pretend it didn't happen. It happened, and I'm so sorry." My voice broke, but I refused to look away from the kids' faces. "I know I left and that was wrong. I thought you kids would want me gone. I thought your mom would never be able to forgive something that big." I tightened my grip on my Layla's hand. "The thing is, she did. She showed me that love can heal this. It's better than time, and it's better than truth. It can cover ugly things and open hard ones. We could all use a lesson from your mother on how to love," I finished, looking over at the woman I loved, and she leaned forward to stroke my face, her eyes reflecting how much she wanted this.

I was in love, in lust, in over my head.

"With that said, I want to ask you kids for permission. I want to know how you'd feel about me joining your family. I plan on asking your mother to marry me eventually, and I plan on being someone you can count on, someone you can depend on, someone who's there. I never ever want or plan to replace your dad. He has a place here, in this house. I want you to talk about him, to remember him. I want to take you back to visit where he's buried, and I want you to feel like you can miss him." I looked over again and found Layla crying silent tears with a smile on her face. I continued, needing to get it all out. "If you feel like this is too fast or you don't want me here, now's the time to tell me. I won't be mad, but I do need to know. If you want me here, I'm going to move in, and I'm going to be here with you guys, day in and day out, a part of your lives." I stroked the side of Layla's leg to put myself at ease.

"We want you here. We don't want you to leave," Henley mumbled from under his blanket.

"Yeah, we want you to move in and be here," Jovi added with little tears in her brown eyes as Steven and Michael nodded.

"We want you here, and we, uh…" Michael cleared his throat. "We missed you."

I nodded at them. "The key here is communication. I still struggle with feeling worthy of being here. I still struggle with wanting to run for the hills because I don't deserve you guys, but I'm trying. I might have a bad day here and there, and you know what? That's okay." I leaned forward, searching their faces. "It's okay if you have a day where you're mad at me, mad about what I did and you need to vent or yell. It's okay, and we can work through it. Never keep that stuff in. I love you guys, and I want this to work." I nodded my head to get everyone's agreement, and they all moved in to do a big group hug. We were together and healing, slowly but surely.

I HAD JUST FINISHED my shower and was walking back into the bedroom when I stopped short near the closet. Layla was moving hangers to the side and making room for me. I leaned against the door frame and smiled. "Looking for snakes?"

She jumped a bit, clearly having been in her own little world. I smiled at her outfit, her tiny shorts and thin sleep tank. My eyes devoured her body, but my heart thrashed in my chest for her words, for her eyes. I hated that I still needed reassurances, but I still felt out of place.

"Tonight, I'm only looking for one snake, sir." She smiled and looked down toward my waist. She waggled her eyebrows suggestively and laughed.

"That was the worst joke I've ever heard." I chuckled, moving toward the duffle bag she'd set in the closet.

"Why do you need clothes?" She moved my bag back with her foot.

I laughed. "You're wearing some."

She eyed her outfit. "Touché."

"Plus, what if the kids need something in the middle of the night?" I asked while leaning down to snatch the bag from her.

When I stood back up, she had tears brimming in her eyes. At first, I panicked, not sure what I had done wrong, but a second later she launched herself at me, kissing my neck and chest, jumping into my arms like she had that time in the tool shed. I caught her and walked us toward the bed.

"What?" I inquired as she kept kissing me, tears falling freely down her face.

"I love you so much, so much, and the fact that you'd think of the kids and what's best for them when I mentioned being naked with me —it's just so freaking sexy." She pressed her lips to my mouth before I could respond, and after her groping me and moving my towel away, I realized I didn't need to.

I might not have had any of her firsts and I certainly didn't deserve her bests, but I was going to enjoy all of her lasts, all the rest of her, down to every smile, laugh, and freckle.

EPILOGUE

Layla

Three and a half years later

WHISPERING WOKE ME—LOUD, OBNOXIOUS KID WHISPERING WHERE THEY think they're being quiet but they aren't being quiet at all.

Since I was awake, I decided to try to hear what they were saying.

"She's going to love it," Scarlett whispered in her three-year-old little timbre, full of confidence.

"I'm not saying she won't, but..." Jovi started, but Henley interrupted her.

"Scar is right—she's going to love it. Move out of the way, Jov." He was eight now and full of opinions, bossiness, and pranks.

The door opened just as I heard Jovi say, "Scarlett, wait for your dad..." but it was muffled as Scarlett made her way into the room. I kept my eyes closed, not sure what exactly they had in store for me and a tad nervous because Jovi wasn't entirely on board. She was twelve now, my wise little helper.

"Mommy?" Scarlett whisper-shouted.

I felt behind me for Reid, to see if he was going to help me out of this. His daughter was ambitious, strong-willed, and fierce; I loved every damn inch of her, but the girl made me stress.

"Mommy?" she whispered louder. I cracked my eyes open and looked down to see my little girl standing there in a princess dress with chubby cheeks, green eyes, and light brown hair a ratted mess. My room was dark because Reid was responsible and knew how to not only measure for blackout shades but purchase and hang them too.

"Yes, baby?" I asked, not moving from my place in bed.

"It's your birthday," she whisper-yelled.

"I know, sweetie, and what was the one thing Mommy wanted for her birthday?" I asked with as much patience as I could muster.

"Sleep," she answered confidently.

I turned my head an inch to catch sight of the alarm clock. The red numbers reflected off the glass from my wedding photo, indicating that it was just past seven in the morning.

"Look what I got you, Mommy!" Scarlett shoved something hard in my face.

I leaned back a bit and tried to sit up. "What is this, sweetheart?"

"It's a rock." She beamed, bringing her tiny hands together.

I turned the stone over in my hands but couldn't see what made it significant.

Scarlett must have recognized the confusion on my face, because she walked over to my shades and pulled the string until they flipped open, letting in bright light and nearly blinding me.

"It's a birthday rock, Mommy. I wished for it, just for you. Henley says Daddy is your rock and I wanted to give you a rock from me, so I could be your rock too." She smiled up at me with all those little baby teeth.

My heart melted, forcing me to abandon my warm blankets and wrap her in my arms. "Baby, where is your daddy?"

"He's talking to Henley's daddy in the barn. He asked what he should do for your birthday and how to get you to some place called Hawwee when you're so scared of spiders and voconos," she lisped in her little three-year-old dialect.

Three years later and Reid was still stealing my breath away. The kids often found him talking out loud to Travis. Steven had asked him about it once, and Reid had grinned, saying, "Your dad gives the best advice on how to deal with you kids."

It had broken me then, and over the past three years, it had never gotten any easier to wrestle with how good I had it, how sweet of a man I had married and how perfect he was for us.

We'd gotten pregnant with Scarlett just two months after we came home from Oregon, which was such a happy surprise, and I knew her being a girl helped to heal something that had been taken from him by his ex.

Scarlett fit into our group like a champion. She was feisty, which came in handy being the youngest of five. She walked with so much confidence that sometimes she made me question my own.

Male voices started laughing and joking from downstairs, which meant Reid had come back inside. He was the life of every party, the one who always stole the show, and every single one of the kids clung to every word he said.

I grabbed Scarlett's hand and slowly made my way downstairs. Just as my feet landed on the wooden floor, those green eyes found mine and I nearly fell back from the love I found there.

Reid flicked a disappointed glare down to his daughter, who was ignoring both of us for whatever show was on television. He walked over to me and wrapped me in his strong arms.

"Guess sleeping in is off the agenda?" he rumbled into my neck, holding back a bit of laughter.

I nodded and held up my present. "Yep, she got me a rock."

He tossed his head back, laughing.

"It's your fault," I accused him, poking him in the chest.

"How?" He wheezed, still laughing.

"She said she wanted to be a rock to me like her daddy is." I glared at him, trying to shove past him.

He stopped me with a solemn face. "You call me your rock?"

I rolled my eyes. "You and Jesus, baby."

That made him laugh some more. "Well then, I guess this makes more sense now."

I stopped and watched him pull a necklace from under his shirt, a plastic pink heart attached to a long chain.

"She said she wanted to be my heart..."

I pulled the plastic pendant in between my fingers, rotating it around, and then stood on my tiptoes and kissed my husband.

Our kids were distracted, so I took the moment and pressed my body into his until his hands were at my waist and tugging me toward the stairs.

I smiled against his lips and said, "Looks like she's wanting the rest, huh?"

He laughed, nipped at my mouth, and let out a sigh. "Looks like it. We're going to have to watch that one." He kissed me hard before walking us forward, toward the stairs. "I think it's time you get your birthday present, Mrs. Harrison."

I smiled as he pulled me upstairs with him and shut our bedroom door behind us. "What exactly is my gift, Mr. Harrison?" I crawled backward onto the bed as he closed the blinds.

"Sleep, glorious sleep," he whispered and then kissed my forehead.

I groaned and fell backward. "You're such a tease!"

As he was about to shut the door, he whispered, "And you're the rest of me, all of it...forever, babe."

ALSO BY ASHLEY MUNOZ

Enjoyed *The Rest of Me*?

Please consider leaving an honest review on Amazon- it is so helpful, in more ways than you might know.

More from Ashley-

(All free with Kindle Unlimited)

Glimmer

At First Fight

Fade

What Are the Chances

COMING SOON:

Tennessee Truths: A Second Chance- Lovers to Enemies Standalone
coming spring 2020

Add it to your Goodreads TBR Today!

Sign up for my shout outs so you don't miss any updates

A NOTE ABOUT THE BOOK

I had jotted down the idea to write this book on a coffee stained post it note, while I waited for my kids during school pick up.

It was just an idea.

A thought.

Something to honor my dead father who left us tragically and way too soon.

While I was one of his adult children, he'd remarried and left behind four young kids with my stepmother. The funeral scene was a near replica to my fathers, with the young four-year-old being my younger brother.

This book was a therapeutic journey, one that I'm glad for but gutted just the same.

He lived in Wyoming and when we spent time with him in the summers, he'd take us to the Walker's Rodeo grounds, where we'd get lost on the farm and see the huge bulls, tucked away in the back of the property. This entire book is essentially a still photo of pieces of my life. Reid and Layla just managed to find a way into it.

I hope you enjoyed it. - Love, Ashley

THANKS:

No book is possible without a massive team of people helping.

First and foremost: Thank you, God. The helper, healer and perfection of peace. Thank you for loving me perfectly and fully.

Secondly: My husband, Jose. Thank you for believing in me, hugging me and building me an office so my dreams can flourish.

To my children: Thank you for keeping me entertained and laughing. I love you and I'm sorry that my head is always in the clouds.

To my sister, Rebecca: I wouldn't even be writing books if it weren't for you. The depth and extra characters are all thanks to you. Thank you for your input and your encouragement with this book. If you hate the ending, you have no one to blame but yourself.

To Brittany- Thank you for hours of voice clips, random pictures DM'd at the most insane times. I love you and couldn't be more thankful for your friendship. I'm glad I have you.

To my beta readers: Katie, Gladys, Leah, Rebecca, Amy and Krystal- Thank you isn't enough. It will never be enough. I adore you each and couldn't be more grateful for your support.

To my street team: I couldn't do this without you- your shares, excitement and dedication to me and Brit, is insane. Thank you so much for all your hard work.

Book Beauties: I adore you all. Thank you for loving my words and for constantly encouraging me.

To my PA, Tiffany: I. Could. Not. Do. This. Without. You. Thank you for being on top of everything!!!

To my cover designer and creative genius behind all the images for this book: Thank you for working so hard on this while your family went through the plague, I adore you.

To my editor and proofreader, this was our first journey together, but I couldn't be more thankful for your help in perfecting my words. Thank you so much.

To Wildfire Promotions, and Enticing Journey, thank you for your support and help with getting my book into the hands of bloggers.

To my readers, new and old: I'm sitting on this side of the computer and feel so strange. I started writing because of my obsession with kindle and all the amazing books there. I wanted to write a story that I wanted to read, and Glimmer was born. It's been pure craziness since. Write. Read, never stop dreaming. -Love, Ashley

FOLLOW ASHLEY:

Facebook- Ashley Munoz Author Page
Instagram -(@ashleymunoz_author)
Reader Group: Book Beauties
Website: www.ashleymunozbooks.com

ABOUT ASHLEY:

Ashley was born in Nebraska but raised in Oregon where she lives with her four children and husband.

If she's not helping her husband with DIY projects around the house, she's writing or sneaking off to a corner to read.

She likes to write happily ever after's for real life people that have inspired her but haven't necessarily gotten their happy ending yet.

She's an avid believer in building others up, grabbing hands to help others and encouraging women to be who they were destined to be.

Feel free to message her, she basically lives on Instagram and in her reader group- Book Beauties.